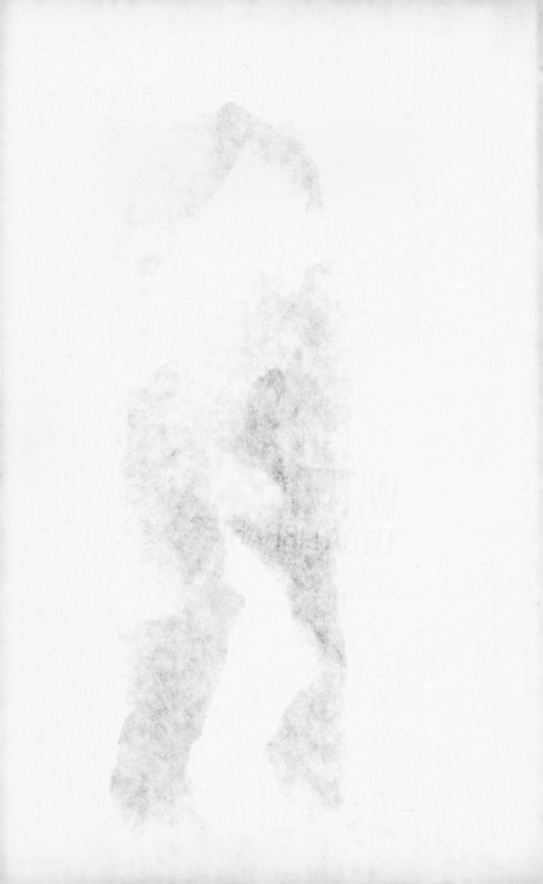

THE
SIXKILLER
CHRONICLES

OTHER BOOKS BY PAUL HEMPHILL

Too Old to Cry

Long Gone (a novel)

The Good Old Boys

Mayor: Notes on the Sixties
(with Ivan Allen Jr.)

The Nashville Sound

THE
SIXKILLER
CHRONICLES

PAUL HEMPHILL

MACMILLAN PUBLISHING COMPANY

NEW YORK

Macmillan Publishing Company
866 Third Avenue, New York, N.Y. 10022
Collier Macmillan Canada, Inc.

Library of Congress Cataloging in Publication Data
Hemphill, Paul, 1936–
The sixkiller chronicles.
1. Cherokee Indians—Fiction.   I. Title.
PS3558.E4793S5   1985   813'.54   84-23425

ISBN 0-02-550910-1

10 9 8 7 6 5 4 3 2 1

Designed by Jack Meserole

Printed in the United States of America

"Amazing Grace," traditional, arranged & adapted by Joan Baez,
© 1978, Chandos Music ASCAP. Used by permission.

For SAFPH,
qui a racheté une génération perdue.

CONTENTS

PROLOGUE

All through the black Appalachian night the wind, messenger of death, howls and shrieks and circles like some giant mythical Ulsterian vulture, raging against the ageless log house, hurling hickory limbs and pine cones at the skittery tin roof, rattling frail windows, cartwheeling loose pails across the yard, tearing gates from rusty hinges, throwing icicle darts at the creaking barn, blowing its hoary breath at terrified animals cowering in the naked orchard, demanding a word with the survivors. *Let me in, let me in, I have news, I have news,* says The Messenger, crying out with malevolent glee, howling, moaning, cackling, circling, beating his great black wings against the fortress of tree and clay. Clay. *Only two, only two, only two.* And then, finally, he retires, as he has many times before, soaring away to his lonely aerie high above the valley, far away on the bleak ridges of Clingman's Dome, leaving only his calling card of stark white nothing.

The boy, still wrapped tightly in blankets and sprawled out where he fell asleep beside the hearth, awakens at dawn. The fire is nearly out. The battery radio, once tuned to the Grand Ole Opry, now crackles with static. He gets up and goes to the window and sees a high blue sky and dazzling sunlight and the thick blanket of snow left by the storm. The pickup truck is gone. He throws more logs on the fire and blows out the flickering kerosene lamp and slumps toward the back room, his parents' room, just to make sure that is how it happened. The room is still in disarray, just as it was when his father wrapped her in blankets and ran out into the night with her in his arms, saying he would be back when he got back, and the boy closes the door and goes back to the fire.

The Indian is on his feet now, stirring a pot of coffee in the fireplace, smoking a cigarette, worrying. The brilliant light coming off the snow outside heightens the deep crevices on his burned face. Except for agreeing that it would be nice to have a telephone, like the people in town, they have little to say. The Indian pours coffee and they stand together at the window, waiting, listening, lost. Finally the boy says, *How long does it take?*

For you it was only an hour.
But it's been all night.
Sometimes it is different. Sometimes all night.
Will they be all right?
Don't worry. Don't worry.
I want a brother.
A boy needs a brother.
I could name him Robin. Like the spring.
Robin. Good name.

Then they see the truck slithering down the narrow drive to the house, its chained tires biting into the snow, its tailpipe wheezing ashen steam. They watch, wordlessly, as the father turns off the engine and remains in the cab for a few minutes, his head bowed over the steering wheel, his shoulders jerking in spasms, then see him slide from the cab, letting the door shut behind him, and crunch toward the house without bothering to pull the hood of the parka over his head. Shoulders slumped, head still bowed, boots and hair covered with snow, eyes red, the father enters the room. He asks the Indian to bring the whiskey and stands before the fire, rubbing his hands together, trying to find something in the flames. The Indian brings the whiskey and the father takes a long drink from the jug. *She's gone*, he says. *So's the boy. They hardly got here.* The boy goes off to his room to cry. The father looks for answers in the jug and the fire. The Indian, born old and wise as the mountains, stands by.

Business. Pieces of paper to be signed, holes to be dug, boxes to be nailed and closed forever, flowers to be picked, marble to be cut, words to be said, Bibles to be read, hymns to be sung. Amazing grace how sweet thou art. Up on a distant hillside, the friends and the neighbors and the ladies from the church all gone now, the boy and the father and the Indian quietly work in the gloaming. They do not speak as they gently lift the two sparse pine boxes, first the mother and then the baby, and softly plant them into the wet black earth. They take turns at the shovel, slowly ladling the dirt until each hole is topped with a soft black mound, in stark contrast with the field of snow, black-and-white/ good-and-evil, then settling the markers of glossy marble. Two more for the hill. Molly O'Hare Clay, 1911–1945. Boy Baby Clay, 1945.

And in the starry evening, the Indian gone off alone some-where to be with ghosts of his own, the father and the son sit together, alone together, in front of the fire shared by six generations. The boy aimlessly whittles on a stick. The father, bony fingers squeaking over guitar frets, whispers the words, trying to get them right—

> Molly my love,
> Molly my love,
> Molly my fair sweet lady . . .

—putting them to a tune brought over centuries before from the lush rolling hills of Ulster, in another place removed only by time, the boy's tears streaking his face, the father's voice cracking, high blue flames leaping in the fireplace, the night now still and The Messenger chuckling in the mountains.

Why, Pa?
Nobody knows, son. Nobody ever knows.
What'll we do?
We'll live.

> . . . They took you away
> And left me alone,
> They even took the baby . . .

BOOK ONE

Bluejay

CHAPTER I

YEAH, we keep up with politics pretty good around here. Why, just t'other day we took a poll of all the foxes. Three was for chickens and two was undecided. Better hold on to that hat you got there. Sally's getting ready to jump this crick." Bluejay probably never had so much fun as he did the time *The New Yorker* dispatched a writer to Sixkiller Gap for a series of stories on life in the Appalachian Outback. That was about the time Bluejay, thanks to his hit song "The Longer You're Gone (The Harder It Gets)," had been invited to join the brotherhood of regulars, right there alongside Roy Acuff and Ernest Tubb, on the Grand Ole Opry. The writer's name was Sean Shaughnessy, of a Boston address, a Harvard man, and in his letter to Bluejay he had said he was "interested in staying for a few days in order to paint a portrait of the quaint Southern Highlanders in their environs." Bluejay liked that. "Paint-a-quaint, paint-a-quaint," he kept chirping around the farm. So he figured he would oblige by wearing his Southern Highlander costume, the buckskins and plowing boots and coonskin cap, and riding the mule to the train depot in Andrews, on the grounds that the pickup wouldn't crank, to meet this Yankee writer. Shaughnessy, as though he had caught the spirit through mental telepathy, also showed up in uniform— red handlebar moustache, three-piece white suit, wire glasses, straw boater, black high-heeled button-up boots, bulging elephant-hide suitcase—and it was thusly that the two men, leaving the boys agog in their chairs at Jack the Clipper barbershop across the street from the depot, set forth atop Sally for the four-mile journey back into the hollow. "Don't get many Catholics around here," said Bluejay to Shaughnessy, once the issue came up. "Matter of fact, we probably got more virgins than we got Catholics in Andrews."

By all accounts the visit of Mr. Shaughnessy of *The New Yorker* to that corner of western North Carolina, which turned into a liquid two weeks, topped everything in Cherokee County history except the time in the thirties when a New Yorker named Roosevelt dared bring his presidential whistle-stop campaign through Andrews, right there in the midst of the Depression, and was hailed with rotten cabbages and signs saying COMINIST GO HOME and NO DAM DAM, the train not stopping again until it reached the relative safety of Chattanooga ninety miles down the track. Shaughnessy, who turned out to be a pitiful match for Bluejay when it came to drinking and lying, was given the run of the place. He gorged himself on gargantuan meals laid out by Bluejay's wife, Molly, she serenely blossoming in her fourth month of pregnancy. He gathered eggs in the dawn light with Bluejay and Molly's son, Jaybird, a gangly nine-year-old who was out of school and free to explore for the summer. From Sam Sixkiller, the ageless Cherokee whose ancestors had given the land its name, he learned the rudiments of taking bushels of corn and miraculously turning them into the meanest whiskey he had ever dared taste.

So he was thoroughly admitted into the fold, this educated man of the East, and every night when he tucked himself into the feather bed of the one-room log cabin to which he had been assigned, a cabin hewn from hickory and chinked with clay more than a century earlier by fathers of fathers of fathers, foreign sounds of wild dogs and owls and cicadas serenading in and out of the forbidding gaps and coves and hollows, he would raise the wick of the kerosene lamp and scribble with a mechanical pencil, on lined pages of spiral notepads bought at the Harvard Co-op in Cambridge, Massachusetts, notes on the day. "Simplicity overwhelming," he would write. *Inbred birth defects. Isolation. Pride. Ask Sam about Cherokees, Trail of Tears. Jaybird's future. Poor educations. Beyond Sixkiller Gap. Molly, the women. Electricity, appliances, television, planes.* Then, before shutting down the lamp, Sean Shaughnessy of Boston would write a short note to his wife, Abigail, a professor of sociology at Radcliffe, often ending with Bluejay's latest witticism. "He told me today that the only surprise he experienced upon actually hearing the Grand Ole Opry in person was, 'There wadn't no static.' "

And so they made the rounds, the Southern Highlander and the Yankee Writer, and once Shaughnessy had gained entrance to Bluejay's world he thought he would never shut him up. They stopped for a rest one afternoon on a bare knoll, far away from the main house, and sat in the grass beside the family burial plot. Granite boulders two feet high formed a square, some thirty feet by thirty feet, and inside the square was an odd collection of tombstones in every size and shape. There were granite stones and marble stones. Tall ones, stubby ones, simple flat ones slapped even with the ground and ornate angels soaring toward the sky. Beneath the monuments were fathers, sons, grandfathers, great-grandfathers, great-great-grandfathers, mothers, sisters, cousins, brothers, uncles and all of the rest. The only constant to the headstones was the last name: CLAY.

"I don't know how it is with y'all up there where you come from," said Bluejay. "Maybe you got books and what you call 'family trees' to tell you everything about your family and all. Only thing we got is old family Bibles and what's in our heads. I was joshing you about being Catholic the other day. Irish Catholic, at that. Well, it seems like that's how the Clays got started. The way I heard it from my daddy was that back there maybe three centuries ago there was this king over there, King James the First, and he was King of England and Ireland and Scotland all at the same time. Ireland was full of Catholics, especially up there in the northern part in a place called Ulster, and old King James didn't care much for Catholics. So he talked thousands of these old boys from Scotland into coming on down to Ulster for two reasons. He needed some more people to farm the land up there, number one, and number two the Scots were Protestants. So that's where we got the name 'Scotch-Irish,' best I can tell. Back then the Clays spelled it Klaegh, K-l-a-e-g-h, something like that. They were mean as hell. Drank whiskey, made music, worked like dogs, didn't take nothing from nobody, started up clans and all. Well, that didn't last more'n a century over there in Ireland. They got mad at the government for trying to tax their whiskey and generally messing with their lives so they got on boats and came to America. Most of 'em wound up in Pennsylvania, which was wild and had some hill country like they were used to, and they were still so mad at the English and so good at killing folks that they got to be just about George Washington's favorite troops during the Revolutionary War. I mean, hell, it was them and a bunch of Irish who'd been born in Pennsylvania and a few what-they-called 'Pennsylvania Dutch' that kicked the Indians out of the mountains and then turned around and beat up on the English. We got it in the Bible that Molly keeps at the house that my great-great-grandfather, Elijah Clay, was born in March of 1776, the same year the United States was born.

"So that's when what you might call the modern period began for us Clays. All of a sudden it was getting too crowded and the government was trying to tax their whiskey again, just like it had happened over in Ireland, so Elijah and them up and left. Some of 'em headed south and west and wound up populating what's East Texas now. But most of 'em came down here, right here to these mountains you're seeing, believe you call it the 'Southern Highlands,' where nobody but Indians had ever been. Talk about wild country. Even up around Asheville was too crowded for Elijah's taste so he and his brother, Jubal Clay, took their families and kept to the ridges, riding horses and beating off the Cherokees, until they came to this place you see right here. It was already called Sixkiller Gap back then, after Sam's great-grandfather, fellow they called 'Uwani Sutalitihi.' Means 'killed six men with arrows' in Cherokee. Good story about that. Know that crick back there in the hollow where Sam's got his moonshine still? This Uwani Sutalitihi was a wild buck who didn't cotton to the white men he saw coming into here around 1800, so he holed up in a cave overlooking what's now Sixkiller Creek and started knocking 'em off with his bow and arrows whenever they were out hunting and stopped there for water. Killed half a dozen of 'em before they finally got him. So there you got Sixkiller Gap, Sixkiller Creek, Sixkiller Farm and Sam Sixkiller. About all Sam knows is that when they found gold around here in the 1830s and started rounding up all the Cherokees so they could send 'em to Oklahoma and keep all the gold to themselves, that 'Trail of Tears' you read about, Sam's folks got away and headed for the hills. Sam says he was born around 1900, he guesses, because he was ten and more or less a member of the family when I was born in 1911. One time I asked him how come he wound up coming down out of the hills and living with white folks and he said he got tired of eating rattlesnakes and ramps.

"I got to back up here a little bit. Okay, 1810. Now that's when my great-grandfather, Buford Clay, was born in the house where me and Molly and Jaybird are living now. At first that old house was nothing but a one-room log cabin made out of hickory and clay by Elijah and them, the ones who came down from Pennsylvania. Over the years every generation has added something to the place. Buford came along and added another cabin next to it, making a dogtrot between the two, and somebody put in a place to cook and somebody else tacked on extra cabins for bedrooms. My grandfather was Newt Clay, the hell-raiser in the bunch. Born in, lemme see"—Bluejay stood up and craned his neck to find the gravestone—"yeah, 1840. Newt Clay, 1840. Built the first real good moonshine still on the place, drank about half of what he made, always into fights, laying ambushes for the excise men, had a couple of kids by squaws but kicked 'em out, got his leg shot off fighting the Yankees over there at Moccasin Bend. Came back from the war and had my daddy—that's Boone Clay, 1871—and put up most of the little buildings you've seen. If you look real close under the boards of that little cabin you're sleeping in you can see where he left his mark in the clay. There's a boot print and a round hole next to it. That was Grandpa Newt's peg leg. And I already told you most of the particulars about me and Pa. He was Boone Jubal Clay, named after the Jubal that first came to Sixkiller with Elijah, and he was into about everything—cutting timber, preaching, making whiskey, making music. Every Sunday, up there on the front porch at the big house, he'd put all four of 'em to work at once—sit there on the steps with a jug of whiskey and a Bible and this fiddle he'd made and by sundown everybody was full of whiskey and music and the Lord. So that's partly how I grew up. Henry Buford Clay, August 18, 1911, named after the famous Henry Clay up in Kentucky. Pa said he started calling me Bluejay because I was always raising hell and butting into other people's business. Probably right. Probably right. Come on, Mr. Shaughnessy, let's get back to the house. Molly's probably got supper on.''

Shaughnessy of *The New Yorker* was staggered by all of this material. He had played a crude form of lacrosse with Jaybird, Bluejay and Sam. He had sat in the kitchen watching Molly put up fresh vegetables in Mason jars for the rude Smoky Mountain winter. He had tested more than his share of Sam's superb whiskey. He had tagged along with Bluejay one night to hear him sing at a roadhouse between Andrews and Murphy, a steaming cinder-block building off the main road dubbed The Bear's Den, Bluejay running through his repertoire of what he called "my fightin'-and-dancin' songs," much fist-fighting and foot-stomping and manly challenging the order of the evening, all of the patrons asking Bluejay when was the next time he would be on the Opry. The writer had filled nearly a dozen of his spiral notebooks, front and back sides of each page, and when Bluejay dropped him off in the pickup truck at the depot fifteen days after his arrival he was too giddy with fresh knowledge to know how wrinkled and hung over and "just plain bone-tired," as Bluejay would put it, he really was. He felt as though the notebooks in his elephant-hide suitcase were the Dead Sea scrolls.

As the two men stood at the depot, waiting for the Chattanooga-to-Asheville train to come wheezing around the bend in the valley, the boys at Jack the Clipper once again froze in their chairs to gawk. Sean Shaughnessy was back in his three-piece cotton suit, washed and ironed by Molly, and Bluejay was back in his buckskin outfit. While they shared a ceremonial last drink from the jug Bluejay carried in the back of the pickup they tried to make small talk.

"How's that war doing over there?" said Bluejay.

"I beg your pardon?"

"One over there in Jay-pan. We got some boys there."

"It's only a matter of time. You don't keep up?"

"Aw, we get it in the *Citizen-Times* now and then."

"We're bombing Tokyo now," Shaughnessy said.

"That Jay-pan," said Bluejay. "That near China?"

"Why, yes. They're both in the Far East. Why do you ask?"

"Ginseng."

"Ginseng?"

"Yep. Might explain why we're gonna win that war."

"I don't understand."

Bluejay was patient. "Remember that tiny little root I showed you? That little bunch back in the woods, ones I asked you not to tell nobody about? Ginseng. Down at the hardware store old man Floyd gives me ten dollars for a shoebox full of it. Then he sells it to somebody else and sooner or later it winds up in China. Chinamen think it'll make your dick hard."

"So it's an aphrodisiac?"

"Whatever."

"So?"

"Well," Bluejay said, "if a Chinaman's that dumb and he's next door to the Japs then I figure the Japs are dumb, too. And anybody that thinks ginseng makes your dick hard ain't got no business winning no war."

"Are you serious, Mr. Clay?"

" 'Course not, Mr. Shaughnessy. But it's a thought. So's ramps."

"Ramps?"

"Pull 'em up out of the ground like onions, except they smell worse. If a boy wants to play hookey he eats ramps for breakfast and the teacher won't let him through the door."

"So your plan is to sell ramps to the Japanese, then?"

"You got it right. They'd get to where they couldn't stand to be around each other."

Shaughnessy enjoyed the first full-bodied laugh of his visit. *These mountain people,* he thought. Each man took another sip from the jug and it was then that Shaughnessy remembered something which had been puzzling him. "Mr. Clay," he said.

"Bluejay. Just call me Bluejay."

"All right. Bluejay. There is something I meant to ask."

"Let 'er rip, Mr. Shaughnessy."

"Well. For two weeks now I've noticed something curious about your place. The light bulbs and the wiring. In the cabin where I stayed, for instance, there was a bulb hanging from the ceiling. There were electrical outlets in the walls. There was a lamp on the table. There was a light switch beside the door. But when I tried the switch there was no electricity. The same I found to be true all over the farm. Light bulbs, you see, but no electricity. I thought perhaps you're behind in your payments to the power company."

"Naw, naw, naw," said Bluejay. "We're just ready."

"Ready."

"Yeah, see, Andrews and all the other little towns around here, they've had electricity ever since the TVA came. But the people up there in all those little hollows, us folks in places like Sixkiller, they ain't bothered to run the wires out to us yet. So I guess for about two years now me and some of the other fellows that get around some, like old Smead Holly the mail carrier, we been taking petitions around with us. Everybody we see we get 'em to sign up to bring the electricity to places like Sixkiller. One night at the Opry I got about sixty names. Even Red Foley signed it. We probably got about three thousand names already. Next thing we do is show it to the Nantahala Light & Power. Then we'll have 'em treed like a 'coon."

"So the lights are installed. Just 'waiting.' "

"Right," said Bluejay. "Fellow down at the light company gave me a book that showed how to do wiring and the next time I got a big check for my record I went down to the hardware store and 'bout bought old man Floyd out of wires and switches and bulbs. Every switch on the place is sitting on ON, just waiting for the juice. I hope it goes on in the middle of the night. Make some of these Holy Rollers think the Lord really *has* come this time. Drive the chickens crazy, thinking they forgot to lay their eggs. And Jaybird, he'll start dressing for school and it won't be but three o'clock in the morning."

They had another good laugh and another good sip of whiskey. Bluejay went to the truck and brought out the clipboard he kept amid the pile of road maps and royalty statements and fan letters in the front seat. He had personally gathered better than seven hundred signatures and he asked Shaughnessy to add his to the list. "Put down there that you're from Boston and maybe it'll mean something extra," Bluejay said. Shaughnessy obliged, adding "Harvard" in parentheses, and the train came and he got on it and headed back to "civilization," as he defined it.

Late in the fall, when Sean Shaughnessy's report from Sixkiller Gap, North Carolina, appeared in *The New Yorker* under the title "U.S. Journal: Appalachia's Wilds," it had people talking. The editors at the magazine gave Shaughnessy a bonus and promised him more free-lance work. Shaughnessy even put together a lecture tour for himself, hitting all of the Ivy League schools and the smaller ones in between, becoming the resident expert in New England on the charming rigors of life in the Southern Outback. There was a brief demand for the records of Bluejay Clay, since he was the primary focus of the article, but interest died before RCA Victor could get any country music into eastern stores. Bluejay liked the story all right—he left a copy of *The New Yorker* at the post office so everybody could read it—figuring Shaughnessy had described Sixkiller as it had been and was and always would be.

Then came the letters from the East. They commiserated, thanked, applauded, wept and laughed. They sent money for food. They mailed packages containing hand-me-down clothes for Jaybird. Somebody even mailed a new steam iron for Molly. Bluejay had neither a typewriter nor a secretary nor the time and inclination to respond to the mail, it being so overwhelming, but he did answer one letter. It was from a woman in Baltimore who wanted to spend her two weeks' vacation at Sixkiller Farm ("I am prepared to pay all of my expenses, of course, plus a generous gratuity") in order to "better understand the plight of our downtrodden." And so it was that one night Bluejay hunkered down beside the kerosene lamp and, using one of Jaybird's school pencils and a lined sheet of paper torn from a composition notebook, wrote the lady in Baltimore that since Mr. Shaughnessy's visit he had been forced to abandon his career and most of the work around the farm because so far three toes and four fingers and all of his hair had mysteriously left him during the nights. "It's the Smoky Mountain Wobbleys," he wrote. "Runs in the family."

CHAPTER II

MUCH had transpired during the years following the visit of *The New Yorker* to Sixkiller, not the least being the deaths of Molly Clay and her son-to-be on that fierce January night of The Messenger, and it had been a crowded time on the pages of the Clay family Bible. One night, in his despair, before the lights came on, Bluejay had taken the quill pen kept next to the kerosene lamp on the table beside the great fireplace and written, on the ragged opening page to Genesis, "Molly said there was a God but there ain't." Bluejay's days, since the death of his Molly, were occupied well enough by the mundane matters of the world—tending to the farm, keeping the machines and the books in order, turning out the crops, making his assignations at the Opry at least once a month, answering fan mail when he felt like it ("Me and my husband Merle drove all the way from Denton to see you on the Opry and you was the best"), fishing with Sam, rooting on winter nights for the Andrews High Raiders basketball team (Jaybird, now fifteen, was a reluctant starting forward whose mind was more on the cheerleaders)— but the nights were another matter. It was at night, when the wild dogs howled and the cicadas laughed and the laurels beckoned, that Bluejay had to deal with forces he couldn't understand. In the feather bed in the back room of the big house on Sixkiller Farm, in that bed Bluejay Clay had shared with the only woman he had ever known, there came the voices of the past. *Goddam Catholics*, said King James I. *A Klaegh kin whip any Irish*, shouted some sotted Scotsman. *Our land, our land, rhymes with Ireland*, spake a Clay to William Penn. *Sixkiller, sixkiller, he killed six*, said the Cherokees. *Jaybird is the last, the last, the last*, said Molly, screaming and clawing, from her deathbed.

So Bluejay stuck with what he knew. It was a fact that Molly and the baby had died at stillbirth and were buried on the hill with the others. It was a fact that the electricity had come on one late afternoon in the summer of '45, as Jaybird took a nap, touching off a celebration of drinking Sam's best and shooting Jaybird's basketball and playing Bluejay's records on the brand-new electrified RCA Victor phonograph and going out to the henhouse now and then to see how Clucky, the head hen, liked Mr. Edison's warming invention. It was a fact that the well worked, the hogs fattened, the cows gave milk, the pickup started on cold mornings, the rhododendron blossomed in the spring, the sun rose above Standing Indian Mountain in the morning, the Asheville *Citizen-Times* still cost a nickel and was stuck into the mailbox by four o'clock every afternoon by Smead Holly atop his swayback horse, Don McNeil's "Breakfast Club" came in over WCHT from Chattanooga every morning at daybreak and at night on television you could watch this big-chested woman named Dagmar make a fool of herself on "Jerry Lester's Broadway Open House." Simplicity was the key for Bluejay, now in his forties, and he liked it that way.

Around Andrews and Murphy and Hayesville and the other towns in that corner of western North Carolina, an inquiry as to the whereabouts of one Henry Buford Clay, whether coming from a bow-tied Internal Revenue Service agent or a family of goggle-eyed Opry fans who had stumbled into Sixkiller Gap, always brought the same general exchange. *You talkin' 'bout Bluejay Clay, one plays the Opry?/We thought maybe he wouldn't mind, I mean the kids been promised/Well, he's awful busy/But we come all the way from Danville just to meet him/ What you do is head toward Cherokee and turn right at the filling station/We bought all his records/And then you go 'bout*

two miles out on the paved road/We seen him one time in
Blacksburg/And then follow the dirt road about two football
fields/Even hear him on WWVA/And you can't miss it.

And they couldn't miss it. When he got the time and some
money Bluejay took a hickory log and rived it three inches thick
and hewed out the letters SIXKILLER and burnished the letters so
they would stand out against the sky and when you passed beneath that archway, suspended between two poplar trunks over-
come with ivy, split-rail fences heading either way to surround
the one-hundred-acre spread, you knew you were there. Two
dozen chickens had run of the place. Everywhere in the rich
black bottom there were the tools of the farm. Plows and tractors
and pickup trucks and harrows and tin pails, each with the hand-
painted *imprimateur* 6-K, were left abandoned where they were
last used. There was the two-seat A-Model Ford runabout and
the barn painted with a SEE ROCK CITY sign and the stark blue
'46 Bluebird bus, the chariot used by Bluejay and his band as
they lurched about the country taking joy to the people, decorated with the simple message BLUEJAY CLAY & THE SIXKILLERS.
STARS GRAND OLE OPRY. SIXKILLER, NORTH CAROLINA. "THE LONGER
YOU'RE GONE THE HARDER IT GETS" & OTHER HITS.

So it wasn't hard to find Bluejay's spread, Sixkiller, and you
had to be blind to miss the man himself. He was a towering
scraggly pine tree, well over six feet tall but only one hundred
and sixty pounds heavy, with the amiable wobble of a woodsman
who had wandered into town looking for supplies. His eyes were
as blue as the Smoky Mountain sky on a June day, his face as
creased as a relief map of the Applachians, his legs as thin as
saplings, his hands as gnarled as ginseng roots, his ears as floppy
as butterfly wings, his elongated feet as uncertain as canoes
slipping into a stream, his hair as sleek-black as a raven's coat.
You could see Bluejay Clay coming from two hundred yards
away, the way he shuffled along the dusty main drag of town,
puffing on a roll-your-own Bull Durham cigarette, cowboy hat
tilted forward, high-heeled Opry boots dragging behind him, not
exactly walking toward Jack the Clipper's as much as being drawn
to it. "Yeah, well, I can explain about how come my left leg's a

foot longer than the right one," he would drawl to Sage and Hink and the other men lazing away the afternoon in the barbershop, repeating the line he always gave in interviews, "as could anybody who tried to plow behind a mule on these hills we got around here."

It was a simple place in a simple time, the Appalachian hollows in the middle of the twentieth century, and few people along the streams and on the high passes and in the deep-gap crossroads communities there showed any awareness, or even cared, of what was going on beyond their particular corner of the world. They vaguely knew, from their daily perusals of the day-late newspapers, that in some place called Korea there was a new war going on and the President, Harry S Truman, was stomping mad at one of his generals for not doing what he was told to do. They didn't pay much attention to news of that sort, anyway, the boys at Jack the Clipper, they being more titillated by what John Parris, the columnist for the *Citizen-Times*, had to say about home remedies for "the fever," the mountaineer's coverall for every disease from menstrual pains to alcoholism, and such fine arts as raising 'coon dogs and keeping the bears out of the beehives. They were not nearly as impressed by the latest spring creations from Paris as they were by Mindy McFeely, Abner and Minnie's daughter, who won first prize in the state Future Homemakers of America contest with a wardrobe made entirely of burlap bags.

One Sunday night, over the radio, they heard Ted Mack of "The Original Amateur Hour" warmly welcome a mechanic from Paducah, Kentucky, who could slap out "Dixie" on his cheeks. Simple places, simple times. Tusquitee, Nantahala Lake, Hiawassee Dam, Granny's Squirrel Gap, Bug Scuffle Creek. The day the lights came on. Amos 'n' Andy, the Opry, "John's Other Wife" and "The Life of Riley" on radio. Loretta Young and John Wayne at the picture show. "Smilin' Jack" and "Gasoline Alley" and "Terry and the Pirates" on the funny pages. John L. Lewis, Dean Acheson, Ike, Alger Hiss, Grantland Rice, Professor Backwards, Roy Acuff, Ted Williams ("Way I hear it, he sees so good the umpires ask *him* whether it's a ball or a strike," Hink opined one day). Paper for a nickel, breakfast for a quarter, man's suit $65, fanciest new car $2,149 (Nash Ambassador Airflyte, makes into twin beds, man could drive all the way to Texas and back without stopping for a hotel). Exchange Club in Fairmont, West Virginia, offers $500 one-way passage to Russia for anybody who'd rather live there. Junior Stephens tells the Red Sox he won't play for less than $50,000 a season. Actress named Jane Russell practically takes her clothes off in a hayloft in *The Outlaw*. Young preacher named Billy Graham, not but thirty-one, tries to warn the Georgia Legislature about all of this. But how about that fellow from Paducah who could slap out "Dixie" on his cheeks.

It took billions of years for the glaciers, inexorably grinding south-by-southwestward down from the frozen Arctic, to create North America's oldest mountain chain. By the middle of the twentieth century the Appalachians—dark, forbidding, hazy from gasses expended in the birth-to-decay process of vegetation (thus, the Smoky Mountains)—was a jagged forested spine of the eastern United States which meandered more than two thousand miles from Mount Katahdin in uppermost Maine to Lookout Mountain at Chattanooga, Tennessee, roughly where the states of Tennessee, Alabama, Georgia and North Carolina rub up against each other. The personality of the Appalachians, and of the people like Bluejay Clay who lived there, was formed by its geography. Quite simply, it was hard to get from one valley to another. One's valley created the boundary for one's life. One was born and educated and married and employed and buried in the same valley, as evidenced by the Clays of Cherokee County in western North Carolina, and that wasn't likely to change much faster than it had taken the ice to change the land.

But now, with the coming of electricity and automobiles and television and superhighways and airplanes and thousands of other seemingly minor accoutrements (*things*, like Mixmasters and automatic transmissions and electric razors), the people of Appalachia were about to be dragged unwillingly into the American mainstream. Bluejay Clay would be able to look back, nearly three decades later, to the very moment when he realized that life for the Clays would never be the same again.

It was on a day soon after Shorty Hunsinger, Bluejay's manager in Nashville, had called to say it might be a good idea to
drive on up for a few days and do the Opry and talk some business
and maybe cut another record. Bluejay hadn't been to Nashville
for a while and the trip seemed to be an altogether plausible
idea. The bus needed some work done on it, for one thing, before
he could make the swing through Alabama and Mississippi laid
out by Shorty for most of the month of June. He hadn't played
the Opry in a month, for another, and he knew how picky they
were at WSM about Opry regulars fulfilling their quota of appearances. And as far as he could recall the last time he had seen
the inside of a recording studio was two years earlier, at least,
when he caught Owen Bradley at the Tulane Hotel from a pay
phone at Frankie's Pool Hall and zipped on over to the studio at
the hotel and walked out three hours later with the makings for
an album called "Best of Bluejay." The album "didn't do pig-
squat," Bluejay remembered Shorty's reporting, so there was no
reason to doubt the perspicacity of the trip.

He would take the bus, going it alone because Jaybird was
still in school, so he could leave it with his mechanic for a couple
of days. He would stay at Mom Upchurch's, where Carl Smith
and some of the other younger Opry stars lived out of the re-
frigerator, so he could cut expenses and bum rides to downtown.
He would drop by Linebaugh's Cafe on Broadway to make some
"homemade 'mater soup," as they called it— *Bring me some ice
water, hold the ice, need some soda crackers, and I notice the
ketchup's 'bout out*—for old times' sake. He would see Grant
Turner and Ernest Tubb and all of the other Opry people and
experience all of the joys of being on the Grand Ole Opry on a
Saturday night, not the least of them being the pleasure of darting
across the street from the Ryman for a quick beer between shows
at Essie May's Blue Room and catching up on the latest gossip
like what *really* happened to Hank Williams from Essie May
Strunk herself.

So going to Nashville for a few days was an altogether fine
idea, Bluejay was thinking, as he shoved his traveling clothes
into two spangled suitcases once given him by the Bluejay Boost-

ers fan club of Crestview, Florida, Bonnie Butler, President, Bluejay being careful not to wrinkle his Opry "suit of lights" so the sequins would crumble and making sure the buckskin suit he would knock around Mom Upchurch's in looked reasonably humble. That done, a note left to Sam about the fellow at the farmer's market in Asheville who wanted to buy the entire lot of Christmas trees from Sixkiller Farms this year, he stepped out onto the front porch of the house and surveyed the place. Sixkiller. Everything Bluejay Clay had been, was, and would be.

It was a beautiful spring day. Sally, the albino cat Bluejay had named after the swayback horse he had traded in for an Airflyte, was being bombarded and dive-bombed by screeching bluejays. A moist pungent smell hung in the air from the rich black over-turned dirt. Chickens scratched and clucked. A stickety-stickety-stickety came from the new asphalt road above the knob. Bluejay swore he could hear the corn growing, it being such a day for life, but he wasn't quite sure what the noise was which came from where Jaybird, down to his bathing suit and shaking his head to a rhythm, stood barefoot and hosed down the bus.

> My daddy's got a long (*unh*) Cadillac,
>   An' when he puts it in (*anh*) th' garage;
> It's just the way he (*umhh*) slides it in,
>   That makes me wanna (*oohhh*) watch again . . .

Bluejay froze. *Me and Molly*, he felt, *well, I never, I mean, me and Molly*, stomping down the steps and mowing through the high grass toward his son, this son of an Ulster, this son of Clay, *the very idea*, now standing half-naked in the sun beneath the shade of bright green elms planted by Elijah and Boone Clay and the others, *I don't know, about the time of the Trail of Tears*, and here he was.

"Son," Bluejay shouted.

"Oh, hi, Pa," said Jaybird.

"Oh, hi, Pa? What's that?"

"What?"

"What? The music. That *noise*."

"Just some music."

"Music? Good godamitey, boy. Since when's *that* music?"

"Aw, Pa, it's just WERD over in Chattanooga. They used to play your songs all the time, remember?"

"WERD? Playing that stuff?"

"Kids listen to it all the time."

"Well, by God, *you* ain't," said Bluejay. His son flushed, bent over, the garden hose spraying his father in the chest as it passed, and turned off the portable radio at his feet. Jaybird went back to hosing the bus. Bluejay pointed to a spot the boy had missed, picked up the radio and stomped back to the house. He couldn't help himself: he turned on the radio and heard the voice of the disc jockey from WERD. "Sam the Bird, gang, with the word from WERD. Yes, sir, the Bird from Word . . ." Bluejay found the button that said OFF.

CHAPTER III

NOT EVEN the disconcerting scene with Jaybird could spoil the day for Bluejay as he shoved the bus into gear and left Sixkiller for Nashville. "Middle Tennessee," a fellow from *Newsweek* had written, "with its funny little hills that blip across the horizon as though a kindergarten child had scrawled them with a crayon." It never looked lovelier, in spite of the scarred red hills abandoned by the strip miners around Copperhill and the smoky back alleys of Chattanooga littered with winos' desperate smashed half-pint bottles and the bulldozers' carvings for new subdivisions along the banks of the Tennessee River near Jasper, as Bluejay pressed on along old U.S. 41. In the valleys, meandering with the two-lane asphalt highway, the bus cruised past SEE ROCK CITY signs and rickety log cabins and chenille bedspread stands and homemade signs tacked to pine trees praising everything from God to birdbaths, onward through the spooky Sequatchie Valley. Bluejay took lunch at Monteagle.

"Excuse me?"

"Sir?"

"I was wondering."

" 'bout what?"

"That your bus out there?"

"When everything's working, it is."

"You Bluejay? Bluejay Clay?"

It wasn't noon yet. Bluejay looked through the plate-glass window of the cafe and saw the bus sitting in the gravel. BLUEJAY CLAY & THE SIXKILLERS. He wondered when they were going to bring him his iced tea and his napkin and how long it would be before they brought him his chicken-fried steak. The fellow who had asked if he really was *the* Bluejay Clay, "one on the Opry," said his name was Joe Frank something and would it be all right if his wife and their two girls came over to meet him. Bluejay said fine and they waddled over, Joe Frank's wife and daughters, and he signed his name to several picture postcards of Rock City and ate lunch fast and ran across the lot to the bus while it was still there. An hour or so later, just after passing the exit for Middle Tennessee State University, he heard the disc jockey for WLAC in Nashville say the next hour would be devoted to Golden Oldies. "Now," the DJ said, "here's Bluejay Clay with his greatest hit, 'The Longer You're Gone.' Need I say more?" And the air rushed through the open window of the bus and Bluejay licked his lips and the music played. Roy Acuff's "Wabash Cannonball" was on when Bluejay saw the billboard saying OPRY MOTEL and turned off the highway and drove the bus around to the rear and parked next to the purple Cadillac with a license plate saying SHORTY.

Shorty Hunsinger's office was the house trailer next to the Cadillac. Shorty didn't want to hear about "funny little hills" scrawled by kindergartners because he had seen more than enough of each. He was a squat dark-skinned man with a greasy black crewcut and purple Western-cut suits from Nudie's in Hollywood and dazzling rings on his fingers and the foulest vocabulary Bluejay had ever heard. It was Shorty's aim in life to live in a big brick house in the middle of Kansas with a horny wife whose "daddy owns a mess of Cadillacs and the Jack Daniel distributorship." When somebody asked Shorty how that would be, what kind of life would that be, riding around the Great Plains forever in a purple Cadillac with a case of Black Jack in the back seat and a sex machine in the front, he blinked in disbelief. "Heaven," he said, "you talkin' 'bout fuckin' *heaven*." In order to reach the promised land he represented three dozen "recording artists," all the way from Bluejay Clay to a foul-mouthed country comic named Bama Red, and for his services he grabbed twenty percent right off the top.

Bluejay shut down the engine of the bus and unfolded from the cab, making sure to lock the door, then crunched in his high-heeled boots through the pungent gravel of the lot to the door of the trailer. J. MORTON HUNSINGER said the nameplate on the door to the trailer, and Bluejay blew open the door with his right hand and produced a jug of Sam Sixkiller's finest with his left. Shorty was on the phone. He waved his eyebrows when he saw Bluejay come in.

"That's it," Shorty was saying on the phone. "Who the hell else is gonna go to fuckin' Lubbock on Saturday for a goddam two hundred bucks? You got any idea how far it is to Lubbock these days? Shit. Fuckin' George Morgan'll cost you nine hundred, easy . . . All right. Naw, I'll call *you*, you ass-hole . . . Bet your sweet ass, pal. I'll get back to you . . ." Shorty slammed the phone and belched and stood up. He wore a see-through lavender nylon shirt and a skinny white suede belt and shiny black gabardine slacks and pointy-toed high-heeled boots. "Well," Shorty said, "fuck a rubber duck. They let you out for the weekend?"

"Now and then."

"How's your hammer hanging?"

"Fair to partly cloudy," Bluejay said.

"And my, my, what the hell's *that*?"

"I don't know what you're talking about."

"Jug there."

"Jug? I don't see no jug."

"Goddam jug in your hand."

Bluejay said, "Oh, *that* one. I don't rightly know what's in it. Sam give it to me as I was leaving. Said it was a present for Mister Shorty. Why don't we see what's in it?" The two men shook hands and Shorty broke out a pair of motel-room tumblers wrapped in cellophane and Bluejay pulled the cork from the clay jug and poured whiskey. "Here's to your Mama 'n' them," said Bluejay. A disheveled young girl stumbled out of the door from the bedroom of the trailer—*Wanda*, Shorty said, *ain't no trouble, just wants to know what day it is*—and they drank to that and praised Sam and pure spring water and Jaybird's basketball and how Eisenhower would make a perfect President and the price of corn and, finally, what Shorty had called about in the first place.

"You been listening to the radio lately?" Shorty said.

"Some."

"What you been listening to?"

"Aw, WSM. WAVE, one in Asheville."

"What they playing?"

"Heard 'em do 'Longer You're Gone' while ago. Had the radio on down around Murfreesboro. Picked up WLAC."

"I'll be damn. When'd you cut that song, Blue?"

"About '43, I reckon."

"Made a lot of money, didn't it?"

"Enough to pay the rent."

"Nineteen and forty-three, you say."

"Best I can remember." Bluejay took another belt from the jug. "You know, Short, this songwriting's the biggest racket I ever heard of. Molly was over in Chattanooga for about a week looking after things when her Mama died and I got to missing her and just sat down and made up some words about it. Bet it didn't take me twenty minutes. Longer she stayed away the harder it got to keep up with things around the place. Just sat down there with my guitar and everything started to work. 'Longer you're gone, the harder it gets.' I didn't do much thinking about the words until the Baptists brought it up. Swear to God I didn't."

"Blue," Shorty said, "you're as full of shit as me."

"I don't think that's possible, coach."

"You knew goddam well what you were doing."

"Well, yeah, maybe, but then I got too rich to quit."

Shorty Hunsinger hunched back deeply into his swivel chair and yelled over his shoulder, to Wanda, to hold the calls. When he found his box of English Ovals and fumbled through his pockets for a light, the cigarette dangling from his mouth, he acknowledged Bluejay's striking a kitchen match on the desk and offering him a light. Shorty leaned to one side and farted, a ploy

that always worked in crucial moments of poker games at the
Drake Motel when it was three o'clock in the morning and everybody was drunk, and then he rocked back in the swivel chair
and he spoke.

"See that guitar? One under the window?"

"Noticed it. Nice instrument. Where'd you get it at?"

"Play it."

"How come?"

"I want you to play me that song they tell me you been
singing down there in the clubs. One about Molly. Stink told
me he stopped by one of them places outside Hayesville one
night to get a beer and you was playing and there was a bunch
of people there." Bluejay, nonplussed, shook his head and Shorty
waggled his hand at him. "Now wait, Blue. Wadn't nobody paying attention while you sang all that Hank Williams shit so then,
now this is according to Stink, Stink says the minute you stood
up and threw your stool down on the floor and told everybody
to shut up"—Bluejay was rolling his eyes now—"now, Blue,
goddamit, just stay with me here. Stink says you got 'em quiet
and then you started singing some sick thing about your wife
and your baby dying at the same time. He says you started crying
and everybody else cried. I'd like to hear what you did."

Bluejay shrugged. It took one giant step for him to reach the
guitar propped against the wall, his bony fingers taking the neck
as gently as a fisherman reaches for the perfect rainbow trout at
the end of the line, the same giant step for him to move back
in front Shorty's desk and finger the frets and begin to sing, as
he had sung years ago, not in a skittery metal trailer in the middle
of nowhere but in front of a fire shared by generations, in front
of a fire with a boy whittling and the bluejays squalling and The
Messenger laughing out there in the dark, blue flames and tears
and winds and coyotes and Cherokees all a part of the plot,
Bluejay's song.

> Molly my love,
> Molly my love,
> Molly my fair sweet lady.

They took you away,
And left me alone,
They even took the baby . . .

"Sad," Shorty said when Bluejay had finished. "Damned sad. I always liked Molly. Hell of a cook." Bluejay took the bandanna from his hip pocket and used it to clean the frets. While he was at it he wiped his face. "Hell of a *woman*," Bluejay said, placing the guitar against the wall, blowing his nose into the bandanna and looking through the grim window at the bus dormant in the gravel.

Shorty rapped on the door to the bedroom of the trailer while Bluejay was looking through the window. Wanda, dyed black hair tousled, jaws working Juicy Fruit, leaned through the crack. "Busy," she said. "Wake the sumbitch up and get him out here, right now," Shorty told her. " 'kay, in-*see*-ust." Rustling of clothes, words passing, trucks passing, jeans zipping, Bluejay waiting, door opening and closing.

"Got the tape?" Shorty said.

"It's somewhere."

"Blue, you know Stinky Bohannon."

"Sure."

"What's up, Blue?"

"Okay."

"Where's the goddam tape, Stink?" Shorty ran through piles of press releases and letters and "demo" tapes and panties and all of the other clutter a personal manager comes across in his day while Stinky Bohannon, lead guitarist for a new band calling itself Stinky & The Gang, stuffed his shirttail into his jeans and tried to get his day organized. Wanda whined through the door, Bluejay sat in bemused silence, Stinky belched and Shorty threw records and newsletters and tapes all over the floor of the trailer until he found what he was looking for.

"Want you to hear this, Blue," said Shorty.

"Yeah," said Stinky.

"Got a demo here. Heard about that song you did about Molly. Hired Stinky and them to kind of change it a little. Thought you

might like it. Got a nice modern beat to it." Shorty stuck the
tape into a tape recorder on his desk. "Call it 'Molly-Molly.'"

> Molly-molly
>   Will you be mine,
> Molly-molly
>   You're so divine . . .

Bluejay bolted straight up out of his chair when he heard it.
Stinky was snapping his fingers and rolling his eyes. Shorty was
saying, "Wait, now, Blue, just wait"—

> Molly-molly
>   Where you been hid,
> Molly-molly
>   Won't you have my kid . . .

—"Give it a chance,
now, Blue"—

> Ah-hah, ah-hah,
> Molly-molly . . .

—until, finally, Bluejay had heard enough. He came
down on the tape recorder with the heel of his fist, causing plastic
shards to fly. Shorty banged backwards against the wall, Stinky
began groveling on the floor in search of the tape and Wanda
wailed from the bedroom, "What y'all doin' in *thay-uh*?" Bluejay
beat Stinky to the tape and began to rip it from its spool like a
crazed kitten tearing into a ball of yarn. And suddenly there was
silence. The men, Bluejay and Shorty, stood face-to-face.
    "Well?" said Shorty.
    "Well, what?"
    "What do you think?"
    "For starters," Bluejay said, "you're fired. Not that you was
ever exactly hired."
    "Fired? After everything I've done for you?"
    "I didn't hear you singing. I didn't see you driving. I didn't
hear you snoring on no bus in Texas. All I saw was 'twenty-
percent, twenty-percent,' and the inside of more fightin'-and-

dancin' clubs than Oklahoma's got oil wells. 'Personal manager,' you say. Well, old buddy, you've just personally managed to fuck yourself out of twenty percent of whatever this old hide's worth. I figure the longer you're gone the easier it's gonna get. Gimme Sam's whiskey back. I might be needing it."

The foray into Nashville, with that as a beginning, turned out to be a dreggy affair. He left his bus for overnight repairs with his mechanic, an erstwhile stock-car driver *cum* moonshine runner named Pig Lipscomb, accepting a ride in Pig's pickup across the river to Mom Upchurch's boardinghouse, where he was greeted with backslaps and a mess of turnip greens and pinto beans and cornbread. He swapped stories of the road with the boys from George Morgan's band— "The goddam fog was so bad I had to get out and *feel* the sign to see which way it was to Roanoke"—called Owen Bradley at the studio in the Tulane Hotel to say he would have a song to record on the next trip, had a beer and signed some autographs at Essie's before running across the alley to sing "The Longer You're Gone" at the Friday Night Opry, picked up the bus the next morning, sang his song again on Saturday night and then, fighting off a crowd of fans trying to block his bus in the parking lot behind Ryman Auditorium, shoved the bus into gear and headed home with only the sounds of the Opry coming in over WSM to keep him company. He tried to build an analogy between the winding lonesome road and his career, giving a blast of the horn as he sped past Shorty Hunsinger's trailer, but all he could come up with was that at least he knew where the road went.

CHAPTER IV

SAM SIXKILLER, Bluejay was thinking as he hoisted the dusty old television set onto the bed of the pickup truck, had to be the most complicated man God or whoever created. He was, on the one hand, undeniably a full-blooded Cherokee with all of the attendant traits: hawkish eyes, sleek-black hair, wind-burned bronze skin, prominent cheekbones, the passivity of a true stoic who has seen it all. On the other hand, though, he could be as outrageously Scotch-Irish as any man in western North Carolina: moonshiner, womanizer, brawler, practical joker, horse trader and all-around good old boy. Somewhere between Uwani Sutalitihi and the Andrews Public Library, where Sam was the most frequent customer, a hybrid had been formed. Here was an Indian who refused to kill his game with a rifle—stalking off into the woods, instead, at the first hint of autumn, in search of his deer with a single arrow and a pair of moccasins and a night's supply of cornbread and chocolate—but knew the most intricate details behind the new F-86 jet fighter planes the United States Air Force was using in Korea. As a consequence the boys at Jack the Clipper, as mean a bunch of Indian-baiters as there was in the valley, laughed not *at* Sam Sixkiller but *with* him. It had been that way ever since John Parris, the roving columnist for the Asheville *Citizen-Times*, had lionized him as western Carolina's "Renaissance Redskin."

35

Bluejay was giving the Motorola TV to Sam that morning, having bought a new and larger one for himself and Jaybird, but that was more a pretense than anything else. He and Sam needed to talk. Jaybird was approaching a critical time in his life, a time when long-range plans such as a college education had to be considered, and then there was the matter of the changes in Bluejay's own life brought about by his firing of Shorty Hunsinger. He negotiated the pickup along the rutted path leading to Sixkiller Creek and stopped beside the old log cabin Sam called home. Already parked beside the cabin was a '46 Dodge coupe with a Tennessee license plate.

"Ho, Chief," Bluejay called.

"How," came the voice of Sam.

"Got peace offering here."

"No war. No need peace offering."

"Well, I'm paying in advance. Come here and help me before I get a hernia." Sam came out to the truck and helped Bluejay with the television set. They carried it through the door and set it on the floor of the front room of the cabin, which Sam, over the thirty years he had lived there, had partitioned into three rooms: one for living, one for sleeping, one for junk. Bluejay had given up trying to talk Sam into moving in with him and Jaybird in the main house, on the grounds that the telephone and the television and the shower stall and the electric range and all of the other modern amenities were there, because the cabin was Sam personified. The main room alone was an indescribable collage that only the Smithsonian Institution could appreciate— earthen moonshine jugs, cheesecake calendars, bear traps, prophylactics, assorted war bonnets, ratty books on everything from Chinese culture to *The Family of Ants*, axes and bows and boots and buckskins and dirty clothes and dishes—and only Sam could abide.

"Why don't you get a rake and clean up the place?" Bluejay said.

"Then I wouldn't know where anything was," said Sam.

"Makes sense, I guess."

" 'The messier the desk, the clearer the mind.' "

"You read that somewhere? Who said that?"

"Sam Sixkiller."

Sam cleared one end of a hand-hewn oak table with the sweep of an arm, half of his collection of 78-rpm records clattering to the floor, and the two men placed the Motorola in the clearing. Bluejay plugged in the set and they stood back to observe snowy images—it looked like a wrestling match—drifting in and out from Chattanooga. An aerial could come later. Sam poured generously from a jug of whiskey he kept on the hearth and, when they could find a place to sit, they sat. The wrestling match continued.

"See you got some company," said Bluejay.

"Professor."

"Damn, Sam, what you doing, starting a university?"

"University of Chattanooga. Wants to know about the Trail of Tears."

"What's his name? Maybe I heard about him."

"Name's Brenda."

"Brenda? Why, you old fart. Last week it was that little preacher's girl, what's-her-name. Ain't you ever gonna learn that they all taste the same?"

"Not finished with my research yet."

"Well, I finished mine a long time ago."

"Ten years ago," said Sam.

Bluejay eased up from his chair, snapped off the television set, poured another shot of moonshine from the jug and sat back down. The subject of Molly seldom came up. He thought about her every night, sure, especially on the cold nights when the wind was tossing pails across the yard or the slashing Appalachian rain was tearing at the corrugated tin roof—on those nights like Molly's last one on earth—and now and then Jaybird would come across some old family photographs and ask questions like "What'd Mama smell like, Pa?" And, of course, being Bluejay Clay of the Grand Ole Opry, thrust out there amid adoring women who would kill to become mistress of Sixkiller Farm, was a constant reminder that he was, as Essie May Strunk would say, available. But he resisted. It was easy.

"Lot of people can't figure it out," Bluejay said, to himself as much as to Sam. "They see this fella, got lots of money and a place, star on the Opry and all that, running around without a woman. Essie got to talking about it the last time I was up to Nashville. I told her it's like a fine guitar. Once you've played one of them Gibsons you'll never want to play anything else. Molly was a Gibson."

"What if you lose it?" said Sam.

"You've just lost it, that's all."

"But you could go out and get another one."

"Wouldn't work."

"Why not? They make lots of Gibson guitars."

"No, they don't. They make one per man. I've had mine."

The dismissal of Shorty Hunsinger had given Bluejay cause to stop everything and evaluate his situation. His next birthday would be his forty-third. Jaybird would graduate from high school soon, the first Clay to do so, and Bluejay wanted him also to be the first in the family to go to college. The boy was precocious, all right, having gotten almost a second education from hanging out with Sam—hearing Sam's Indian stories, reading his books, learning how to live on the land—and he was going to need every edge because he was going to see more abrupt changes in the next ten years than most Clay men had experienced in a lifetime. All Bluejay had to see in order to make that prediction was what was happening to the music. Maybe Shorty was right. *Molly-molly will you be mine, Molly-molly you're so divine.* The teen-agers, the ones the record people in Nashville had decided they would have to please, were giggling behind their parents' backs when Bluejay sang "The Longer You're Gone" or Ernest Tubb did "Walkin' the Floor Over You" or Little Jimmy Dickens stomped into "Sleepin' at the Foot of the Bed." The kids wanted to hear this crap, this "nigger music" they played on WERD, and for all Bluejay knew his own son was giggling with them.

"It'll never be the same again, Sam," Bluejay said.

"That's what the professor kept saying last night."

"Naw, I ain't talking about that anymore. I'm talking about life around here. You and me and Jaybird. Minute I drove away from Shorty's place I knew it was gonna change. I ain't so sure I want it to change. Thinking about gathering the wagons and holing up. Right here at Sixkiller."

"What you mean?" said Sam.

"Incorporate. Look out for ourselves."

"Seems like that's what we been doing."

"Well, sort of," said Bluejay, "but I just want to kind of make it official. Getting tired of giving twenty percent of everything I make to somebody I can't trust, anyway. Besides, I figure you've been my personal manager for nothing ever since I took my first breath. How do you like it? I had 'em print up a couple thousand of 'em."

Bluejay reached into his pocket and produced a calling card for Sam. It was in pale blue stock with raised black letters—

THE HOLY GHOST, INC.

J. Sam Sixkiller

Personal Manager   P.O. Box 1
BLUEJAY CLAY   Andrews, N.C.

—and when Sam read he began to grin. He stood up and read it again and he began to snigger. He poured himself another shot of whiskey and read it a third time, this time aloud, and now he was howling with laughter. When a female voice came from the "bedroom," Sam, choking on his laughter, said, "Okay. Pale-face make joke."

"Not bad, huh?" said Bluejay.

"You're crazy." Sam sat cross-legged on the floor.

"Makes perfectly good sense to me."

"You're going to get somebody killed. Mainly me."

"Ah. How do you figure that?"

"Indian calling around making dates for Bluejay Clay. What do I do, call up some redneck in Birmingham and say, 'This Chief Sixkiller. You no pay big wampum hear Holy Ghost sing I burn teepee, take woman'? Hanh?"

"Well, come to think of it, it might work."

"Work? Damned right it'll work. I'll get to participate in my first lynching."

"Aw, come on, now, Sam."

"And what's this 'J.' stuff? 'J. Sam Sixkiller.' "

"I never knew anybody important that didn't start their name with a 'J.' You can look it up. J. Pierpont Morgan, for starters."

"And what's this 'Holy Ghost'?"

"Aw," said Bluejay, "I was just looking for something different to call the fund. Seems like we're always talking about—"

"The fund."

"The fund. I'll tell you all about that. Anyway, seems like we're always talking about ghosts around here. If it ain't you making up stories about your great-grandfather Sutalitihi I'm talking about old Jubal Clay. Or I'm thinking about Molly. So I figure I'll just call the corporation 'The Holy Ghost, Inc.' Winnie Dalton over at the bank says anything's okay with him. That's J. Winfred Dalton in case you didn't know. But let me tell you about the fund."

Bluejay's plan was simple. His only son was coming of age and he wanted to be sure that if any sort of calamity ever struck— like, say, Bluejay got killed on the road while racing from one date to another—Jaybird would be taken care of. He was asking Sam to read up on taxes and estates and investments, knowing that the minute Sam saw his new calling card he had begun spinning schemes through his head, and then get with Winnie Dalton at the Cherokee State Bank to draw something up. Bluejay didn't want to be as rich as Roy Acuff, who was busy becoming the biggest millionaire in Nashville, he just wanted what he had to be safe.

"Yeah," Bluejay said, "I reckon that's the way it's supposed to work. It's like I told that fellow from that magazine that time.

Each generation's supposed to do something for the next bunch. If my daddy didn't teach me anything else, he taught me how to make music. It was *his* daddy built up most of the farm here, and it was Grandpa Newt's daddy that cleared out the Indians. And so forth. So this is what you might call *my* part. Legacy. That what they call it?"

"All right," said Sam. "So I'm your manager now."

"Right. Take yourself a big salary."

"You want to open a bank account?"

"Might as well. It's 1954, ain't it?"

"I heard about a deal over in Copperhill where you could invest maybe $20,000 and within three years you'd—"

"Don't want to hear about it. Do it."

"I guess I'll need a phone down here. File cabinets."

"Get 'em."

"Well, I'll be damned," said Sam, looking one more time at the calling card. "Return of the red man."

Bluejay hopped up and stepped out the door of the cabin to the truck. In a moment he returned with a potato sack and emptied the contents onto the floor. "Mail call, almost forgot," he said. "After Saturday you'll have to start going in to the post office and get it yourself. Smead says he's getting too damn old for riding all the way back into here, what with all the stuff you get in the mail." The mail included Sam's Sunday edition of *The New York Times*, a Donald Duck watch from Sears, Roebuck and a book sent by a friend on the reservation up the road in Cherokee.

"Ah, good, it's here," Sam said, stripping off the wrapping paper.

"I thought you stole all your books from the library."

"I *borrow* 'em. But they won't even stock this one."

"What is it, one of them 'hot' books? Naked women?"

"No. It's called '1984.' Ken Two Trees sent it."

"He the one that believes in that 'levitation'?"

"Yeah. You met him at the county fair one time."

"Anybody believes he can pick up a cow just looking at it's crazy," said Bluejay. "What's the book about?"

"Englishman wrote it a few years ago. It's about what things might be like in 1984. Government takes over everything. Can't have sex unless they tell you. 'Big Brother' runs everything. Robots do the work. Everybody spies on everybody else."

"You don't believe that kind of stuff, do you?"

"Anything's possible, Bluejay."

"Sometimes I worry about you, Sam. Ain't no way I'm gonna believe a book written by an Englishman and recommended by an Indian that thinks he can look a cow off the ground. By 1984 you'll be so damn tired you'll be begging 'em to tell you *not* to have sex."

CHAPTER V

I T WAS him against the machine and the machine was winning. *Wheeeeuuuwww-cheiew-uckit-uckit-wheeeuuuuwwwww*, the tape would say in Reverse. "Shit, goddamit," Bluejay would say. *Click*. Another click as he put it on Forward. *Maoorlee moaey waoffe, maoorlee*. "Sumbitch." *Click*. *Wheee-wuuuwwwchieew-uckiet-uckiet-wheeeuuuuwwww*. *Click*. Fast Forward this time. *Mollymylove Mollymylove Mollymyfair-sweeladi* . . . *Click*. "I'll just be a goddam suck-egg dog." Alone, around midnight in the main room of the big house, with a fire going and only the distant wailing of a wild dog in the hills to interrupt his concentration, Bluejay sloshed another helping of whiskey into his coffee mug before making a final assault on the tape recorder Sam had bought for him at Floyd's Hardware. Medium Forward. *Click*—

> . . . They took you away
> And left me alone,
> They even took the baby . . .

—click. He reached for the guitar and strummed it, at the same time locating the red button for Record, then pressed the button and sat back in the rocker to strum the refrain and speak the recitation.

The cold wind was a-howling
  On that awful winter's night,
The night the devil came
  A-spoiling for a fight.

The three of us were happy
  For soon we would be four,
But little did we know
  What the devil had in store . . .

"Pa?"

"In here, son. By the fire."

Bluejay turned off the tape recorder and leaned back again in the rocker, strumming and trying to memorize the words, as Jaybird stomped the snow from his boots and slammed the heavy door behind him. He clomped across the oak floor, leaving a trail of water in his wake, to rub his hands in front of the fire and begin peeling off the blue parka and the Andrews High jacket with a block letter "A" over the heart and a basketball emblem on the sleeve. He raked his right hand through his flat-top crew-cut, plastered to his scalp from wearing a ski cap, to make it stand up again.

"Probably got some hot chocolate in there," Bluejay said.

"Believe I will. Snow's piling up. You want some?"

"No. Got some of Sam's tea here. Y'all win?"

"Nah. Hayesville's tough. Too big a school for us."

"So late, I figured you'd gone into overtime with 'em."

"Nah," Jaybird said, "everybody went to Briscoe's for hamburgers."

"I see Becky was there."

"Sir?"

"Pretty good copy of a kiss on your neck there."

"Yes, sir." The boy, growing gangly and angular and loping in the manner of Clay men, walked to the kitchen to find an apple and something hot to drink.

Bluejay's approach to fathering was much the same as that of his own father and the others before him. "About all I ever did," he remembered his father, Boone Jubal Clay, telling him one time when it appeared he was going to escape adolescence without any serious consequences, "was let you have a lot of rope and jerk on it now and then. Same as raising a good horse." It had been necessary for Bluejay to work hard at practicing *laissez-faire*, seeing as how he had to be both father and mother to the boy during his most intense years of growth, but what he saw now was a seventeen-year-old boy with more than a decent head on his frail shoulders. Just like Bluejay, who had dropped out of high school when his father died of "the fever" but could work Sam's *New York Times* Sunday crossword puzzle with a ball-point pen, Jaybird seemed to have been born to intelligence. He made "B" grades at school without having to study. He began averaging twenty points per game for the Andrews High Raiders the night he first started in his sophomore year. "I swear, Blue, the boy looks just like you," people on the street would say. "Well, the boy can't help it," Bluejay would respond, winking and draping an arm around Jaybird's shoulder as they sat at the counter in Valley Drugs eating ice cream together.

"Together" was the working word. Molly's last words in the delivery room, when she had seen them set aside the lifeless fetus and begin frantically trying to save her life, still cried out to Bluejay. "Jaybird's the last . . . the last . . . the last." That was another reason he had forsaken all other women and, for all intents and purposes, most other people and interests. He regarded Molly's last words as a trust. He would raise the last boy, the last Clay, to carry the banner properly. If that cost him, Bluejay Clay of the Grand Ole Opry, a career beyond musty old Ryman Auditorium and the cinder-block fighting-and-dancing-club circuit—kept him from spending more time on the road, muffled his desire to even find out about the changes beginning to come over Nashville, stifled his energy to at least cut a new record every now and then—so be it. Jaybird—Henry Buford Clay Jr.—was Bluejay Clay's life.

"You get it finished, Pa?" Jaybird came back into the main room, chomping on an apple and carrying a mug of steaming cocoa, and sat on the sofa in front of the fire.

"Huh?"

"The recitation for the record."

"Oh. Caught me thinking."

"Saw you working the tape recorder when I came in."

"Aw," Bluejay said, "I'm working on it. Found out how come those engineers up in Nashville make so much money."

"How's that?"

"Songwriting's nothing. Recorder's driving me crazy."

"Aw, Pa, that's simple. Let me work that while you sing."

"Some other time," Bluejay said. "Owen said we'll just cut the record when I've got it ready. Trouble is, every time I think I've got the words right and get the recorder working I forget what I wrote. Well, anyway. One more day won't hurt. I've waited ten years to do it. How'd you do tonight?"

"Didn't score but thirteen points," Jaybird said. "They were all over me. That man from East Carolina was there, too. The coach."

"One talking about a scholarship?"

"Yeah. Great timing. When we came out for the second half he was gone. Guess I won't be an East Carolina Pirate."

"Well, you won't need a scholarship, anyway."

"Guess not."

"You still thinking about Middle Tennessee?"

"Pretty much. Becky and I were talking about it tonight."

"That where she's going?"

"If I do."

Bluejay was in the midst of swallowing a good slug of whiskey when Jaybird said it. The whiskey had started down his throat when he coughed. It sprayed all over Bluejay's buckskin britches and the coffee table and the guitar propped against the table. Some of it had made it to the fire, where little puffs of steam popped from the front log. Bluejay, still coughing, stood up and began wiping up the mess with his bandanna. He looked at Jaybird. The boy took another bite of apple.

"Let's see if I got this right." Bluejay finished wiping off the rocker and sat back down in it. "You been thinking about going to Middle Tennessee State University for college. 'MTSU.' One up in Murfreesboro. Gonna study business. Take that new course they got where you learn about screwing singers out of their money."

"Aw, Pa."

"Well, that's what it amounts to if Shorty's in on it."

"They call it 'The Business of Music,' Pa. It's an elective."

"What the hell does that mean? An 'elective'?"

"You don't have to take it if you don't want to."

"If Shorty Hunsinger's teaching it, I think I'd elect to set his car on fire." Normally Bluejay was a calm man who understood that life was a long haul, an extended tour of one-nighters, but the idea of Shorty Hunsinger's having any effect whatsoever on his boy's life made him livid. "I figured you'd already learned enough about Shorty and his kind, anyway, after what happened between me and him. If you want to know about the music business you don't even have to leave Sixkiller. If I don't know the answer, Sam does."

Jaybird couldn't argue the point. He didn't much care where he went to college, or whether he went at all, but Bluejay had been so insistent that he become the first Clay to see the innards of a lecture hall that the boy more or less flipped a coin and it came up Middle Tennessee. A flyer from MTSU, a small four-year college in Murfreesboro, less than an hour's drive south of Nashville, told of the new courses dealing with music management—"Directed by J. Morton Hunsinger, highly successful Nashville talent agent . . . Ins and outs of the music industry . . . Field trips to Nashville recording studios and the world-famous Grand Ole Opry . . . Guest lectures by Minnie Pearl, Roy Acuff, Carl Smith & other Opry stars"—and that was that. Bluejay tried to talk him out of it, to no avail, but now there was another problem. A big one.

"Say Becky's gonna go if you do," Bluejay said.

"Yes, sir. She's thinking about it."

"Sounds like she's more than thinking about it."

"Well, yessir. We've been talking about going together."

"Becky Rollins. The rich kid."

"Aw, now, Pa."

"One that lives up on the hill. One in the mansion."

"It's just a big new house, Pa. Not a mansion."

"Any place got servants and a swimming pool, that's a man-sion."

"They *need* all that, Pa. Becky's folks have to entertain a lot. People from Mr. Rollins' company come down a lot from Chicago and places like that. He figures it's better for them to just stay at their house while they're down here, that's all."

"Down here seeing which trees they're gonna cut down next."

"I don't know about that," said Jaybird.

"Well, you ought to be learning. Time they get done there won't be a blade of grass between here and Chattanooga."

Even *The New York Times* had paid attention two years earlier when it was announced that Diversified Enterprises, a conglomerate based in Chicago, had bought huge swatches of timber land in the southern Appalachians for the purpose of "meeting the needs of the nation's bourgeoning post-war housing industry." Those were the words Bluejay and Sam read on the front porch the day Sam's copy of the Sunday *Times* came in the mail. There was an interview with the Vice President of Southern Operations, H. Kennerly Rollins III, photographed wearing a three-piece suit and sitting behind a desk in the Chicago offices. "Mr. Rollins," said the *Times*, "views the acquisition of the rugged Appalachian forest land as 'an important step toward filling the housing industry's needs *vis-à-vis* rare Southern hardwoods.' His company, said Rollins, would be acquiring more land in western North Carolina and Middle Tennessee 'as it becomes available.' " Bluejay Clay and Sam Sixkiller said nothing as they read the story, over and over again, on the business page of *The New York Times*. "Diversified Enterprises," H. Kennerly Rollins III was quoted, "envisions a prosperous future not only for itself but for the people of the region. Golf courses, for example, and weekend hideaways. Ski slopes, chalets, new roads, tourist attractions. We go there as friends and partners." Sam shrugged. "Same thing they told Uwani Sutalitihi," he said.

At first the people of Cherokee County, whose only marketable assets were their own strong backs and fierce wills, welcomed the coming of Diversified Enterprises. The county's unemployment rate had always hovered dangerously near twenty percent, even during the post-World War II years, but suddenly there were jobs for loggers and truck drivers and clerks and secretaries at the sprawling complex of mills and warehouses and offices stuck back in Wolf Gap off of U.S. 19 between Andrews and Murphy. The smoke from the sawmills began to obscure the view of Standing Indian Mountain on still summer days, and now and then a fellow would check out sick from his shift at the mill and come home to find his wife in bed with a neighbor who worked a different shift, and the Game & Fish rangers had to close down a trout stream from time to time, and once there was a killing at the Diversified railroad siding when some union organizers came down from Raleigh. But that was all right. Diversified had brought jobs to the valley. Kids didn't have to leave home and go to Asheville or Chattanooga or Atlanta anymore when they got out of Andrews High. There were plenty of trout streams clear of pollution. That smoke up there on the mountains was a modern-day sign, a smoke signal of the mid-twentieth century, that Cherokee county had joined America. *And anyway, that fella got shot that time, one came around stirring up things, one talking 'bout "minimum wage" and "working conditions," wasn't he a New York Jew? Hell. Man can make $1.25 an hour sawing boards. Even charge groceries at the Valley Co-op.*

The people didn't notice in the beginning, so busy were they at making money and spending it, but steadily changes began to ooze into the social fabric of that corner of Appalachia. It had happened only once before, more than a century earlier, when the white man moved into the hills and proclaimed his superiority and drove the Cherokee out. Since the Trail of Tears there had been, essentially, but one class of people: poor, white, Scotch-Irish, semiliterate, provincial, honest, industrious, rooted to their land and proud of it. But now, with the pervasion of "the company," as everybody referred to Diversified, there were two classes of people. One class worked for the company. The other class *was* the company.

"Lord, son. Lord, Lord. Where's your Mama now?" Bluejay felt the boy slipping away, without any warning, and he wasn't sure whether he could do anything about it. "I don't think you know what you're getting into, son." *Oh, shit.* "Look. The Rollins people, they're different. It's not *money* that makes 'em different. I probably got ten times the money Becky's daddy's got. I don't know how much money I got. Maybe *that's* the difference. It's how you make your money and what you do with it that's important." Jaybird started to cut in but Bluejay held up his hand. "About all a man needs is some clothes for his body and a roof for his head and enough cornbread for his belly and something honest to do with his hands. But then you got these other people. They got to have more than that. One pair of pants ain't gonna do when they can go out and buy 'em by the dozen. One car might not start one morning, so they got to have a backup. It goes on and on like that until it gets to where they spend more time thinking about things than thinking about people. You see what I mean? See what I'm trying to say?"

"Sure," Jaybird said. "I guess."

"I want you to do something for me," said Bluejay.

"Okay."

"Next time you take Becky home."

"Yes, sir?"

"You know them fancy rocking chairs they got out there?"

"On the front porch? Sure."

"I want you to look at 'em real close."

"Sure, Pa. But why?"

"They got 'em chained to the floor."

CHAPTER VI

ALL it took to shake up Bluejay, to get him moving on the record he wanted to cut about Molly, was to listen to the radio. One day he was searching up and down the dial for a country-music station when he stumbled across WERD and there it was. "And now, gang, here it is," Sam the Bird was screaming, "WERD's Hit Pick of the Week. 'Molly-Molly,' with Stinky & the Gang. Here she comes"—

> Molly-molly
> Where you been hid,
> Molly-molly
> Won't you have my kid . . .

—Sam the Bird singing along with his own "ah-hah, ah-hah, Molly-molly." Before sundown Bluejay had polished his lyrics, finalized the "recitation" part, put it on tape so he wouldn't forget it and called Owen Bradley in Nashville to tell him he was on his way. With a vengeance he drove away from Sixkiller at dawn the next day, rehearsing the song as he negotiated the 225-mile drive to Nashville in the pickup truck, parked in the loading zone of the Tulane Hotel with the hood of the truck raised and bounded up the steps with his guitar to the studio where Owen Bradley and the band Decca had hired were waiting. "What do you want to call it,

Blue?" said Owen Bradley. " 'Molly,' " Bluejay said. "Just 'Molly.' "
The entire process took twenty-five minutes.

By a quarter past one, Bluejay found himself at one of the
Formica tables in Linebaugh's Cafe, on Broadway near Ryman
Auditorium, washing down a BLT with a Jax beer. He felt elated,
burned out, like a sprinter who had just run the best hundred-
yard dash of his life, and it helped to have one of his kind to
share it with. He was sitting with Leon Brasher, a hard-line
fiddler from north Alabama, celebrating his first anniversary as
a member of Ernest Tubb's Texas Troubadours.

"Thought y'all never left the road," Bluejay was saying.

"Ain't that the truth. E.T.'s doing twenty-two shows this
month."

"How in the world do you do it, Leon?"

"It's for a good cause, I guess."

"How's that?"

" 'cause I need the money."

At lease E.T. was carrying on the fight, Bluejay thought, *him
and Lefty Frizzell and Webb Pierce and Acuff and Carl Smith
and even Little Jimmy Dickens.* Ten years earlier, even before
Bluejay had made it with "The Longer You're Gone," Tubb had
gone to the top of the country charts with "Walkin' the Floor
Over You," and he hadn't changed a whit since then. No more
hits had come for E.T.—it was the same, of course, with Bluejay—but he didn't seem to mind. All he had to do was load up
the Troubadours and head west to Texas, where he could probably run for governor and win, and sing exactly the way he sang
in 1943, in those sparse little farming and ranching settlements
sprawled out between the Brazos and the Rio Grande, and he
was the ruler of his own fiefdom. Some of them, like this Eddy
Arnold, were beginning to record behind string sections—*violins*, please, not *fiddles*—but not Ernest Tubb. Around Nashville
they liked to tell the story about the hot young star who made
his first foray into West Texas, as a warm-up act for Tubb, and
came back off the road swearing he'd never go back: "Hell, I got
up there and laid my biggest hit on 'em and they got up and

started *dancing*." E.T. had to explain to the kid that when they danced it meant they liked him.

"E.T. doing all right?" Bluejay said.

"He'll never change," said Leon. "He was tickled to death when he heard about you and Shorty."

"People know that already?"

"*Know* it? Does a whore sweat? It's all over town."

"What're they saying?"

"They're saying you can't keep a good 'billy down."

"Sounds like a good song, there, Leon."

"Yeah, well, don't try it on Shorty Hunsinger."

Almost overnight, it seemed, Bluejay's faith in what he was doing was justified. "Molly" was released by Decca two weeks after he and Owen Bradley recorded it and it shot to the top of the country charts even faster than "Longer You're Gone" had done. Sam Sixkiller, getting the hang of the personal management-and-bookings game, noted that since "Molly-molly" was No. 1 on the new "rock and roll" charts maybe they ought to sue Shorty and Stinky for plagiarism ("Fancy word for stealing," he had to explain to Bluejay) but Bluejay, fascinated as he was by the idea, said he figured Shorty Hunsinger would drown in his own bile in due time. Besides, Bluejay said, he was having too much fun being on top again. The newspaper and magazine reporters and photographers were visiting Sixkiller, "Molly" was on the radio constantly and Bluejay was feeling the faint early inspiration for a new song about all of this—remembering the chat he had with Leon in Nashville—which he would call "Hillbilly Fever" or something like that. *It started in the mountains/ Spread all over town/Dah-da-dah-da-dee-da-dah/Can't keep a 'billy down.* Or something.

So the business, the music part, was looking better than ever. In a few months there would be a rush of fresh money from the new record. The writing of a song touched off a chain of events which developed into an endless cycle. You wrote it. Then you recorded it. If the single did well you slapped it on a "new" album—the only thing new about it was the one song and a different photograph and some kind of title (in this case, Decca had already ordained, it would be "Molly" with a "letter to my fans" written in Bluejay's hand telling how the song came to him)—and then you hit the road while you were hot. Then, if you were lucky or the song was good or both, other singers began to record it and you received royalties every time it was heard on a radio or at a show. Sam Sixkiller had never seen the books before. He couldn't believe it. *Francis Scott Key*, he thought one day while adding up the latest figures, *would have made a killing*.

The situation at home, though, was looking bleak. It seemed that even if he had been gone for a weekend, playing a couple of one-nighters and then doing the Opry on Saturday, when he got back to Sixkiller he would hear more bad news. The bad news almost always emanated from the offices of H. Kennerly Rollins III—Diversified Enterprises had paid fifty dollars an acre for Skag Lacey's place up on the ridge, Diversified was building a nine-hole golf course for its executives where the best trout stream used to run, Diversified had bought the weekly *Cherokee Chronicle*—and the mention of Diversified reminded him of Jaybird.

"Just how've you been doing, Bluejay? I haven't seen you since basketball ended." It was noon, at the Handy Pantry cafe on Main Street, and Harvey Sellers limped across the linoleum floor to shake hands with Bluejay and join him for lunch. The place was crowded with sawmill workers and truck drivers and traveling salesmen and, seated at the round Formica table in the back, a gaggle of Diversified Enterprises executives' wives. Harvey Sellers, an old Andrews High classmate of Bluejay's who had gone on to become principal of the school, wore a short-sleeved see-through nylon shirt with a clip-on bow tie and a row of ball-point pens in the shirt pocket. He winced as he eased into the red plastic booth.

"Pretty busy, Harv, pretty busy," Bluejay said. "What happened? Mule kick you?"

"Might as well have," said Sellers. "Last night after you called I was out back shooting baskets with Harvey Jr. and I must've pulled something. One thing I found out is, we aren't so young anymore."

"Ain't that a fact."

"But you, now"—he opened the copy of that week's *Chronicle*, which he had bought at the counter when he came in, and showed Bluejay his own picture on the front page—"you just keep on going. Says you got another hit record. Haven't read the story yet."

"You mean they actually printed something about me?"

"Why not? You're the biggest thing this town has."

"Ever since Rollins bought the paper and turned it over to that alcoholic brother-in-law of his, all I've read about is Diversified."

"Come to think of it, you've made a good point."

"Your school must be full of 'em."

"Full of what?"

"Them Diversified kids. Yankee kids."

"Well," said Harvey Sellers, "you could certainly say that when the company started bringing in its own people it, ah, it did change the complexion of the school somewhat. The last figure I saw showed twenty-six Diversified children in the top four grades."

"Where they come from? New York?"

"Oh, New York. Oregon. Missouri. All over."

"Must be hard on the local kids. Like your boy and mine."

"Oh, no, Bluejay. To the contrary, to the contrary."

"How's that? Hell, they might as well talk foreign."

"But it's good for them, Bluejay. Broadening."

Somebody put a nickel in the jukebox and played "Molly." Bluejay, giving the *Chronicle* story a skim (he was referred to in the lead paragraph as "local resident Henry Buford Clay, known to his fans as 'Bluejay' Clay"), reddened when some of the old-timers seated at the counter turned around and started hooting and applauding. Harvey grinned at Bluejay and politely patted his hands together. Patsy Snider came over to the booth and took their order, sticking her gum behind her ear before she wrote, and the two men waited for the record to finish playing.

"You said you had something to talk about," Sellers said.

"Aw," said Bluejay, "I just wondered when the dance is."

"The senior dance?"

"Yeah. One me and the band always plays at."

"The same as usual. The last Friday in May."

"Night before graduation? Down at the gym?"

"That's right. May the—let me think—May the twenty-eighth."

"Good. I'll write it down. Wanted to be sure we'd be here."

"Well, uh, Bluejay." Harvey Sellers crooked his finger into the collar of his shirt and straightened his bow tie. "I suppose I should have remembered to call you and tell you. The kids decided they wanted to do something different this year. Sorry I didn't tell you."

"Different," Bluejay said.

"For entertainment."

"They want different entertainment."

"Yes," Sellers said. "They came up to me a few weeks ago and said they'd like to put it to a vote. You know, let the seniors vote on who they'd like to have. I told 'em that you and your band had always done it for free and that it was more or less an Andrews High tradition that Bluejay and the Sixkillers played for the Senior Dance. But then they went ahead and voted and there wasn't much I could do about it."

"Do about it."

"Do about changing their minds."

"Changing their minds, you say."

"Right, well, ah"—Sellers was fiddling with his bow tie again—"it seems they wanted to get somebody from out of town so they voted to ask this group from up at Asheville. I think they call themselves 'Sammy and the Slicks.' Something like that. They sing this new 'rock and roll' music."

"Damn, Harv, how come you didn't stop 'em?"

"Nothing I could do, Bluejay. That's the way they voted."

"You coulda called me or something."

"I assumed that Jaybird would have told you."

"Jaybird. That's right. He vote?"

"Becky said everybody voted."

"Becky. The Rollins girl?"

"Quite a little lady. She's the senior president. All-'A' student, 'Who's Who,' head cheerleader, everything. Don't know why I'm telling *you* all of that. Understand Jaybird's pretty sweet on her."

"Yeah, well, I'm working on that."

Harvey Sellers leaned over the hamburger Patsy had placed in front of him and lowered his voice. "Remember what we used to say, don't you, Bluejay? 'Stiff dick's got a mind of its own.' Remember that?"

"Seems like that's *my* business." Bluejay had no stomach for lunch. *Sammy and the Slicks, for God's sake, it's a wonder it wasn't Stinky & The Gang.* "Lemme ask you something, Harv. Don't know if I want to know the answer. But, ah, how'd the vote go? I mean, ah, any holdouts for ol' Bluejay and the Sixkillers? How'd they vote? Hanh?"

"It was unanimous, Bluejay. Unanimous."

"Sonofabitch. My own boy."

CHAPTER VII

I DON'T KNOW, Sam. Fifty dollars, that's a lot of money."

"Not for TiHi."

"How's she spell that?"

"Bit 'T,' little 'I,' big 'H,' little 'I.' Like 'tee-hee.' "

"That an Indian name? Like your granddaddy Sutalitihi?"

"I don't know where it came from. She giggles a lot."

"Well, she *better*. For fifty dollars."

"It's a bargain, Bluejay. She gets more than that in Gatlinburg."

"That where she works? Gatlinburg?"

"She and her mama both. Wigwam Lodge. Yankees love 'em."

"Her mama, too?"

"Tom-Tom Tompkins."

"I don't believe you. Tom-Tom and TiHi Tompkins."

"Stage names. If you can call yourself 'Bluejay' they can call themselves 'Tom-Tom' and 'TiHi.' "

"Reckon you're right. You want me to stoke the fire?"

Sam and Bluejay sat on the damp mossy bank of Sixkiller Creek beside the still. After a supper of rabbit and collard greens and black-eyes and cornbread at the main house with Jaybird and TiHi Tompkins, the two men, blatantly repeating how they intended to stay up all night stirring a fresh batch of moonshine, noisily gathered up blankets and snacks before bidding the kids

58

a good night and trudging off toward the creek. From where they sat, under a full moon, they could look through the trees and see the lights of Sam's cabin.

"You say this is a Cherokee thing? A tradition?"

"Maybe some tribes still do it. I don't know. I read about it."

"Where?"

"I don't know where I read it. *National Geographic*, maybe."

"No, I mean where do they do it?"

"Oh," said Sam. "Africa. Young boy gets circumcised and they pick out a girl for him. Make 'em go up in the hills for three nights."

"And he comes back a man. That the thinking?"

"Part of it."

Bluejay said, "Part of it."

"Important part. Then he'll know what it's like."

"Uh-huh."

"And if he knows what it's like, he won't have to get married to find out. Damn, Bluejay. Don't you remember any of that? Don't you remember your first time?"

"Well, that was a long time ago."

"Come on. What was her name?"

"Pa called her Blackie."

"What'd *you* call her?"

"Same thing. Blackie."

"What was she like?"

"Actually," said Bluejay, "she was a sheep."

"A sheep? Did white men really do that?"

"This one did."

They heard sounds and stopped talking. Jaybird, with a flashlight, was leading the young Indian girl to Sam's cabin. They entered. The door closed behind them. Sam and Bluejay could make out their shadows through the window. Either Jaybird or TiHi put on a record. It was one of Sam's favorites, the "William Tell Overture," the theme song for the "Lone Ranger" radio show. Bluejay and Sam made sure the mash was bubbling and the fire was all right, poured themselves some whiskey and sat back to let nature take its course.

"I don't know, Sam," said Bluejay, flipping a cigarette into the white foaming rapids of the creek, "this whole deal smells bad. Lying to my own boy, sitting out here spying on him. Maybe it'll backfire. Maybe he'll like it so much he'll want *TiHi* to marry him."

"Doesn't work like that. That's why the first one's a whore."

"Well, you never know."

"Believe me. TiHi enjoys her work too much."

"But, see, if he likes it so much that he can't stand doing without it, then he'll sure as hell want to get married to this Becky, and then I'll be the one that caused it. See?"

"Bluejay," said Sam, "you and I have done an honorable thing tonight. Ooop. Look there. Lights just went off. She's right on schedule. Yes, an honorable and noble thing. We have introduced an innocent young paleface to joys that only the great TiHi Tompkins would know. Should Jaybird ever get inside this prissy little rich girl's pants, after what he's about to learn from TiHi, he'll find her about as exciting as Blackie the sheep. Have some more whiskey and go to sleep. Some Clay blood is about to spill."

CHAPTER VIII

THE BUS had been the first visible sign of Bluejay's success in the music business. When "The Longer You're Gone" bolted to No. 1 on the country charts, in the midst of World War II, Bluejay and his odd collection of music-making friends known as "The Sixkillers" were caught by surprise. All of that time, before he became a star, the five of them had been riding from honky-tonk to honky-tonk in a battered old '41 Dodge sedan. But then the record hit and calls came for Bluejay Clay and the Sixkillers to make longer trips to more distant points, the most memorable being a two-thousand-miler to Iowa and back in the middle of the winter, so he avoided a mutiny by taking $12,000 in a flour sack to the factory in Middle Georgia and negotiating the purchase of the first 1946 model Bluebird school bus off the line. The bus had metamorphosed as inexorably as had the farm. First there was a coat of navy-blue paint (thus, "Ol' Blue"). Then the legend, in white, on both sides: BLUEJAY CLAY & THE SIXKILLERS, STARS GRAND OLE OPRY, SIXKILLER NORTH CAROLINA, THE LONGER YOU'RE GONE THE HARDER IT GETS & OTHER HITS. Then the gutting of the seats and the installation of bunk beds by Buddy Brumby, regarded good-naturedly by Bluejay as "a damned sight better carpenter than you are a fiddler," followed by calico curtains fashioned by Ethel McGahee, followed by a shower stall and toilet, followed by a battery-powered

61

hot plate and an icebox and a sink. The bus had become as much a part of Bluejay's life as his old guitar. It was his home away from home, a motel-diner-office on wheels, and he showed no inclination to trade it in for a new one.

It was eight o'clock on the first Saturday morning of May, a bright and promising day full of robins and playful puppies and high puffy clouds and clicking grasshoppers, and Bluejay sat on the front porch watching Jaybird and Sam finish readying the bus for the trip. This would be a short one, only to Nashville for that night's Opry, but it was an important one for Bluejay. It would be his last chance, before it was time for college to start, to show Jaybird what it was really like to be Bluejay Clay. They would do it all—Linebaugh's, Frankie's Pool Hall, Essie May's Blue Room, Mom Upchurch's boardinghouse, Ryman Auditorium, Ernest Tubb's Record Shop—with the hope that Jaybird, about to enter a new phase of his life, would remember.

"I reckon I know what you're going through, Blue. My boy's about the same age and it's all I can do to get him to feed the chickens anymore." Floyd Watkins, who worked the graveyard shift at the Diversified mill and had been the Sixkillers' drummer since the band's creation, had parked his pickup in the yard and joined Bluejay on the porch. They sipped coffee and watched Sam and Jaybird.

"I don't know what to make of it, myself," Bluejay said.

"It's that damned nigger music, if you ask me."

"Could be, Floyd. Could be."

"Damned 'Sammy and the Slicks.' Even *sounds* dirty."

"Probably the way they want it to sound."

"I hear the kids was anonymous."

"What's that?" Bluejay motioned for Jaybird to wipe the windows.

"Anonymous," said Floyd. "Every damned one of 'em voted that way."

"*Unanimous.* Twenty-three to nothing. Becky Rollins, president."

"She behind it?"

"That's the way I see it."

"Sonofabitch. My own kid."

"*Everybody's* own kid." The others were gathered around the bus now—Buddy Brumby, the carpenter from around the mountain in Hayesville; Skeeter McGahee, the lead guitarist and bootlegger from Tusquitee; Floyd Watkins with his drums; Claude Owenby, the farmer from Buck's Creek, with his dobro and steel guitar—and when Sam, going along as the driver on this trip, edged in behind the steering wheel and gave the horn three blasts it was the signal for them to clamber aboard. Sam revved the engine of the old Bluebird, startling the chickens milling around in the yard, and abruptly bolted away from the farm. Soon they were on the asphalt of U.S. 64, the sun shining and the radio playing and the whiskey flowing, Ol' Blue, their chariot, rushing them to the end of the rainbow. Nashville. Hillbilly Heaven.

What Bluejay Clay knew about the history of country music had come to him, like what he knew about the evolution of his own family, by word of mouth. The Nashville he knew in 1954 had its roots, as far as he could tell, back there on a night in November of 1925 when the Grand Ole Opry was born. The National Life and Accident Insurance Company of Nashville had opened a radio station with the call letters WSM, which stood for "We Sell Millions," broadcasting at 50,000 watts into the deepest coves of Appalachia and even into the most forlorn farm hamlets of the Midwest. They hired a former Memphis newspaperman by the name of George D. Hay as program manager. Hay had fallen in love with the pure hard music of the Southern Highlands, and he figured it might be good for business if he capitalized on it, so on that night he sat an old mountain fiddler named Uncle Jimmy Thompson in front of a carbon microphone and let him have at it for more than an hour. The weekly program became known as the Grand Ole Opry shortly after that, according to a story Bluejay had read in the program sold every weekend at Ryman Auditorium, when George Hay came on the air following a program of grand opera music and said, "For the past hour we have been listening to music largely from grand opera, but from now on we will present grand *old* opry." And there it was. The Grand Ole Opry.

It was like stumbling across a single nugget of gold and then finding that it represented a mother lode. Suddenly the people at WSM radio in Nashville couldn't beat away from its doors, even if they wanted to, the hordes of mountain pickers and singers who descended upon Nashville demanding to be on the radio. Within five years, when the Great Depression had plunged the Deep South into its deepest pit, the hills were crawling with record producers and small radio stations and musicians who were now being paid to do what they once did for fun on the front porches of their cabins in the hills. By the beginning of World War II, when Bluejay Clay had joined the dash to Nashville, what the up-East folklorists were now calling "hillbilly music" was rivaling the music of Tin Pan Alley in popularity. As many as ten million people listened every Saturday night to the broadcast of the Grand Ole Opry, now housed in an old downtown Nashville tabernacle called Ryman Auditorium in honor of the born-again steamboat captain who built it for his favorite Bible-thumping evangelist, and there was no accounting of how many more danced and farmed and made love to the music all across America.

In spite of the ominous rumblings that Bluejay and the other old-line country performers like Tubb and Acuff and Hank Snow were hearing—the noise of Sammy and the Slicks and the violins, rather than fiddles, in the background of the newer country songs— they were faring better than ever. Upwards of ten thousand people were showing up at Ryman Auditorium every weekend to see the Opry in person and the radio broadcast was still one of the most-listened-to live shows in America. Country music was being performed in New England and Carnegie Hall and even in Europe now. There were sixty-five "country" recording companies and about 650 "country" radio stations across the land. The business was still one for people like Bluejay Clay and the Sixkillers, who could make more than a comfortable living by playing and singing their kind of music for their kind of people Out There during the week and at the Opry on Saturday night, so 1954 seemed to be no time for panic. No matter what Shorty Hunsinger—and, up to now, Jaybird Clay—had to say.

"It ain't exactly like I was *making* you do it, understand? I mean, you're old enough now to be doing what you want to do. But I just figured it'd be nice." Bluejay and Jaybird sat across from each other at the fold-out table toward the front of the bus, the table used for dining and poker-playing, as Ol' Blue skirted Chattanooga and plunged northward into the hills leading to Nashville. Sam was driving. The Sixkillers, some of whom had worked at their regular jobs through the night, were asleep in their bunks. "You don't mind, do you? Be your first time."

"Naw, Pa, it's okay."

"It's just them four chords. C, F-sharp, A, D."

"I know, Pa. It's easy."

"I'll borrow a guitar for you."

"Okay."

"Maybe one of the fellas in the stage band."

"It doesn't matter."

"Yeah," Bluejay said, "figured it'd be real nice. Me and you up there on the stage, father and son, singing and playing together about your Mama and what was gonna be your little brother. They ought to like that. Don't know why we never did it before."

"Sing? I thought I was just going to strum."

"Yeah, that's all. Just strum. Why, you scared?"

"Naw, Pa. Just checking."

"Gotta be a little bit nervous, anyway."

"Not really," said Jaybird.

Bluejay turned the afternoon into a guided tour of Nashville for his son. Sam parked the bus on Boscobel Street, about a mile across the Cumberland River bridge from the Ryman, in front of Mom Upchurch's two-story stucco-and-rock house. Mom Upchurch was sixty-three now, the widow of a Texas farmer who lived to be ninety-seven himself, and the five years since her husband's death she had taken in so many struggling country musicians that she had lost track. There had been Pee Wee King and the Golden West Cowboys at first, followed by the likes of the Carter Family and Grandpa Jones, and now there were a half dozen like Carl Smith and Faron Young. She would take in only country musicians as boarders, she told Jaybird, "because they don't mix too good with people in other livelihoods. And besides, I just like good old hillbilly music." She charged Depression rents, darned their socks and cleaned up their rooms and took messages for them if they were out on the road. Bluejay winked at Mom and turned to Jaybird: "One time I was staying here for the weekend, son, and about two o'clock in the morning some old boy was upstairs in his room picking and singing, making a lot of racket, so I yelled, 'Hey, don't you know some folks are trying to sleep?' Know what he said? 'Naw, but maybe if you'd hum a couple o' bars I could get the hang of it.' That's the kind of place Mom runs."

Sam and the others wanted to stick around the house, playing cards and talking with the other musicians, so Bluejay borrowed a car and he and Jaybird drove across the river bridge to downtown Nashville. For the next two hours Jaybird's head swam. Music blared from the Ernest Tubb Record Shop. Early arrivals for that night's Opry were already set up in parking lots, biding their time, napping in the cabs of their pickup trucks or cooking steaks on portable charcoal grills. The ticket line already wound from Ryman Auditorium to Margaret's Chops & Steaks two blocks up Opry Place. At Linebaugh's, where George Linebaugh couldn't keep up with the orders for hamburgers, Bluejay taught Jaybird how to make "homemade 'mater soup." At the Tulane Hotel, packed with Opry fans, he had to autograph his way through the lobby in order to show his son the studio where he had done all of his recording. They stopped by Essie May's Blue Room, where Bluejay had a ceremonial beer and Jaybird a Nehi Orange, Essie May Strunk mussing the boy's crewcut while Bluejay regaled some fans from Iowa: "I'd o' learned to play the piano with *both* hands if they hadn't shot the Pony Express. Injuns got him in Buck's Gap while he was bringing me my left-hand book." Hank Williams had died less than two years earlier, dead from booze and pills in the back seat of a car taking him to a show, so Bluejay drove by Hank's house to show Jaybird the ornamental-ironwork fence with the notes to "Your Cheatin' Heart" on it. En route back to Mom Upchurch's, stopped by a traffic light at the bridge, Bluejay stuck a ten-dollar bill through the window to an unkempt kid with a guitar on his back who said he'd just hitchhiked in from Mississippi.

When they got back to the house Mom invited Jaybird back to the ktichen for some apple pie and told him where he could take a bath and change clothes for the Opry if he wanted to. Sam was sitting on the glider on the front porch reading *The Upper Room*, that being the only reading material left after *Life* and *Reader's Digest*, and Bluejay joined him. They would leave for the Opry around dark, in order to make the Goo-Goo Candy Bar portion at 8:15, riding in the bus so they could head back home to Sixkiller after making an appearance on Ernest Tubb's Midnight Jamboree.

"Well?" Sam said, putting aside the magazine.

"Hard to tell, Sam. He's a quiet boy."

"Not surprising. Been alone most of his life."

"Yeah, I know," Bluejay said. "I wish it could've been different. I've done the best I could to be with him. Been different, I guess, if I'd just been a farmer or something like most daddies. Two ways to look at that, Sam. You can be dull but always there, or you can be special but always gone. Not that I'm all that special. But I sure ain't no hardware salesman like old man Floyd."

"Or an H. Kennerly Rollins III."

"Took the words right out of my mouth."

"So," said Sam, "you gave him the tour."

"Saw it all," said Bluejay. "Blue Room, Hank's house, Linebaugh's. Owen and them weren't at the studio but we took a peek at it. Even saw this kid hitchhiking in, looked to be about Jaybird's age, guitar on his back and all. Give him a little money to eat on. Saw him looking kinda funny when I did that."

"The hitchhiker?"

"Naw, Jaybird. Like he was seeing a ghost or something."

At dusk they piled onto Ol' Blue and rolled away from Mom Upchurch's boardinghouse. No matter how many times they had gone through this ritual of playing the Grand Ole Opry on a Saturday—it was Skeeter McGahee's guess that they were closing in on three hundred Opry appearances after ten years as regulars—they went quiet as they passed over the Cumberland

River, muddy and swollen from the late-spring rains, and lumbered into seedy old downtown Nashville. Playing the Opry was a humbling experience, even for a star such as Bluejay Clay, once you started thinking about how many millions of families out there between Savannah and Des Moines had eaten supper early so they could get comfortable in front of the radio and listen to it until midnight. Bluejay Clay and the Sixkillers could be out on the road somewhere like, say, at Panther Hall in Fort Worth, making $1,500 to perform in concert for two or three hours. But they chose to do this—ride for ten hours, round-trip, do two songs on two fifteen-minute segments, collect union wages of $25 per man per show—not only for the inestimable exposure over WSM but because, if the real reason were to be known, they simply loved it. They were hillbillies, and proud of it, and they and their people were coming together in celebration. It was not by accident that Nashville had come to be known as Hillbilly Heaven and the rigid old red-brick Ryman Auditorium, once the home of a fire-breathing evangelist, as the Mother Church of Country Music.

Saturday Night at the Opry. Pickup trucks, sedans, Jeeps, station wagons. License tags from Oklahoma and New Jersey and Alabama and Kentucky and Ohio. A wriggly queue of The Faithful lined up at the box office, twisting and sweating and jostling and murmuring halfway to Church Street up on the ridge of downtown, mamas suckling babies and snot-nosed kids holding to their skirts while the old man tries to make a deal for tickets. *Now Claude, you and Raymond, y'all quit shovin'* . . . *Hey, I think I just seen ol' E.T. walk across the street. . . . Naw, see, me and the little woman and the kids come all the way down from Dayton and we ain't got no tickets. . . . Lord, hon, I wish you'd told me they didn't have no air conditioning in there. . . . Yessir, that Lefty Frizzell, he's been my favorite ever since he done that "Mom and Dad Waltz" song. . . . Well, if you hadn't o' got drunk over there at Essie May's you wouldn't o' lost 'em. . . . Way I heard it, Hank's wife give him all them pills so she could get the money. . . . Yep, he's here tonight.*

Bluejay Clay and the Sixkillers, eight-fifteen. Got it tacked up on the door. . . . Dammit, Horace, will you quit smackin' 'at gum? . . . Neon lights, steel guitars, cold fried chicken in brown paper sacks, pints of Wild Turkey in hip pockets, Opry stars in their spangled suits of light, hoots and hollers, wails and moans, funeral-parlor fans and diaper bags and autograph books and Kodaks and cowboy hats and overalls. And at the corner of Opry and Broadway, he with his Bible and she with her skirt, two people of the street looking for converts.

Sam drove the bus into the maelstrom, hitting the horn and bumping over curbs until they had reached the safety of the fenced gravel parking lot reserved for Opry stars behind the auditorium, and then the seven of them—Bluejay, Sam, the Sixkillers and Jaybird—burst from Ol' Blue like Marines hitting a beach, Bluejay shouting promises over his shoulder to the clawing fans ("I'll be at the alley soon's we do the Goo-Goo show"), the fans chasing them down the cobblestoned alleyway behind Ryman until they could make it up the stone steps and past the balding security guard to refuge backstage. It was almost eight o'clock and the second show, the Martha White Flour show starring Hank Snow, was winding down. Hank Snow, in a lavender outfit twinkling above the footlights of the dusty old stage, went into overdrive on "Movin' On," one of his biggest hits, while Carl Smith, a star who once lived at Mom Upchurch's, stood on the stage not ten feet from Hank Snow, oblivious to it all, tuning his guitar in preparation for the next segment on behalf of Purina Dog Chow. When Snow finished his song and read a commercial from a music stand next to the clutter of microphones at the lip of the stage—the Opry is, foremost, a radio show—he closed out with a couple of more bars of "Movin' On" and drifted off center-stage to where Bluejay and the others stood.

"Well, lookie here," said Snow. "How you doing, Blue?"

"Keeping it in the road," Bluejay told him.

"Fine song you got out. Fine song."

"Figure it's about time. Hank. Want you to meet my boy. Name's Jaybird. This here's Hank Snow, son. Best thing that ever come out of Canada." Jaybird, dressed in starched blue jeans and a fringed leather jacket he had borrowed from Sam, shook hands with the great Hank Snow.

"Not your first time here, is it, son?" Snow said.

"Oh, nossir," said Jaybird.

"I'm gonna put him on tonight," Bluejay said to Snow.

"Going to follow in the old man's footsteps, hunh?"

"Well," said Jaybird, "not exactly."

"He's the boy in my song, Hank. My new one. 'Molly.' "

"Well. That's mighty fine, Blue, mighty fine. Boy's lucky to have a daddy like you. I ought to be an expert about that."

When Hank Snow walked away from them, stepping daintily over the ropes and pulleys and backdrop flats littering the back-stage area, Carl Smith had the younger women squealing—tall, handsome, blue eyes, black curly hair, beige Western-cut suit, chocolate hand-tooled boots—as he did "I Overlooked an Orchid While Searching for a Rose." Jaybird was laughing and pointing to a sight he saw in the front row of church pews—a fat woman managing, all at one time, to suckle a baby and cry at Carl Smith's song and keep herself cool by working a funeral-parlor fan with one hand and flapping her calico skirt with the other—while Bluejay thought ʼbout what Hank Snow had said about fathers. *I ought to be an expert about that*, Snow had said, and everybody in Nashville knew that to be a fact: poor Canadian kid, parents divorced at eight, sisters shipped out to foster homes, beaten by a stepfather, shipped out as a cabin boy in the Atlantic when he was twelve, learned to play on a mail-order guitar, got discovered playing and singing on a Canadian radio show, became a star in spite of his background. The story proved that sons could make it without fathers, Bluejay was thinking, but he wondered what the odds were. He was jolted back to the business at hand as Carl Smith finished up with "Am I the One," and there was a commercial for Purina Dog Chow as the curtains closed and the Purina flat was dropped while burly young stage-hands raised the one for Goo-Goo Cluster Candy Bars, the spon-sor for Bluejay's segment, and the engineer in the glass radio booth high above the stage waved at Bluejay and motioned for him and the Sixkillers to move into place behind the curtains. Grant Turner, the grandfatherly Opry emcee, read out a few upcoming show dates—"Ernest Tubb and his Texas Troubadours will be at the War Memorial Auditorium in Dayton, Ohio, next Friday night, while Webb Pierce and Kitty Wells will be at the armory in Bowling Green, Kentucky . . ."—while Bluejay and Skeeter struck "C" on their guitars to be sure they were in tune with each other. Jaybird, who wouldn't join them until his father announced him, stood peering behind a curtain at stage left with Sam at his side to ensure that he didn't miss his cue.

"And now, ladies and gentleman," Grant Turner said to the thousands in the church pews of Ryman Auditorium and the millions out there in America sitting at their radios, "how about a great big Nashville welcome for one of the biggest stars of the Grand Ole Opry, direct from the hills of North Carolina, the one and only . . . BLUEJAY CLAY." Showtime. As the curtains parted, exposing Bluejay and the band and behind them the huge flat showing a contented customer chomping into a Goo-Goo Cluster, they went into the familiar tune of "The Longer You're Gone" as the people out beyond the colored footlights, hearing the song and seeing Bluejay towering resplendently in a blue and silver suit and tooled gray boots, whistled and stomped as he sang the opening bars—

> Now a bluejay's a strange bird,
>   Not like the rest;
> Whenever he's lonely,
>   He'll leave the nest.
>
> But this time was different,
>   You said it was best;
> You flew the coop, dear,
>   And left me the mess.

—and roared along with him, everybody in the musty old firetrap of an auditorium, as Bluejay and the Sixkillers all sang the chorus.

The longer you're gone,
The harder it gets;
You flew the coop, dear,
And left me the mess . . .

They were on their feet, cheering, and after an encore it was
time for business. Grant Turner read from a script about "that
good old down-home chocolate flavor of Goo-Goo. You can take
it from Bluejay Clay himself." Turner pointed to Bluejay, who
leaned in to the microphone and sang, to the old shave-and-a-
haircut-six-bits jingle, "Go-get-a-Goo-Goo . . . it's good!" Bluejay
brought on the Stone Mountain Cloggers from Atlanta, the men
in shiny black rayon trousers and string ties and the women in
red and white bolero skirts and lacy petticoats, and while they
spun and clattered to a foot-stomping hoedown he drifted away
from the microphones.

"Are you serious, Bluejay?" somebody laughed at him.

"About what?"

"That 'go-get-a-goo-goo.' "

"Naw," Bluejay said, "but *they* are."

The cloggers finished and there was another commercial for
Goo-Goo before Bluejay was welcomed back by the audience.
When the applause died he cleared his throat and said, motioning
for Jaybird to join him, "I want y'all to meet my son here. Henry
Buford Clay Jr.'s his name, but we all call him 'Jaybird.' " The
crowd cheered. "Looks like his old man, but he can't help it,"
Bluejay said, Jaybird blushing, Grant Turner standing in the wings
imploring the crowd to applaud again. Again Bluejay cleared his
throat. "Maybe some of y'all have heard my latest release on
Decca records, song called 'Molly.' " Whistling, clapping, stomping until Bluejay held up his arms. "Thank you, thank you very
much, but let me talk for a minute. Reason I wanted Jaybird to
be here tonight, right here on the stage with me, is because, well,
see, the real Molly was my wife and Jaybird's mama, and, well,
see, all of this really"—Bluejay was having a hell of a time of it,
to his surprise, and many of the women in the church pews were
digging for their Kleenex—"well, it really happened like this.

Molly and what was going to be Robin, Jaybird's little brother, neither one of 'em made it that night and I just"—the Sixkillers, ever so softly, were going into the melody—"well, I just wanted to sing about Molly for you. First time we've done it on the Opry."

> The cold wind was a-howling
>   On that awful winter's night,
> The night the devil came
>   A-spoiling for a fight.

> The three of us were happy
>   For soon we would be four,
> But little did we know
>   What the devil had in store.

>   Molly my love,
>   Molly my love,
>   Molly my fair sweet lady;
>   They took you away
>   And left us alone
>   They even took the baby . . .

It wasn't an Opry record for encores—Hank Williams got that, fourteen, the time he first sang "Lovesick Blues" at Ryman Auditorium—because it wasn't the sort of foot-stomping howler associated with delirium. "Molly," sappy and autobiographical as it was, brought more tears than cheers from the audience of simple rural people. Bluejay was pleased enough with three encores, pleased enough that he could have Jaybird take an extra bow, and the same was true when they repeated it on the eleven o'clock Stanback ("Snap back with Stanback") Headache Powder show. After the Opry they all dropped by the Blue Room for beer and Nehis and autographs and adulation and gossip and entreaties from would-be songwriters ("Blue, you got to hear this song," a red-faced old boy would say, "I wrote the words *and* the lyrics"). Then they walked across Broadway to Ernest Tubb's Record Shop to sing "Molly" again, this time on the "Midnight Jamboree" show following the Opry on WSM. Sam went and got the bus and brought it around to the front door of E.T.'s place and they piled aboard, suddenly very tired, for the ride back home to Sixkiller.

"What's so funny?" Bluejay said to Jaybird. They sat at the fold-down table near the front of the bus, sipping coffee, unable to sleep like the others, while Sam maneuvered the bus southward through the hump-backed hills of Middle Tennessee.

"Sam, at the Opry," said Jaybird.

"Well, he is sort of funny, come to think of it."

"You should've seen him."

"What'd I miss?"

"You were over there talking to Roy Acuff between shows and Sam grabbed Ray Price."

"The 'Cherokee Cowboy'?"

"Uh-hunh. Sam said something like, 'Allow me to present myself,' and gave him a calling card. Said, 'Us Injuns gotta stick together. Call me if I can be of service.' "

"What'd Ray do?"

"Asked him how things were on the reservation."

Sam overheard their conversation and said something about how he was thinking about expanding—new clients like the Cherokee Cowboy, medicine shows, a Rent-a-Squaw scam, authentic Sutalitihi Firewater at ten dollars a jug—as they rolled through the deserted main drag of Monteagle. Sam had dialed the radio to WSM. The guest that night on the all-night "Opry Star Spotlight" was Minnie Pearl, she of the outrageous store-bought hat with a price tag on it and the down-home tales of "Uncle Nabob" and his drinking, explaining one more time how a graduate of Vanderbilt wound up as an Opry regular.

"That Minnie," said Bluejay, "she's a card."

"I guess so." Jaybird drained the cup of coffee.

"What do you mean, you *guess* so?"

"She's corny, Pa. Tacky."

"Tacky? Where'd you learn that word?"

"Never mind. Forget it."

Bluejay said, "I reckon people like Becky Rollins might look at it like that. Probably figure I'm 'tacky,' too. Matter of fact, from what I been hearing, there's some of our own people starting to talk like that. Like that fella that came out in that gold outfit, jumping all over the place, singing about Memphis. If you want to call it singing."

"Bobby Smart."

"Yeah, that's him. Electric guitar. How'd you know?"

"I talked to him," said Jaybird.

"Didn't know they could talk."

"Aw, Pa."

"Okay, son. What'd this 'Bobby Smart' have to say?"

Jaybird crushed the paper cup and began fiddling with his plastic spoon. He spoke with his head down, in a rush. "He said the Opry wasn't going to last much longer. That people like Ernest Tubb and Roy Acuff and Minnie Pearl were going out of style. You, too. Called y'all 'billies.' Said you were too stubborn to change. Said every time an old farmer dies somewhere that's one more fan he doesn't have to worry about. Said y'all are 'tacky.' That's where I heard the word."

"You believe that, son?"

"I don't know, Pa. I'm thinking about it."

"Well, you just do that."

"Look, Pa, I'm sorry."

"I might be tacky, but I notice you ain't starving."

It was daybreak when the bus bumped beneath the archway announcing SIXKILLER. The Sixkillers stirred away in their bunks, gathered their instruments and wordlessly went to their own homes. Bluejay told Jaybird to go on into the house and get some sleep, that he and Sam would take care of the morning chores on the farm, and once Sam had parked the bus in the barn he and Bluejay went about collecting eggs and letting the cows out to the pasture and looking in on the new lambs. That accomplished, all quiet on the home front on a dewy Sunday morning, Bluejay went to the house and brought his guitar out to the front porch and began—in earnest this time—working on "Hillbilly Fever." *It started in the mountains/Spread all over town . . . Can't keep a 'billy down . . .*

CHAPTER IX

A T MIDMORNING, with Jaybird in school and Sam off to Cherokee in the pickup on some vague mission, Bluejay lolled in a hammock strung in a grove of elms and went through the mail. This, he was thinking as he plunged into the mail pouch, was exactly why one of Sam's duties under the new arrangement was to serve as sort of unofficial postmaster for Sixkiller Farm. *Sam . . . fan letter . . . fan letter . . . Jaybird . . . advertising . . . fan letter, fan letter . . . light bill . . . Sears . . . Sam . . . royalty check . . .* As he sorted through the dozens of envelopes he deftly flipped them onto the proper pile in the deep green spring grass—a pile for Sam, a fan-mail pile, a pile for farm business, a pile for pure junk—as expertly as a card sharp would deal blackjack in Reno. The only one he bothered to open and read, on the assumption that Sam would cull the rest, was one addressed to "Mr. Henry Buford Clay Sr." from Diversified Enterprises Inc.

Dear Mr. Clay:

I am authorized on the behalf of Diversified Enterprises to discuss with you a proposal which should be, in my opinion, beneficial to both parties.

Will you, at your earliest convenience, please contact my secretary, Mrs. Adele Griggs, so a meeting between the two of us can be arranged? Lunch, perhaps, in our new Executive Annex?

Besides, darn it, if I may be personal for a moment, it seems about time that I met the most famous citizen of Cherokee County!

Yours Truly,

(Signed)
H. Kennerly Rollins III
Vice President, Southern Operations

P.S.: Congratulations on your latest record!!

It seemed to Bluejay that they would never give up. Three times in the last month he had gotten a letter from a Frank M. Segrist, "Senior Purchasing Officer," trying to set up a meeting and three times he had tossed the letter aside. He knew what they wanted. Diversified had been buying up land in and around Andrews so voraciously that the company now owned an estimated thirty percent of what didn't belong to the federal government. They were moving in on widows and small dirt farmers, easily winning bankruptcy auctions with their big Midwestern money, and it seemed as though they could get their hands on anything they wanted. The day the membership on the Cherokee State Bank board of directors went top-heavy with executives of Diversified was the day the bank stopped giving ninety-day loan extensions. Now, it was clear to Bluejay, Diversified wanted a piece of Sixkiller Farm. A proposal "beneficial to both parties," Rollins had written, reminded him of Sam's reaction to the story that time in *The New York Times* about the coming of Diversified. *Same thing they told Uwani Sutal-itihi.*

So Bluejay rolled the letter into a ball and was taking aim at one of the stray cats on the place when Billy Wingo rolled up in his new patrol car, gave the siren a wail, then got out grinning and tipping his gray ranger's hat as he ambled toward where Bluejay lay in the hammock.

"What in the pluperfect hell's going on here, Billy?"

"Got me a new wagon, Blue."

"Well, hell, I can see that. Steal it from Franklin?"

"Naw. County bought it for me."

"New uniform, too, I see."

"Yep. New everything."

"But that new gun, Billy. What happened to your six-shooter?"

"Well, that's the bad part," said Billy Wingo. He sat down in the grass, hitching up the belt holding a shiny new .38 police revolver, and leaned back against an elm. "Tried to tell 'em it was my granddaddy's gun, one he used to shoot squirrels with, but they said I couldn't wear it on the job no more. Said it wadn't good for my image, walking around town with a six-shooter on my hip. Give me this little ol' water pistol here"—he slapped the .38—"and told me to hang the iron on the wall."

"That what this is all about?" Bluejay said.

"What?"

"Image. Y'all got to look like gentlemen of the law now?"

"I reckon," Billy said. "Next thing you know they'll make me and Wesley take down the speed trap."

Billy Wingo, like most of the other men of the valley who were now in their forties, had been a friend of Bluejay's since the days of shooting marbles and flying kites and skinny-dipping and playing hookey. Bluejay had grown up to become a star of the Grand Ole Opry, Harvey Sellers had become principal of the high school and Billy Wingo had become sheriff of Cherokee County. On the night Billy played his last game at tackle for the Andrews High Raiders, meaning he quit exercising but kept on eating, he went to fat. He wasn't six feet tall but weighed nearly three hundred pounds—a perfect match for his wife and mother of six children, the former Evelyn Hooks, so fat now she used a cane to get around—giving him a decided advantage when it became necessary to calm down a drunk, say, at the Bear's Den on a Saturday night. Billy simply sat on them, when such occasions arose, bringing peace without undue violence and furthering his image as an all-around good old boy. Billy Wingo, in short, was one of them.

"So what brings you out here, Billy?"

"Oh, just thought I'd visit. Been a while.'"

"Reckon it has been," said Bluejay.

"Yep. Sure has," said Billy.

"Evelyn all right?"

"What?"

"Your wife. Evelyn. She doing all right?"

"Oh, sure. Sure. She's okay."

They watched two bluejays dive-bomb the scraggly striped cat. Billy pulled at weeds. Bluejay rolled a Bull Durham. Billy cleaned his new .38. Bluejay batted at some gnats and finally said, "Okay, Billy, what's on your mind? If you came here for small talk you ain't doing a very good job of it."

Billy blurted it out. "Sam here?"

"Naw," said Bluejay. "Over in Cherokee. Why?"

"Seems I got a warrant for his arrest."

"A warrant? For Sam?"

"Yep. In the car there."

"What in the devil for, Billy?"

"Moonshine."

"Good godamitey, Billy. Usually you want to *buy* some."

"I know," Billy Wingo said. "But that's all changed now."

"Changed."

"Changed. They say we got to bring him in."

"They," said Bluejay.

"They," said Billy.

No Sam, no arrest, it was agreed. Billy said there was no particular rush about it, Bluejay said he'd be sure to mention it whenever he saw Sam, and Billy trundled back to the new blue and gray Cherokee County Sheriff's car. As he eased away from the farm to drive back into Andrews, giving the siren another short blast, Billy Wingo could have seen Bluejay Clay flipping out of the hammock and slamming his cigarette to the ground and stalking off to the house. Bluejay slapped his cowboy hat on his head, the one that went with his desert-tan fringed jacket and blue jeans and chocolate boots, grabbed a jug of Sam's finest and cranked the old AirFlyte and fish-tailed beneath the SIXKILLER arch. Ten minutes later he was standing in the paneled and carpeted foyer of Diversified Enterprises' executive wing.

Adele Griggs, who had been one of Molly O'Hare Clay's best friends during high school nearly thirty years earlier, sat at the walnut desk—behind glass double doors, in a frilly pink blouse, beneath air conditioning—typing a letter. Behind her was an oak door with a bronze nameplate saying H. KENNERLY ROLLINS III. When she looked up from her typewriter to see Bluejay she froze. "Why Bluejay—"

"Where's the sonofabitch at?" said Bluejay.

"What a surprise, Bluejay."

"Yeah, it's been a day full of 'em. Where's he at?"

Adele, flustered, said, "He's in conference right now, Bluejay, but if you'll take a seat I'll—"

Bluejay rushed around her desk. "Think I'll join him."

"Bluejay, you can't go in there."

"You ought to be ashamed of yourself," Bluejay said. He blew open the door to Rollins' office and stood in the doorway—feet apart, jug in hand, cowboy hat tilted forward, Adele jabbering in his wake—to confront the enemy. He wished he had brought a pearl-handled six-shooter, slung low on his hips, for effect.

What Bluejay saw reminded him of the scene in all of the World War II movies where John Wayne and a bunch of other battlefield commanders stand around a map in what they called the "war room," pushing toy tanks and soldiers here and there with long-handled sticks, planning their next battle. In this case there were two men in three-piece Palm Beach suits and paisley ties and two-toned wing-tip shoes, deep in conversation, using long batons to point out various shaded areas on a large relief map mounted to a three-quarter-inch plywood table occupying half of the room. When the door flew open the men, startled, froze for a second and looked over Bluejay's shoulders for an explanation. Adele babbled about how she had tried to stop him. The man whom Bluejay guessed to be Rollins told her it was all right, laid his baton on the map and excused the other man, and then stepped toward Bluejay with his right hand extended.

"Well, now. Bluejay," he said.

"Only my friends call me Bluejay." Bluejay's hands didn't move.

"Sorry, Mr. Clay. I'm like a fan, I suppose. Feel like I've known you ever since your son gave my daughter one of your records."

"Let's leave them out of this."

"As you wish. Care for a cigar? Some iced tea?"

"No, thanks," said Bluejay. "I brought my own. Genuine hundred-and-twenty-octane Cherokee Firewater. Guaranteed to blow your brains out. Just found out it's illegal as hell, something I figured you might o' heard about, but I like it so much it's too late to quit." In one move Bluejay uncapped the jug, hoisted it to his shoulder and took a drink mountain-style, tamped the cork back in and plopped the jug on Rollins' mahogany desk. "It's yours. Give you something to write home about."

"Well, my stars, Mr. Clay."

"Yeah, well, you'll be seeing stars when you try it."

"It's the real thing, you say? Real 'moonshine'?"

"Might be the last batch ever run around here."

"I'm afraid I don't follow you."

Bluejay, still standing, folded his arms across his chest. "Look, Rollins," he said, "why don't we cut out the bullshit? I'm no more some ignorant hillbilly than you are a city slicker who don't know his moonshine. I don't like you worth a damn and I figure you're gonna feel the same way about me in five minutes. You and me are like oil and water. Right?"

"Well," said Rollins, "I feel that perhaps, with time—"

"Goddamit, don't you understand me, man?"

"All right, Clay. All right."

"Good. Now show me that goddam map over there."

They stepped to the map. It was an official United States Geological Survey relief map of Cherokee County, North Carolina, showing every ridge and every fold in the mountains. Bluejay had never seen one before and he was fascinated. He ran his fingers over Hanging Dog Mountain and the low-lying part west of Murphy signifying Hiawassee Lake. All of the towns and villages in the county and nearby were there—Tusquitee, Brasstown, Ranger, Marble, Hothouse, Hayesville—and in the larger towns of Andrews and Murphy there were clusters of tiny black dots denoting houses and buildings.

"What's all them different colors?" Bluejay said.

"It's coded," said Rollins.

"For what?"

"To show us the disposition of the land."

"The green, now," Bluejay said, "that would be for the national forest. Right?"

"Correct. As you see, the majority is shaded green."

"And the white part. What's that stand for?"

"Clay," said Rollins, "this is company business. It's secret. It's our game plan, so to speak. I shouldn't be showing you this."

"Ain't you in charge?"

"Well, yes, technically."

"Didn't you invite me up here? Didn't you keep writing?"

"Yes."

"Here I am. Tell me how you're gonna win the war."

Rollins took the baton in his hand. Bluejay, who had decided to let him go, stuffed his hands in his fringed jacket. "All right," Rollins said. "The areas shaded in green, as you pointed out, signify the Nantahala National Forest. The white means city or county land. The areas which have been shaded blue represent land we have purchased since we began our operations here two years ago. And the pink areas are known as TAP."

"TAP, you say," said Bluejay.

"It's an acronym for 'Target Acquisition Properties.' "

"What do you know. Forty-three years and I thought it was green."

"I'm afraid I don't understand."

"Sixkiller," Bluejay said. "You got it painted pink."

'Well, yes, that's why I wanted to talk to you."

"Course, sometimes in the winter it's white. Real bright green around April. Turns a pretty orange about late September. But I'll be a sonofabitch if you ain't got it pink here."

Rollins flipped the baton onto the relief map, jiggled at his tie and walked back to his desk. Bluejay followed him and placed his fingertips on the desk and said, as coldly as a gunslinger, "You can't touch me, Rollins, and I figure you sort of know that deep down in your gut. I got more reasons to stay than you got engineers to try taking it away. That map you got over there looks real nice and orderly, all them plans laid out like it was a drawing board, but there's a lot of things that map don't show. It don't show that my great-granddaddy was born where you got it painted pink. It don't show that old man Henry Bottoms died with a heart attack plowing behind a mule last year, trying to feed his kids, and y'all wouldn't extend his loan because you wanted to paint his land that pretty blue. Y'all ain't just messing around with the land around here. You're messing with *lives*. And I'm one that ain't gonna put up with it. About the only way you'd ever get your hands on Sixkiller would be if Jaybird and that little girl of yours was to get married and something bad happened."

"I don't believe that will happen, Clay," said Rollins.

"I sure as hell hope not."

"So do I."

"You mean that?"

"Of course," said Rollins. "I don't think your son is, ah, quite *right* for my Rebecca."

"Well, I'll be a sonofabitch," Bluejay said. "At least we agree on *something*."

CHAPTER X

BLUE JAY looked at the summer of Jaybird's eighteenth year, a one-hundred-day period during which the boy would become the first Clay to graduate from high school and then the first to attend college, as his last real opportunity to leave his son with something to think about. "Got to put that Clay brand on him, Sam, just like you do a colt," he said on the night of the Senior Dance, parents not invited, while he and Sam played checkers in the big house and Jaybird was at the Andrews High gymnasium jumping to Sammy and the Slicks. Except for the next night, graduation night, when the two men did too much celebrating *before* the event and nearly broke up the ceremony by standing on their metal folding chairs and cutting loose with blood-curdling *Yeeeeaaaayyyiiiieeeee!!!* Rebel yells when Harvey Sellers called out the name Henry Buford Clay Jr., Bluejay and Sam spent the summer as indulgent co-fathers. Bluejay canceled all of his appearances, except for two obligatory trips to do the Opry (Jaybird had good excuses not to go each time), in order to stay on the farm with the boy. Jaybird was allowed, for the most part, to do anything he wanted. He slept through the chores, went on a ten-day hike alone to Clingman's Dome and back on the Appalachian Trail, caught trout with Bluejay, trapped and skinned a black bear with Sam, drove all the way to Atlanta with a buddy one day just to see what the

big city looked like and, of course, saw all of Becky Rollins that
he could.

It hadn't been easy for Bluejay to hold his tongue on the
subject of Becky, on those honeysuckled midnights when Jaybird
would quietly return to the farm after spending the evening with
her in the back seat of the AirFlyte at the Carolina Drive-In, but
his only hope seemed to be that maybe the boy would see enough
of her to see what he saw. Now and then Bluejay couldn't contain
himself. "Never took up golf, myself, mainly 'cause I don't like
the people that play it," he would blurt at the supper table, Sam
going rigid and Jaybird dropping his fork in his plate, the father
quickly moving on to discussing the weather. He was better at
speaking in parables, anyway, so he learned to talk about Judas
goats when he had something to say about Rollins and sirens
luring sailors to death on the shoals when he meant Becky. On
rainy nights, with a modest fire going and raindrops dancing on
the tin roof and the father and the son aimlessly watching Dagmar wiggle across the harsh gray television screen, Bluejay was
wont to take out the leather-bound family Bible and see the name
of an ancestor carefully inscribed by Molly—Elijah Clay, 1776–
1816, Fever—and begin rambling. "Elijah, now, my daddy told
me about the time Elijah and them took this revenuer by surprise
up there in Pennsylvania and hung him up to this tree by his
ankles and . . ." Bluejay garnishing the story, Jaybird nodding
and trying to listen to Milton Berle and his father at the same
time.

It was on such a night in August, when they had been counting on going with Sam to the county fair before a sudden rain-
storm roared over the ridge, that Bluejay made what was, to him,
a remarkable discovery. Jaybird was munching popcorn and
watching the ventriloquist Señor Winces when Bluejay, who had
been rummaging through an old suitcase stuffed with everything
from bills of sale to snapshots of Molly, suddenly slapped his
thigh and said, "By God, there it is."

"There's what?" said Jaybird.

"What I been looking for all along."

"Didn't know you'd lost anything, Pa."

"I didn't, either, until I found it."

"Found what?"

"Turn that thing off," Bluejay said, "so I can read you something. I'll be damn. First time I read it I didn't pay much attention. It's that story that fellow did on us one time, that Shaughnessy fellow with *The New Yorker*, one that came down here before your Mama died." Jaybird turned off the television set. Then Bluejay began to read aloud.

. . . for never, in my scores of interviews with Southern Highlanders ranging from Bluejay Clay, the country singer in western North Carolina, to the last remaining grandson of Devil Anse Hatfield in southwestern West Virginia (Henry Hatfield, in a grim irony, is now the tombstone supplier on the infamous Hatfield-McCoy feuding ground), did women figure prominently in the mountain folks' recounting of family histories. Whenever there was a special mention of a wife or daughter or aunt or grandmother it was because she had somehow caused a disruption in the orderly progression of the male bloodline. "Way I see it," a farmer in northeastern Tennessee told me, "Adam came first and the only reason he needed Eve was so he'd have some boys to pass things on to." The Hatfield-McCoy feud began, according to Henry Hatfield, in a dispute over a voluptuous McCoy girl. Bluejay Clay, like most of the Appalachian men I interviewed, never so much as hinted at the possibility that his enduring wife, Molly, might bear a daughter. "When Jaybird's brother gets here," he would preface his expectations for the future of the Clay family. In the mountains a woman is expected to serve as a mere conduit through which passes the male blood . . .

"The boy wrote fancy," Bluejay said when he finished reading.

"I'll say," said Jaybird. "You don't see 'conduit' much."

"Means a sort of passageway, don't it?"

"Yes, sir. Like a telephone wire. Or a gas line."

"What I thought. Maybe that's why they pay them writers so much money. They got to be smart enough to explain things you been thinking all along. The fellow Shaughnessy was right. Says here, wait a minute, yeah, says, 'Whenever there was a special mention of a wife or daughter or aunt or grandmother it was because she had somehow caused a disruption in the orderly progression of the male bloodline.' And that's right. My daddy didn't quite come right out and say it, but the reason *his* daddy, that's Newt, one with the peg leg, got all messed up for a while was because of his wife. She was one of them Townsends. She was just plain sorry. That's what drove ol' Newt to drinking and messing around with squaws. But when his wife gave him my daddy he kicked her out. Kinda said, 'Thank you, but the Clays'll take over now.' And then he straightened out and raised my daddy by himself."

"I don't know, Pa," Jaybird said, "I don't think your theory holds up. What about Mama? You talk about Mama like she was the only woman in the world. You go and sing 'Molly' on the Opry and it's all you can do to keep from crying. Didn't my Mama count?"

"You don't understand what I'm trying to say, son."

"Afraid I don't. And I don't like to hear it."

"But it's *there*, boy, it's *there*. It's in the blood. It's in the Clay blood. O'Hare blood didn't have nothing to do with it."

"I guess now I'm gonna get a lecture about Rollins blood."

"Naw," said Bluejay, "naw, you won't. Now that I think about it, it ain't gonna make a bit of difference. She might slow you down a little bit. You might wind up losing about ten years off your life like Newt's daddy did. That's Buford, one I'm named after, the one that died with the fever because his wife was one of them Holy Rollers that didn't believe in doctors."

"You never told me about that," said Jaybird.

"I just forgot," Bluejay said. "That was about 1845, more than a hundred years ago, right here in this house. Their boy, Newt, wasn't but about five years old. Buford's wife was another sorry one. A McAlister from Murphy. Didn't matter, though, don't you see, because the Clay blood had already been passed through that 'conduit' to Newt and it was too late to stop it. See, boy, it's simple."

"Things aren't that simple, Pa."

"They are, son, they are. You'll see."

"What about if I married Becky. Becky *Rollins*."

"Fine with me," said Bluejay.

"Fine?" Jaybird was flustered. "Ain't she 'sorry,' too?"

"Way I'm thinking now, it won't matter. *Clay* matters."

"Yeah, yeah. 'It's in the blood.' "

"I'd kinda like Robin," Bluejay said, closing and strapping the old suitcase full of Clay family memorabilia. "Robin Clay. Got a nice sound to it. We never had a chance to use that one."

An unlikely sort of serenity settled in with Bluejay after that talk with Jaybird about fathers and sons, as though he had finally been able to articulate his feelings about life, so much so that on the eve of his son's departure for the alien world of classrooms and dormitories and exams he felt no particular urge to give any final last-minute fatherly advice. *What will be*, was his mood, *will be. He's a Clay.*

"Smartest thing to do, the way I see it, is just take him up there on the bus." Bluejay winked at Sam and the two of them kept straight faces, acting as though Jaybird weren't there with them. It was nearing dusk, the fireflies already playing in the yard, and the three of them sat on the front porch after supper.

"Probably the easiest way to carry everything," said Sam.

"Figure it'd impress his new friends," said Bluejay.

"Maybe the boys would want to go along."

"Damn, Sam, you're right. That's a good idea."

"Roll up in the bus with BLUEJAY CLAY & THE SIXKILLERS on it."

"Yeah. And then we do 'The Longer You're Gone.' Right there in front of the dormitory. That's a hell of a way to send him off." Bluejay paused to glance at Jaybird. The boy was prepared to walk to Middle Tennessee State University. "But then, on the other hand, if we did that he wouldn't have anything to drive around school."

"That's right," said Sam. "I forgot about that."

"Where's that old pickup at, Sam? I ain't seen it around."

"In the barn, far as I know."

"It still working?"

"Far as I know."

"Why don't we just go down there and check it out? Pickup

ought to be just about right for carrying things to Murfreesboro. Old thing's about had it, anyway."

Sam walked ahead of Bluejay and Jaybird, in order to throw open the barn doors and turn on the lights, and when Jaybird saw what they had been up to he couldn't believe his eyes. The faithful old '46 Dodge had been transformed into the most wondrously bizarre chariot an eighteen-year-old boy could imagine: new wide racing tires, jacked up in the back, radio aerial with a squirrel's tail on the tip, fringed curtains for drive-in privacy, a camper body furnished with a bunk and a toilet and a hot plate, bearskin seat covers, an AM-FM radio with a total of four speakers front and back, new chrome, Twin Smitties, a horn that went *my-dog-has-fleas*, a chrome hood ornament of a soaring eagle with a six-inch wing span and—the topper—a very-blue paint job and four-inch letters on each door spelling JAYBIRD.

"Might as well take it," said Bluejay. "I wouldn't be caught dead in it."

"Y'all do that?" said Jaybird.

"The lettering, too."

"Yeah, the lettering."

"I figured ain't nobody likely to steal it with your name on it."

"Well," Jaybird said, "we'll see about the lettering."

"Just keep it in the road, son. Keep it in the road."

"I'll try, Pa. I'll try."

BOOK TWO

Jaybird

CHAPTER I

TELL you one thing, Jay, if somebody was to drop a bomb on one of Gordy's Christmas parties there'd never be another country song come out of Nashville. Now that's a fact, my friend." Jaybird Clay and Buck Moon, the drummer in Bobby Smart's band, were standing next to one of the half-dozen bars in the penthouse of TopRank International's sleek new glass and concrete building on Music Row as the stars and hangers-on and executives and groupies streamed through the wide glass double doors for the annual "Holiday Hoo-Hah" thrown by Gordon Mock and TopRank. Jaybird, ordering another bourbon on the rocks, surveyed the crowd and acknowledged Buck's perception. Swirling about the room, ogling the leggy secretaries and swilling booze and trying to top each other with show-business stories, was just about everybody of any consequence in what was now being called "Music City U.S.A." There was Johnny Cash, wearing his *de rigueur* black, being interviewed by Bill Williams of *Billboard*. Ralph Emery, the powerful disc jockey and host of WSM's late-night "Opry Star Spotlight," was laughing out of control at a Jerry Reed joke. Tex Ritter and Bill Monroe, two of the old-timers, stood in a corner together and looked lost. John Hartford, about to bid farewell to blue jeans and ratty Volkswagens and follow Glen Campbell to Hollywood since "Gentle On My Mind," was saying good-bye to Chet Atkins. Porter Wagoner in his rhinestones, Dolly Parton with her cleavage, Eddy Arnold wearing a tuxedo. Everybody was there, indeed, including Jay Clay of TopRank, Inc.

"So," Buck Moon said, "you enjoying the single life?"

"Much as I did when I was married," said Jaybird.

"Hah. You scoundrel. I been reading about you."

"I don't know what you're talking about."

"Bullshit. That thing in the *Music City News*. That broad that writes the gossip column. How'd it go? 'What rhyming son-of-a-bird is holding P-TA meetings in Demonbreun lovenest these nights?' If that ain't you and Jeannie C. Riley I ain't Buck Moon."

"You better check your ID, then."

"Aw, come on, Jay, you can tell *me*."

"That could've been anybody," said Jaybird.

"Anybody, my ass. 'Rhyming son-of-a-bird,' tell me that ain't Jay Clay, son of Bluejay. 'P-TA,' as in 'Harper Valley PTA.' Your pad's on Demonbreun, ain't it?"

"For Christ's sake, Buck. Number one, she's married. Number two, the only place I've seen her was getting out of that awful purple Cadillac behind Hubert's office one day. Number three, she can't sing a lick. And number four, I'm too busy."

"What I heard."

"So many women, so little time."

"What say?"

"So many women, so little time."

"Sounds like a good song to me," said Buck.

"Good," Jaybird said, "I'll live it, you write it," chucking Buck under the chin, winking, swallowing his bourbon and ordering another, spying Red O'Donnell of the *Banner* across the way, excusing himself to Buck, weaving through the crowd, greeting and being greeted, bumping into Danny Davis of The Nashville Brass, stopping long enough to clink glasses and say Merry Christmas to Tootsie Bess of Tootsie's Orchid Lounge, plunging ahead through the maelstrom like a trout moving upstream through familiar waters, overhearing the fervent delicious snippets of a world he wanted now more than ever before— *Five encores at Cobo Hall ain't to be sniffed at. . . . See, it's*

what I call the old "What woman?" theory. . . . Audrey's made
damned sure everybody knows who she is. . . . Who would've
ever thought they'd close the Ryman? . . . Pills, booze, you name
it. . . . And then Minnie, she says . . . Hag told the Opry they
could go to hell. . . . Dylan's supposed to be here next month—
a world he thought would never end.

In the ten years since he had graduated from Middle Tennessee State University and gone to work as a troubleshooter for
TopRank—talent agent, publicist, artists-and-repertoire man,
talent scout—Jaybird had seen the Nashville music industry climb
from its deepest pit and soar to its highest pinnacle. When he
first arrived to work for Gordon Mock the country music business was in disarray because of rock 'n' roll. His father and the
others of that generation, the Ernest Tubbs and Hank Snows and
Webb Pierces, had refused to acknowledge the "baby boom"
which followed World War II. Those babies were now reaching
their teens and, thanks to the remarkable changes which hit the
South after the war, they were the region's first generation to
have any degree of affluence and to go to college *en masse* and
to have interests stretching beyond the boundaries of the farms
and the small towns and the honky-tonks their fathers had known.
Bobby Smart had been right, back there in 1954, when he told
a young Jaybird Clay that every time a farmer died that meant
one less fan he had to worry about pleasing. The kids of the late
fifties and early sixties didn't want twangy steel guitars and
yodels and corn-pone Minnie Pearl humor. They wanted Elvis
Presley and electrified noise and blatant sexuality. Nashville was
still Hillbilly Heaven, sure, but there wasn't much demand for
hillbillies anymore.

What one heard on the radio was a good barometer. In 1961
there were only eighty full-time "country" radio stations in all
of North America. Those were still hanging on to the same hard-
line country format which had always succeeded before—Tubb
and Bluejay and Kitty Wells, country preachers, hucksters selling
everything short of autographed pictures of Jesus Himself, songs
about prison and unrequited love and faithful mothers and un-
faithful wives—while the rest of the world went ahead without

them. Tubb, content to work the same round of fighting-and-dancing clubs in West Texas, still banged around the two-lane black-topped roads in an old bus and played in front of three or four thousand hell-raising ranchers and farmers on Friday nights before racing all the way back to Nashville for the Opry to play for peanuts. In the meantime the men like Bobby Smart, with their tight lamé suits and hard-driving electric guitars and leering libidos showing, were flying off to play in front of some twenty thousand people at Cobo Hall in Detroit for $7,500.

It didn't take long for Nashville to recover. By the mid-sixties men such as Chet Atkins, a brilliant guitarist who had been weaned on the stage of Ryman Auditorium but saw the need for change, created what became known as the Nashville Sound. It was a hybrid which retained the aching emotions of country music but added string sections and became sweeter and more palatable to people in the city, which is where the majority of Americans lived now, and by the end of the decade "countrypolitan" music was the rage. Countrypolitan was "The Glen Campbell Goodtime Hour" on CBS-TV, Dean Martin and Ray Charles and the like recording in the new studios up and down "Music Row" in Nashville, the Public Broadcasting Service running a ninety-minute perspective on Johnny Cash, a Japanese version of the Grand Ole Opry cranking up in Tokyo, regular "country" concerts at places like Carnegie Hall in New York and the Palladium in London and the Hollywood Bowl.

Nashville, then, had become everything this son of an old-line "hillbilly" had hoped for when he left the farm in western North Carolina. It had been dizzying for Jaybird—the abrupt affluence, the cars, the women, the high times, the merry-go-round—and it had cost him. Now, at thirty-two, he was divorced from his childhood sweetheart, Rebecca Rollins of Andrews, North Carolina. So bitter had she become over the womanizing which had led to the divorce, she had become most effective at keeping Jaybird away from their son, now nine and living in Andrews with his mother and her new husband, a young executive for Diversified Enterprises by the name of Siebert. And this divorce, this breaking of the natural progression of the generations, had created the greatest problem of all. It meant that Henry Buford Clay III, known as "Robin," the last of the Clay men, was being systematically plucked from the roost.

"Jay, over here." Jaybird found a clearing in the crowd and made his way to Red O'Donnell, the columnist for the *Banner*, who stood beside another of the portable bars set up in the penthouse for the party. Through the plate-glass window beyond Red, out on Sixteenth Avenue South, Music Row, the first snow of the winter had begun to collect. "Want you to meet somebody here, Jay," said O'Donnell. Jaybird was introduced to a reedy man, about his age, named David Nelson. "Dave's gonna be spending some time here doing a book. Thought y'all ought to meet." Red waved to Jo Walker of the Country Music Association and left Jaybird with Nelson.

"Red tells me you're Bluejay Clay's son," the writer said.

"Hard to hide it around here," said Jaybird.

"You wouldn't *want* to hide it, would you?"

"Why? What kind of question is that?"

"Oh, don't get me wrong. I didn't mean it like that. But it's interesting."

"What's interesting?"

"The sons of the stars," Nelson said. "So far I've talked with Justin Tubb and Hank Jr. Both of them told me essentially the same thing—that it's been hard for them to make the transition."

"Well, for starters, I'm in the business end. Not a star."

"Yeah, but still you're sort of caught in the crossfire."

"I don't look at it like that," said Jaybird.

"Hank Jr. says he's having a hell of a time living it down."

"So be it. My old man's a 'billy. I'm not. So what?"

"That what you call him? A 'billy?"

"Look"—Jaybird was trying hard not to dislike this man— "it's a word even my old man uses. He's got it in a song he cut almost ten years ago. He even called the song 'Hillbilly Fever.' You ought to get a copy of it. He was just saying what *he* felt."

"You see much of him?" Nelson said.

"Not enough. But, yeah. I'm here and he's there. You know."

"Where's 'there'?"

"Little farm in North Carolina. Place where I grew up."

"You go back often?"

"Going tomorrow, for Christmas. My boy's down there, too," Jaybird said. He reached for his billfold and produced a calling card for the writer. "Hey," he said, "I do believe I see some quail over there that need flushing. Here's my card. Maybe we can talk some other time, okay? Keep 'er in the road."

Jaybird Clay moved as deftly as Sam Sixkiller stalking a deer, cutting a lissome brunette from her two girlfriends, dazzling her with the gold pendant hanging against his bare chest, taking her down to the next floor to show her the framed gold records lining his office ("I was Bobby Smart's A&R man on each one"), suggesting a steak at the Red Lion, ordering the best wine, boring through her with his sleepy blue eyes, being first-named by the *maître d'*, recommending music and cognac at his place, she beginning to giggle and lean on his shoulder as he did his Tex Ritter "High Noon" imitation on the drive through snow-slick streets, parking the new white Thunderbird behind the condominiums on Demonbreun, up a flight of stairs, soft opening of the door, home at last. *Rita! Rishia! Rhonda! / Golly, what a nice apartment / Cognac! / Sure / Music! / Glen Campbell / Married! / Used to be / Didn't everybody used to be! / Get comfortable / Ummmmmm / Let me help you.* It was too easy. Much too easy.

CHAPTER II

HER NAME, not that it mattered, was Roxie. XXX ROXIE 451–2793 she had scrawled with her lipstick on the mirror above the bathroom sink, with a PS—IOU $5, probably meaning she had taken a five-dollar bill to pay for a cab. *Be my guest*, he thought as he wiped the mirror clean in order to shave. *Love me or leave me but don't let me be lonely, dah-de-dah-de-de-dah-dah* . . . A pint of Guinness Stout and two Excedrin for the head. Louis Armstrong turned up full-power on the stereo—*Hello, Roxie, well hello, Roxie*—shaving, showering, assessing the damage in front of the full-length mirror. *Don't you ever die, you devil.* Faded jeans, the gray alligator-skin cowboy boots, STOLEN FROM VANDERBILT sweatshirt, cowboy hat, sheepskin parka. Christmas Eve. *To Grandpa's house we go.* Gifts in the trunk of the car—Flexible Flyer for Robin, Nikon camera for Pa, pearl-handled hunting knife for Sam—and a fifth of Southern Comfort for company.

It was only ten o'clock in the morning, Nashville time, when Jaybird parked his white T-bird in front of Linebaugh's on Broadway. The snow of the night before, with its promise of a white Christmas, was melting fast but had been sufficient to leave downtown Nashville all but deserted. When he walked inside the cafe he shouted an order of ham and eggs and biscuits to George Linebaugh and then walked over to one of the red Naughahyde booths against the far wall to join Lew Glock, an erstwhile songwriter, for breakfast.

"What you doing," Lew said, "driving a herd somewhere?"

"How's that?" said Jaybird.

"Goddam outfit you got on."

"Naw, that's just my traveling clothes. Going to see my boy."

"What you got him for Christmas?"

"Flex Flyer. Brand-new red one."

"What the hell's that?"

"Jesus, Lew, a Flex is the Cadillac of sleds," Jaybird told him.

"Wadn't much market for sleds where I grew up."

"Where you from?"

"Miami."

"Miami? I didn't know that. What're you doing in Nashville?"

"Starving," said Lew.

George Linebaugh brought Jaybird his breakfast. Lew asked for more coffee. A wino came in from the cold, and George, who normally would have rushed him straight back onto the street, invited him to sit down at the counter and have some hot chocolate. The sun suddenly burst aflame.

"I got ambivalent feelings about the sun," Jaybird said.

" 'Am' what?" said Lew.

"Ambivalent. Means mixed feelings."

"Oh."

"Sun means I got a clear road to Andrews, but there won't be any snow so I can see my boy on his sled."

"If you meant 'mixed feeling,' why didn't you say so?"

"Lew, what the hell's eating you? It's Christmas Eve."

"Yeah, I know," said Lew. "Sorry. It's the worst time of the fuckin' year for me. Same thing happens every Christmas. I start off with breakfast here so I'll have a little something on my stomach and then I get blind over at Tootsie's and somebody carries me to my room and I try to get unconscious for Christmas. Usually works."

"I thought you had a boy," said Jaybird.

"Used to," said Lew.

"How can you 'used to' have a kid?"

"Took him away from me. Changed his name on me."

"Come on, Lew, they can't do that."

"Get a woman pissed off enough, she can do anything she damned well pleases," Lew said. "I got behind in my payments after we broke up. She went back to Miami and married this fellow. Blumberg. They're both raising hell, talking about abandonment, said some psychiatrist told 'em little Lew Jr. was getting all messed up because he had one last name and his Mama had another one. Kept wanting to adopt him and change his name. Here I was up here broke and messed up, myself, and I just got to where I couldn't fight it no more. That's why we ain't got a Lew Glock Jr. anymore. Got a Lewis Blumberg."

"Jesus H. Christ," said Jaybird.

"So you better watch it, Jay Clay."

"Sonofabitch."

Lew Glock's story, plus the monotonous four-hour drive to Andrews, gave Jaybird plenty of time to think back over his life as he found the new interstate highway and pointed the white Thunderbird south toward Chattanooga. He was due at the home of Becky and her new husband, Mr. and Mrs. Rex Siebert, up on Cloudland Ridge Road, to pick up his son, Robin, for the Christmas weekend at four o'clock Eastern Time. So there was plenty of time. Too much time. He put on an eight-track tape of Roger Miller's latest, "Little Green Apples," and, knowing better but doing it anyway, poured himself a liberal shot of Southern Comfort in a coffee mug. There would be hell to pay if the cops were operating spot checks on driver's licenses. He'd been driving without one ever since his last drunk-driving arrest back in September.

Becky. Jaybird wasn't about to admit it, not yet, but he had the gnawing notion that his father had been right all along. He and Becky had gone on to Middle Tennessee State together, seeing nobody but each other, during the entire four years. On the week after their graduation from college they were married in an opulent ceremony at the Cloudland County Club, a ceremony Bluejay managed to escape by booking himself on a string of one-nighters through Arkansas, and H. Kennerly Rollins III staked them to a honeymoon trip to Hawaii and soon Jaybird found himself in Nashville with a job at TopRank. Gordon Mock paid notoriously poor wages—Jaybird, armed with a major in business and a minor in music, started out in 1958 at $7,000 a year—but TopRank appeared to be the coming all-purpose talent agency in Nashville. Jaybird's duties included everything from writing press releases to serving as traveling secretary for acts like, say, Bobby Smart, the same Bobby Smart he had met briefly that night backstage at the Opry in '54, when they went on extended tours. He didn't exactly *use* the fact that he was the son of Bluejay Clay. But it didn't hurt to mention it in certain circles.

Now, more than ten years later, he still couldn't understand what happened with Becky. All he knew was the bare facts. In the beginning, when they were still in that ethereal early stage where dreaming of the future overrides any niggling inconvenience of the present, they were quite content with their $85-a-month duplex and Jaybird's having to stay at a recording studio until three o'clock in the morning and Becky's staying home all day (her college degree was in speech therapy but, as she was wont to tell friends who would drop by for beer and football on Saturdays, "all I really wanted was my MRS degree"). Jaybird didn't mind. He thought a woman's place was in the home, anyway, so he allowed Becky to indulge herself while he struck out every day for Music Row, partaking of what he jokingly called "the daily dazzle," bumping into Johnny Cash on Sixteenth Avenue, having lunch with Chet Atkins at Ireland's, working over material with Bobby Smart, overseeing a recording session.

Then came the baby, whom they named Henry Buford Clay III after much pulling and tugging between the two grandfathers, and after that it seemed as though everything went downhill for Jaybird. Suddenly, no matter how hard he tried to be a loving father, he was left out of it. Becky's telephone bill to her mother and father in Andrews one month came to $181.73. Now she wanted a big house and a station wagon and membership in a country club and Ethan Allen furniture and Dior dresses. Suddenly it was "my kitchen" and "my baby" and "my house," not the *ours* of their dreams, and very quickly the only things Jaybird could call his very own were his friends and his job and his debts. And his women.

His aimless philandering gave her the perfect excuse to take the baby, Robin, and go. She went back home to Andrews to live for a while with her parents, summarily divorced Jaybird, soon married one of the midwestern executives sent south by Diversified, moved into the contemporary palace built to her specifications by Rex Siebert and then began to exorcise Jaybird from her life and her son's life. "As long as you owe me a single penny you'll never see your son," she would shout to Jaybird, who held two tickets for the circus, before slamming the phone. He would catch up on her alimony payments—which seemed ridiculous, in principle, since the fellow she had married earned four times as much as he—only to be kept away from Robin because, this said most motherly, "it'll just break his heart, Jay, to be away from his little friends." Jaybird had been permitted to awaken in the same room with his son, now nine years old, exactly twenty-three times in the five years since Becky had taken him away. Now, on this cold-bright Christmas Eve as he drove into the city limits of Andrews, he shuddered to hear the echo of what old Lew Glock had said that morning. *I just got to where I couldn't fight it no more.*

Cloudland Ridge Road was the name of the meandering boulevard which followed the spine of the ridge overlooking Andrews. The old-timers persisted in calling the ridge Polecat Knob, going back to the days when the road was no more than a logging trail, but now it was the main artery for the subdivision where all of Diversified Enterprises' executives and their families lived. From up there, in their California contemporaries and Swiss chalets, they could both see and be seen. Cloudland Knob, the name of the development, was a collage of high-ceilinged A-frames and cul-de-sacs dubbed Foxtail Circle and kidney-shaped swimming pools and a skeet range and a nine-hole golf course and a fleet of Cadillacs and even a security checkpoint at the only entrance.

Jaybird turned left at the downtown traffic light on U.S. 19 and wound two miles upward on the newly black-topped road, the one he and Becky once took when it was gravel and led to a favorite necking spot known as Owl Hollow, until he reached the gate. CLOUDLAND KNOB read a quiet sign. VISITORS MUST REGISTER. Since there was no one inside the glass and stone gatehouse, no one to register with, he put the car into low gear and slowly negotiated the speed bumps of Cloudland Ridge Road. He thought he had found 342, Rex Siebert's home, when he looked into his rearview mirror and saw the flashing blue lights. He pulled over onto the grass of someone's manicured lawn and stopped. A portly security officer, bald and wearing a nightstick, snuggled a trooper's hat onto his head and waddled toward him.

"Need to see your driver's license, please-sir," the man said.

"Oh, yeah, sure." Jaybird fumbled for his billfold.

"Just a little check. Like to know who's up here."

"Right. Let me just—"

"Wait a minute here." The man backed off for a few seconds and took a better look. "Jaybird? 'at you, Jaybird?"

The air went out of Jaybird. "Billy Wingo. I'll be goddam."

"Where in the hell you been, boy?"

"Up in Nashville."

"Uh-huh. Reckon yo' daddy told me 'bout that. Reckon he did. Doing pretty good up there?"

"Okay, Billy. Okay. How about you? What the hell are you doing up here? Aren't you sheriff anymore?"

"Naw," said Billy Wingo. "Got tired of having to run all my friends in all the time. Company said come on up here and be security guard. Another way to say 'keep the niggers out.' Put me and the wife up in a nice little house. Pays good. Beats hell out o' being sheriff."

"You don't miss chasing after Sam?"

"Shoot, naw. Speed traps, neither." Billy checked his watch. "Little bit early for the party, ain't you? Don't start till six."

"What party?"

"Mr. and Mrs. Rollins. They got a big Christmas party tonight."

"I don't suspect I'm on their mailing list these days, Billy."

"Seems like I heard about that," Wingo said.

"Just came to pick up my boy to take him to the farm," said Jaybird.

"Came to pick him up, you say?"

"Yeah. Got him a Flex Flyer in the back of the car."

"They didn't tell you nothing?"

"What? What's wrong?"

"Hell, Jaybird, I don't *know* what," Billy said. "This ain't none of my business, son. Maybe you better go over to the Rollins' house on this one. All I know is, Becky 'n' them left day before yesterday."

"Left?" said Jaybird. "Robin, too?"

"Like I said, all of 'em. Drove up to the main gate in the station wagon, all loaded down with suitcases, said look out for the house while they was gone."

"I'll be a goddam sonofabitch."

"I figured you'd know."

"I don't know pig-squat, Billy."

Billy Wingo said, "Lookie here, Jaybird."

"What now?"

"How 'bout putting that bottle of whiskey somewhere so I can't see it, son. I ain' got much jurisdiction up here, but I'd sure hate to see my old sheriff instincts rear up on me. Might ruin your Christmas."

"Too late, Billy. Too late." Jaybird fired his car, fish-tailed it across somebody's lawn, and left the smell of burning rubber in his wake as he squealed around the placid curves leading to the white-columned Colonial home of Mr. and Mrs. H. Kennerly Rollins III. Only the ten-year-old BMW, which Mrs. Rollins loved to call "my little scoot-about," was in the brick driveway. Smoke rose from the chimney. The statue of a red-jacketed black boy, like a groom awaiting his master's return from the hunt, stood beside the walk leading from the driveway to the front door. Jaybird screeched to a halt behind the BMW, slammed the door and stalked in livid fury to the front door of the Rollins house. He banged with both fists until the door opened. It was Genevieve Rollins in a red velvet cocktail dress tied at the waist with a green satin bow.

"Why, Jay," she said, "what a surprise."

"Where are they?"

"For a moment I thought it was Ken, but the—"

"Goddamit, where are they?" Jaybird shouted.

"Oh, my. Dear Jay. That language again."

"I asked a simple question, Mrs. Rollins. Where's my boy?"

"Florida, of course. They didn't tell you?"

"Florida?" Jaybird jammed his hands in the pockets of his sheepskin parka. "What in the living name of hell are they doing taking a nine-year-old boy to Florida on Christmas for?"

"Why, to see the porpoises, of course. Jay, Robin was so excited."

"Porpoises? On Christmas?"

"You know, at Marineland. The place near St. Augustine."

"Shit. I'll be a godddam sonofabitch."

"Jay, Jay, Jay. Tsk-tsk-tsk. They didn't tell you."

"Hell, no, they didn't tell me," Jaybird said.

"I guess you were, ah, *out*. Please come in for a minute. It's letting the cold air in." Genevieve Rollins led Jaybird into the living room, decorated with Tiffany lamps and Oriental rugs and paintings she and her husband had collected in their travels. Two young Cherokee women were laying out *hors d'oeuvres* on the fifteen-foot-long dining-room table while, upstairs, a vacuum cleaner whirred. An Indian boy, about Robin's age, stood on a stepladder patiently polishing each teardrop of the glass chandelier hanging above the long table.

"That's a hell of a note," Jaybird said. "Florida. Porpoises."

"We just felt like it was a marvelous idea," said Mrs. Rollins.

"*We?* What's this *we* shit? What about the boy?"

"Oh, Jay, he was so excited. Never been to Florida. First plane ride. Swimming on Christms Day. What with the weather being so bad lately, and Rex being so exhausted from his work, and Rebecca having had to do so much entertaining over the holidays. We just decided it was a marvelous idea."

"You said that already."

"What?"

"That it was a marvelous idea."

"I did?" said Mrs. Rollins.

"Yeah," said Jaybird. "And you said 'we' again."

Genevieve Rollins stood up to smooth her red velvet party dress. She sat back down on a Chippendale sofa. "Dear Jay," she said, holding up her hand when Jaybird tried to cut in, "dear boy. Of course, it's 'we.' It's always been like that, ever since Rebecca came to her senses. You should realize by now that it was all a mistake, you two getting married. Don't you remember the day you left here for college? There you were in that perfectly tacky little blue pickup truck with your name on the side and there was my little girl following you in the new red convertible we gave her for graduation. Don't you see? That, right there, was enough to show the different worlds you and Rebecca came from. Ken and I knew it wasn't going to work. Right from the start."

"Well," Jaybird said, "maybe it *did* work."

"I can't see how."

"The boy. We had a beautiful kid together. We made Robin."

"And just bout ruined him," Mrs. Rollins said.

"Ruined him? Y'all don't let me see enough of him to ruin him."

"Why, Jay. We're not *withholding* your son."

"Well just what the hell do you call it? I've got football tickets, at the last minute he can't go. I want to come and get him for the weekend, all of a sudden Becky calls and says he's sick. And now, right now, out in the car I've got his Christmas present for him but he's in goddam Florida watching porpoises with his mama and this ass-hole she hooked."

"I'll disregard what you said about Rex," Mrs. Rollins said. "He's a fine man. He's an adult. He doesn't come in drunk at all hours and he doesn't have any, ah, women friends."

"Give him time," said Jay. "Give him time."

"Rex treats Robin as though he were his own blood."

"What?"

"He might as well be Robin Siebert as far as he's concerned."

I got to where I couldn't fight it no more. "The boy's name is Clay. Henry Buford Clay III. He was born a Clay and he'll die a Clay. That blood runs so deep in him that nothing's ever gonna change it. No Chippendale sofas, no Tiffany lamps, no plane rides to Florida, no mansions on the hill, *nothing* will ever change that. It's like trying to kill kudzu, you pitiful old bitch. No matter how many times you try to rip it up by the roots it keeps on coming. Nobody's ever found out exactly how to stop kudzu from growing."

"You need help," said Mrs. Rollins. "You really do."

"Somebody does."

Debating Genevieve Rollins was as frustrating as debating her daughter and Jaybird was in no mood to carry on with her. He spun on his heels and walked out the door without saying anything else to her, wanting to avoid the return home of Mr. Rollins and what he feared would develop into a real man-to-man physical fight, and got into his car for the drive to Sixkiller. He hadn't been there since August, when he had managed to wrest Robin away from Becky long enough for a weekend of swimming and general horseplay with Bluejay and Sam, but there were no noticeable changes. It was nearly dusk, Christmas Eve, as he rolled down the deserted main drag of Andrews. The only business still open, for people who ran out of cigarettes or milk or beer, was a new convenience store which had replaced the country store operated by Ed and Grace Wheeler since Jaybird was a kid. The new cars with out-of-state tags, clustered in the yards of the familiar old frame houses of his youth, told him that he wasn't the only son of the mountains who had come home for the holidays.

As soon as he drove through the SIXKILLER arch he saw the front door of the main house fly open and produce Bluejay and Sam. He winced. They were playing the same game they played on him when he was Robin's age. His father was wearing the same old dime-store Santa Claus outfit he had bought in Atlanta before World War II and Sam had added *bona fide* antlers this year to his homemade reindeer suit. They came toward Jaybird, this skinny Santa Claus chanting "Ho-ho-ho-ho" and this sixty-eight-year-old Indian loping behind him on all fours in a reindeer disguise, and before he could cut the engine they were dancing around the car.

"Where's that boy at?" Bluejay called between ho-ho-hos. "Santa's done come all the way from the North Pole to see him. Me and my personal reindeer. Ain't that right, reindeer?" Sam, still not sure how a reindeer was supposed to talk, stood up and waggled his arms and whinnied. "Santa's here to see Robin Clay."

Jaybird rolled down the window. "Hi, Pa."

"All right, I know he's hiding somewhere," said Bluejay.

"He's not here, Pa."

"The trunk. Check the trunk, reindeer."

"Pa. He's not coming, Pa."

They helped Jaybird unload the trunk of the car—his things, the boxes holding their gifts, the Flexible Flyer with a red bow around it—and soundlessly walked to the house. Strung over the big stone fireplace was a crude banner spelling out MERRY XMAS ROBIN and next to the hearth stood a twelve-foot fir they had cut and dragged from the hill near the family cemetery. While Bluejay and Jaybird dumped the gifts at the base of the tree, decorated with popcorn and flashing colored lights and baubles crocheted by Molly some three decades earlier, Sam walked to the stereo and cut off Gene Autry in the middle of "Frosty the Snowman." A round of whiskey was poured. Bluejay and Sam took off the hoods of their costumes and Jaybird peeled down to his gray Vanderbilt sweatshirt. Suddenly the fire and the tree and the banner didn't seem jolly. Nobody had to ask for the jug of whiskey to be passed.

"Florida," Bluejay said after a while. "They make their Christmas trees out of plastic in Florida. Pour sand around it for snow. Turn the air conditioning up so it'll be cold."

"Shit," Jaybird said. "At least they could've told me."

"It wouldn't have hurt so bad then. That's what they wanted."

"What makes people so mean, Pa? Like they are."

"Sometimes I think they can't help themselves, son. Born mean."

"Some horses you never *can* break," said Sam.

There was more whiskey poured. Sam added logs to the fire,

then went into the kitchen to check on the turkey they had killed and cleaned and cooked but weren't likely to eat. They were in no mood to exchange gifts. Jaybird said there was no snow for sledding, anyway, and Sam said he could use a few extra days to put the finishing touches on the saddle he had made for Robin. Bluejay said the colt he had bought for the boy, which he and Sam had named "Sutalitihi," could use a few extra pounds.

"How much money you owe her, son?"

"I don't know," said Jaybird. "Five years' worth of alimony."

"You've been paying for Robin, have you?"

"Everything and more. School, doctors, everything."

"But nothing for her," said Bluejay.

"Hell, no. Why should I?"

"I don't argue with you. But it's the law."

"Yeah, but it's the principle of the thing, Pa. Christ, I don't even see a thousand dollars a month after taxes and that guy she married probably makes fifty thousand a year. How come I got to keep *her* up?"

"It's the rocking chairs, son, the rocking chairs."

"What the hell you talking about?"

"I didn't figure you'd pay any attention to me," said Bluejay. "One time when you was all goo-goo-eyed over that little girl I told you to check out the rocking chairs on the front porch up at the Rollins' place and you'd find 'em chained down so nobody'd steal 'em. I reckon now you know what I was talking about."

"Oh, boy, do I," said Jaybird.

"So how much rocking-chair money do you owe here?"

"Five years, two hundred a month. Ten, fifteen thousand."

"All right," Bluejay said. "We'll pay it. Sam here'll write her a check as soon as you figure it up. You're going to have to start cutting back some so you don't get behind anymore. Sell that car or something. Just don't give her any more excuses than you have to. Then maybe we can do something."

Jaybird looked up from the fire and said, "Do something."

"Go and get him."

"What do you mean?"

"I mean get the boy and bring him here. To Sixkiller."

"Pa," Jaybird said, "now wait a minute. That's kidnapping."

"Same thing she's done, ain't it?"

"Yeah, but she's got custody."

"And you've got what they call 'visitation rights.' Right?"

"But *kidnapping*, Pa. That's against the law."

"Not if you're his daddy. Sam looked it up." Bluejay looked at Sam, who nodded a Yes. "We've been talking about it, me and Sam. Lots of things to look at. Biggest one's whether it'd get the boy messed up. There's some other things like what the new judge down here might think. Used to, I knew all of 'em and they'd do anything I wanted 'em to do. But now, I don't know. Them, the newspaper, the lawyers, even the sheriff that replaced ol' Billy Wingo, they all belong to the company now. We'll just have to see about it. If we don't do nothing else, at least we can scare the hell out of 'em."

They all drank themselves into a stupor that night, forgetting about eating the turkey and opening gifts, and when Jaybird awoke in the morning he found himself splayed on the sofa in front of a smoldering fire. He got the fire going again, went to the bathroom, poured some of the coffee he had smelled in the kitchen and was back in front of the fire when his father stomped in from looking after the animals. He could vaguely recall Sam lurching toward the door in the middle of the night and stumbling into the darkness for his cabin. Bluejay shed his parka and got himself a cup of the coffee and joined Jaybird in front of the fire.

"Sam okay?" Jaybird said.

"Made it as far as the barn last night," said Bluejay.

"I don't see how he does it at his age."

"How 'bout me? Hell, I'm fifty-eight years old."

"Yeah," Jaybird said, "I'm not as young as I used to be, either."

Bluejay hacked. "Everything all right with you, son?"

"I'm okay, Pa, except for Robin. Why?"

"Just asking."

"Sounds like you got a reason for asking."

"Aw, I just heard a thing or two, that's all," said Bluejay.

"Like what?"

"Last time I was up there to do the Opry," Bluejay said, "think you said you was tied up with some singer or something. Anyway, I was having a beer at Tootsie's and she said she was kinda worried about you. Said she thought maybe you was running with a bad crowd or something. And Owen, Owen Bradley, he told me he had to run you off his place one night. Out there at that new Bradley's Barn. I don't know. It just kinda got me worried, that's all."

"Aw, Pa, it's all right. It's all right."

"Ain't found yourself a woman yet, have you?"

"No problem with that," Jaybird said.

"I mean a *good* woman, son. Like your Mama."

"I haven't seen any like that, Pa."

"Well, you ought to be looking," said Bluejay. "I know I do a hell of a lot of talking about how it's the *men* that's important. That the women are just supposed to hang around and have the babies and do the cooking and leave the real stuff to us. But I don't know for sure anymore. I look back at what your Mama meant to me and then I see what this Becky's done to your life and I figure maybe I'm just an old geezer who got spoiled and don't know much about women except what I learned from your Mama. Problem is, I judge every woman I see against Molly. They come up short every time."

There seemed to be no reason to hang around the farm, the joy of it having disappeared with Robin, so Jaybird left the gifts beneath the tree and threw his things in the car and said good-bye without so much as looking at his son's new horse or opening his own Christmas gifts. When he reached his apartment in Nashville he went straight to the bathroom and peered at the mirror over the medicine cabinet. He had done an efficient job of erasing the lipsticked name and number. He turned up the heat and took the rest of the Southern Comfort back to the bedroom and tried to remember her name.

CHAPTER III

EVERY MONDAY MORNING at ten o'clock there was a routine staff meeting at TopRank International, in the ornate office of Gordon Mock, and in most ways they resembled the sort of meetings probably going on all over Nashville at insurance companies and the larger law firms and even in, say, the history department at Vanderbilt University. The purpose, of course, was simply to gather the half-dozen primary executives together in one room for what Gordy insisted on calling "the big picture." The big picture usually didn't take more than twenty minutes—Bobby Smart's newest release was ranked No. 19 with a "bullet" in *Billboard*, Audie Braswell and his band were still snowed-in out in the Texas Panhandle, a new country-music park was opening in north Georgia—and then, over coffee and doughnuts and an occasional dollop of bourbon from the crystal decanter on Gordy's walnut desk, the proceedings took on the air of a minor-league-baseball clubhouse. "I told her, 'If you'll breathe deep for me, honey, I'll pay for the damages,'" Dick Molleson, the TopRank attorney, would end a story, and right up until eleven-thirty it was time out for lies and gossip and cigars and promises.

On this day, though, it was different. When they drifted into Gordy's office they felt they had stumbled into a war room or, at the very least, a sales seminar. The boss sat at his desk with his sleeves rolled up, nervously working the pipe in his mouth, and behind him was an array of easels. Displayed on the easels were charts and graphs with headings like "Bookings" and "Expenses" and "Projection '69." Jaybird, the last man to enter the office, closed the door behind him and sat on the gold shag carpet. For the next forty-five minutes the only person who spoke, the only person who moved, was Gordon Mock. TopRank was no longer No. 1 on Music Row, he said, and he couldn't live with that. He sweated, pointed his finger, jabbed at the graphs and charts, unveiled a new chain of command, pleaded, shouted and eventually screamed.

When he was finished he had fired Buzz Lemmons, who had been there for six years as the chief talent scout, and put everybody else on notice. "I don't figure any of you would have trouble finding another job, anyway," said Gordy, "seeing as how you've been spending more time at other places than you have here. Now get the hell out of here and go to work." They left much quicker than they had come. Jaybird was joining the exodus when Gordy said, "Jay. Sit down."

At least he still had his job, as far as he knew, Jaybird was thinking as he sank into the low avocado chair beside Mock's desk. In the new organizational chart they had been shown, the name CLAY had been grease-penciled out to the side of PRESIDENT. He had no idea what it meant. His hands shook—*tension? booze? the moment?*—as he lit a Winston. Gordon Mock relit his pipe, sighed and plopped into his black high-backed leather executive's chair.

"How was Christmas?" Gordy said.

"Oh, you know, okay," said Jaybird.

"Went down home, did you?"

"Yeah."

"Bluejay doing all right?"

"Same as ever."

"Still don't want to represent him, do you?"

"Oh, no. We don't even talk about it."

"Guess he's doing okay by Sam, anyway."

"Yeah. Sam's mean as hell."

Gordy said, "I assume you drove down."

"Sure," said Jaybird. "Be a long time before Andrews gets an airport. Why?"

"Because you don't even have a goddam driver's license, that's why." Jaybird started to explain, but Gordon Mock cut him off. "Hertz sent me a bill for six-hundred-something by-God dollars for the car y'all used in Newark last November when Bobby played up there and you were with 'em. That's what it cost because the car was just left at the hotel instead of being taken back to LaGuardia where you got it. They couldn't find it for five days. Since your name wasn't on the rental agreement like it's supposed to be, I asked Buck Moon why *his* name was and he said because you'd had your license lifted. I checked with a friend of mine at the state patrol and he said you'd had three DWI's in two months last year."

"Well, that's true, Gordy, but—"

"And that's not all, either," said Mock. "Not only do I have one of my top people running around town without a driver's license, but there's *this* and there's *this*." He spun two letters across the desk to Jaybird. One was a statement from Owen Bradley asking for $314.58 in "damages" incurred at Bradley's Barn in early December. The other was a legal document ordering TopRank to dock $400 per month from Jaybird's paycheck, the plaintiff being Rebecca Clay Siebert, until the $9,800 arrearage in alimony payments had been met. "Hell of a morning at the mailbox, I'd say," said Gordy.

"Becky's being taken care of," Jaybird said.

"Well, that's your business. But the rest is *my* business."

"Where'd that figure come from? The one from Owen."

"I didn't figure you'd remember. Owen says you got into it with one of the 'billies about two o'clock one morning while you were supposed to be overseeing a session and y'all about half tore up the studio, and then when he ran you out you backed into his car. That's $314.58. I'm paying that and I'm paying Hertz. But it's coming out of your paycheck. You better hope you've got an understanding landlord."

Gordon sat back in his chair and relit his pipe while Jaybird

fumbled for another cigarette. Jaybird was being put on proba-
tion, Gordy said, and until he proved he could straighten out
his life he was in charge of writing press releases and nothing
more. He was to put in a full day, every day, five days a week,
in his office. He was to check in to Gordy at nine o'clock to
prove he was there, ask permission to go to lunch, check back
when he returned for lunch and then check out at five as he
was leaving.

"Oh, boy," said Jaybird.

"And consider yourself lucky," said Mock.

"I guess I do."

"Damn, Jay. What's happening to you, son?"

"I wish I knew, Gordy."

"What are you, thirty-two?"

"Be thirty-three next month."

"Supposed to be the prime of life," said Gordy. "Damned
shame. If you weren't Bluejay's son I'd have fired you flat-out
like I did Buzz. I've been trying to figure out what's happened
with you, Jay, but I'll be damned if I can come up with anything.
I'm a great believer in the bloodlines. Your old man and I talked
about that one time. But somewhere in there something got left
out. I hope I'm wrong. Maybe you just got too much too soon.
Maybe I shouldn't be giving you a break. I guess we'll see."

The warning seemed sufficient. Jaybird tried very hard for a
period of several weeks to bring some order to his life. He sold
the sleek white Thunderbird and used the proceeds to pay off
the debts to Hertz and to Owen Bradley and to buy a bruised
1960 Chevy station wagon which a country singer named Red
Samples had driven for 186,000 punishing miles. He passed his
apartment on to Bobby Smart, who was being divorced again,
and took a dollar-a-day room in one of the sagging old frame
houses at the seedy end of Seventeenth Avenue South. For the
first time in his life, in order to save money, he began doing his
own cooking and laundering. He began drinking beer instead of
Southern Comfort. And every day, wearing jeans and boots and
sweatshirts since there was no more need for him to entertain
with credit-card lunches, he showed his face to Gordon Mock

at nine o'clock sharp and then walked down the hall to his office. At a manual Underwood typewriter, with a pot of coffee on his desk, he spent his mornings typing copy for new TopRank promotional flyers and press releases which began, "TopRank International, one of the leading talent agencies in Music City, U.S.A., has just signed 'the hottest young songwriter in America' . . ." He would walk down Music Row to the Paddock for a beer and a sandwich and then return to spend the afternoon on the phone, feeding items to Red O'Donnell or *Music City News* or Bill Williams at the Nashville bureau of *Billboard*, then walk the block back to his room at the end of the day. He would warm up some meat loaf or make a hamburger and, with a beer in hand, drift out to the living room of the rooming house to watch the communal black-and-white television set with the struggling young singers and pickers and songwriters he had always read about.

On one of those dank winter nights, when he had walked from the office to the room in the face of a bitter driving hailstorm and cooked supper and watched "The Glen Campbell Goodtime Hour" on the television set, he was back in his room reading the afternoon Nashville *Banner* (Red O'Connell had used an item of Jaybird's about Gordy Mock's buying a new house next door to Johnny Cash on Old Hickory Lake) when he heard music drifting up the hallway from another room. Bored with the newspaper, anxious to talk to somebody, he put on some sneakers and walked toward the music. The door to the room at the end of the hall was halfway open and a bearded fellow about his age sat on the edge of the bed, barefooted and wearing an olive-green U.S. Army T-shirt and jeans, strumming a guitar and singing about a down-and-out singer.

When the singer stopped, cursed, tried for a different chord and then reached for a Budweiser, Jaybird stepped to the doorway. "Sounds like you've been reading my mail," he said.

"Oh, hey," the singer said.

"Mind if I come in?"

"Pull up a rug. Beer's in the window, staying cold."

Jaybird introduced himself and learned that the man's name

was Kris Kristofferson. He had seen him around, walking the street along Sixteenth Avenue and shooting basketballs in the graveled backyard next door with John Hartford and some of the other songwriters, but until now he didn't know anything about him. Although Kristofferson's story was a bit unusual— ex-football player, Rhodes scholar, Army helicopter pilot, en route to West Point when he listened to the urge to go to Nashville— he was like hundreds of others who had drifted into town. He was writing songs, sweeping floors at the Columbia studios to support himself, trying to make somebody listen.

"What's the song?" Jaybird asked him.

"Call it 'The Pilgrim, Chapter 33.' Story of my goddam life."

"Having any luck?"

"Maybe," he said. "I was sweeping floors the other night and John was recording. So naturally, when he took a break, I made sure he heard me walking around singing. He wants me to make a demo so he can hear the whole thing. Can you believe it? Johnny Cash, man."

"What's the title mean?" said Jaybird.

"Means age thirty-three. When it all happens."

"I don't follow you."

"Jesus was thirty-three when they got him."

"Is that what it's about?"

"Naw," Kristofferson said. "Well, sort of. I mean, like, I'm thirty-three and I've managed to mess everything up so far. Quit the Army, quit my wife and kids, making fifty-eight bucks a week cleaning ashtrays, threw away a Rhodes scholarship, all that crap. Gotta have *something* to look forward to. Ain't we all?"

Jaybird figured if this stranger could open up *his* wounds, so could he. He told him about his father and Becky and the boy, and TopRank, anxious to share his problems with a neutral. He felt better than he had since the TopRank Christmas party, in fact, and accepted another cold beer as he began regaling this Kris with stories from his life which suddenly had some clarity and meaning: his teenaged infatuation with Becky, the coming of Diversified Enterprises to the mountains, the night Bluejay and Sam set him up with a Cherokee prostitute named TiHi Tompkins, his off-to-college camper with JAYBIRD painted on the doors, the agony of being kept from his son.

"Say Bluejay Clay's your old man," Kristofferson said.

"Yeah," said Jaybird. "The original 'billy."

"Hey, now. Yo' Pa oughta be bronzed."

"Well, I don't know about that."

"No, I'm serious. He and Hank and E.T. and Acuff. Those dudes, that's where the music comes from. Like, they're *originals.*"

"I guess I'm too close to know that."

"Could be. Maybe one day you'll understand it."

"So." Jaybird finished his beer. "What else you got working?"

"I got 'em all over the place," said Kristofferson. "Lot like your old man and Hank. Something happens to me, I write it." He took up his guitar, strummed it, and sang. He was calling this one "To Beat the Devil."

Jaybird, when he had finished, said, "Good. Real good."

"Aw, I sing like a goddam frog."

"But the words. It's something to think about."

"You bet it is. I got a great future behind me."

Maybe it was because of the exchange with the songwriter, and the words of the songs he had to sing, or maybe it was what happened later that night on the telephone. Jaybird went to the pay phone in the foyer of the rooming house and called person-to-person to Robin Clay in Andrews, North Carolina, and the boy answered but his mother picked up on an extension a split second later and told the operator that Robin Clay wasn't there and the boy started to protest but then the line went dead. Jaybird went to his room and put on his sheepskin coat and boots and cowboy hat and walked four blocks through the snow to a package store and bought a quart of Gordon's vodka and when he struggled to TopRank the next morning it was eleven-forty and there was a note from Gordon Mock wishing him good luck.

CHAPTER IV

AND SO began a wallowing odyssey which plunged Jaybird Clay, son of the great Bluejay Clay of the Grand Ole Opry, into the pits and hollows and stark days and bleary nights of a Nashville he had thought existed only in the minds of the more creative songwriters such as Kris Kristofferson. He had first heard Webb Pierce sing "There Stands the Glass" fifteen years earlier, the night his father dragged him onto the stage of Ryman Auditorium to sing "Molly" with him and the Sixkillers, and now he was living it. The days and nights ran together in a mush of empty whiskey bottles and strange beds and frozen TV dinners and drunken shoving matches at two o'clock in the morning and car trouble and hangovers and bail bondsmen and letters to his son which were never answered.

There was still a little cash left from the sale of the Thunderbird, although the $400-a-month payments in back alimony and the $200 a month in support for Robin were about to wipe it out, and in order to feed and house and entertain himself he became a sort of "personal manager" for a boggling menagerie of hangers-on. Gordon Mock, being not entirely without sympathy toward Jaybird, let him take over what was left of the careers of a blind black street singer named Amos Threadgill and an alcoholic fifty-three-year-old Italian cabaret crooner who billed himself as "Luciano LaRussa" and had once played the rooftop lounge at the Holiday Inn in Montgomery, Alabama. From Shorty Hunsinger, who had now moved out of the trailer behind the Opry Motel on Murfreesboro Road into an office on Music Row, he drew the foul-mouthed comic Bama Red. There were others—mostly young men and women whose first view of Music City U.S.A. had been of the Trailways bus station— and Jaybird took twenty percent of whatever income he could generate for them. He fed items to *Country Song Roundup* and *Music City News* and *Billboard* and to Red O'Donnell at the *Banner* and at night, mixing business with pleasure, he would comb the places like Possum Holler and Bud's Corral and Sally's in search of what could only vaguely be called "talent."

It was on one of those nights that he met Maureen Barksdale. To celebrate the retrieval of his driver's license, with no little help from Gordy Mock, he had driven out Lebanon Road in the damaged '60 Chevy station wagon for a hamburger and some merriment at a roadhouse called Hank's Pop-a-Top. The owner was Hank Elliott, a ruddy hillbilly for whom the son of Bluejay Clay could do no wrong, and Elliott kept a loose rein on Jaybird's tab. Dark had come two hours earlier and the threat of snow had held the usual boisterous crowd of construction workers and used-car salesmen to a gaggle of about a dozen. The jukebox was stacked with pure hard country—Hank Williams, Bluejay, Tubb, Acuff, Webb Pierce, Frizzell—and Jaybird was aimlessly loading up a second hamburger with catsup and snapping the top from a can of Pabst and listening to the jukebox when somebody pulled the plug on Roger Miller's "King of the Road." There were some halfhearted boos from the dark corners of the saloon where wind-whipped roustabouts still in their hard hats sat with their elbows on littered tables, but then there was a smattering of applause as somebody turned a small spotlight onto the narrow platform where a stool and a microphone had already been put in place. "Do it, Mo, do it," one of the men yelled.

Jaybird hadn't noticed that she had been there all along, pulling draft beers and mixing drinks and running the cash register, but now she was walking out from behind the bar and mounting the platform. She wore white boot-cut Levi's, stretched low and tight over lissome hips and thighs, moving easily in her gray snakeskin cowgirl boots—*Is that it*, Jaybird wondered, *'cowgirl boots'*?—looking like a lost angel amid this circle of rough-handed good old boys, shaking her pig-tailed raven hair and straightening the collar of her frilly white long-sleeved blouse as she deftly looped the guitar strap over her head and then hoisted herself atop the stool and into the spotlight. At first she squinted and waved at the spotlight, as if to wave it away, but then she got used to it and opened her eyes wide. The eyes were large and black, almost luminous, and they held a sadness which belied the dimples and the petite figure and the creamy white skin and the tossing black pigtails. She tugged at the black leather vest, revealing an ample bosom, still not acknowledging the yahoos beyond the spotlight—*WaaaaHooooo, hot-dam/Mo, Mo, gimme Mo/'Cowboy,' Mo, 'Cowboy'*—wiggling gently until she was comfortable on the stool, strumming the guitar with long ruby fingernails, still peering into the darkness with her baleful black eyes, the men suddenly hers. Then, only then, she sang.

> One day he came to me
> And said 'twas his duty,
> He had to go out on the range.
>   So that night I held him
>   And showed him I loved him,
>   And cried away all of my pain.

It was a simple "story song," the kind Nashville thrived on, but there was nothing particularly special about it. The song told of a cowboy leaving his lover and never coming back, an old country theme, the lover pining for somebody to take his place. *So please won't you be/My cowboy tonight?* There were plenty of takers inside the cinder-block walls of Hank's Pop-a-Top that night, to hear the foot-stomping and ya-hooing when the girl had finished, and it was not until she had encored the song three times that she had to stop. She was crying softly, enough to drive any good old boy to gallantry, and after one of them had passed up a clean bandanna and she had wiped her eyes she straightened up on the stool and sang her way through an hour's worth of country standards like "It Wasn't God Who Made Honky-Tonk Angels." Then she bowed and went back to pouring drinks.

Somebody plugged in the jukebox and played a Conway Twitty. She was behind the bar again, helping the two other waitresses fill orders, and the noise level was back where it was before she came on. Jaybird was staring at her from his table across the room when Hank Elliott came by to join him.

"How you like my new singer?" Hank said.

"What the hell is it, Hank, Amateur Night?" said Jaybird.

"Well, the boys love her. You heard it."

"One song. Is that all she's got?"

"She wrote it herself."

"Sounds like it," Jaybird said. "She always cry like that?"

"Aw," said Hank, "it's part show biz. Part's real, though."

"Tell me."

"How old you figure she is?"

"I'd say maybe twenty-two, right off."

"Think again. Thirty-five."

"No."

"Had to see her driver's license when she came to work. Had a hard life, that little woman. Name's Maureen Barksdale but everybody calls her Mo. Took up with some bad boys in her time. Tried to have kids but couldn't. Used to be married, but ain't. 'bout all I've gotten out of her. Pretty little thing, though, ain't she?"

"Suppose I could talk to her?" said Jaybird.

"Talent scout, or a horny no-good sonofabitch?"

"Talent scout." Jaybird fished for one of his old TopRank business cards, which had served him well, and Hank Elliott went to fetch her for him. "And have her bring me a double bourbon," Jaybird yelled after him. He wished he had worn something more impressive-looking than his old MTSU sweatshirt and toboggan cap and hiking boots, he was thinking, but then how is a man to know what might happen when he slams the door behind him. Hank caught her at the cash register and when he pointed out Jaybird she spun her head and the pigtails, with white bows on the end, spun with her. Soon she was taking off her apron and wiping her hands on it and weaving her wonderful hips from side to side, maneuvering her way between the tables full of yahoos who called after, until she made it to Jaybird and said, "Mr. Clay?"

"It's Jay," he said. "Jay Clay. Maureen?"

"Maureen Barksdale. Boys call me Mo."

"So I heard. Sit down?"

"For just a second," she said. "I've got to work and then do another show. Not that we're that busy, but I owe it to Hank. He's been good to me."

She was even prettier than he had thought. But that was under the spotlight, created to flatter, and Jaybird could see the age in her face as she leaned toward the light of the candle flickering from a bowl on the table. There were crow's-feet around the deep black eyes and there was an old inch-long scar not quite hidden by her right eyebrow. Even here, even sitting at a table in a saloon with people talking and a jukebox playing, she emitted the same air of loss.

"I enjoyed your song," Jaybird said.

"Why, thank you. I call it 'Please Be My Cowboy.' It's my song."

"Your song."

"I mean I wrote it."

"You *wrote* it? Well, it's certainly a good song."

"Well, thank you. Thank you again."

"Do you, ah," Jaybird said, "you don't happen to have an agent, do you?"

"Oh, no," she told him, "I used to but it didn't work out. You know. Contract. Twenty percent. I figured, 'Twenty percent of *what*?' Playing a high school dance? Riding all night to do two songs at a rodeo for eighty-five dollars? Who needs it? Oops."

"What?"

"*You're* an agent. I'm *terribly* sorry. TopRank?"

"Not really. Not anymore. I'm on my own now."

"Doing what?"

"Well, it'll take a lot of explaining," Jaybird said. "Maybe we could meet later. If you aren't tied up."

"Oh, no," she said, "I'm free. Good old Mo."

"After the second gig, then."

"Fine, if you can stand it."

"Sure," said Jaybird. "My place or yours?"

"Neither."

"I'm sorry?"

"I said neither." The sorrow flashed again. "I've been around that block and I don't need to see it again. Look, there's a great little all-night place about a mile up the road. Jerry's. Gobs and gobs of coffee. Looks like you're going to be needing some. Okay?"

"Jerry's."

"See if you can get Bluejay to come along." She was up and gone before he could say anything.

Heads turned when Maureen Barksdale walked into Jerry's at two o'clock in the morning. She wore a floor-length coat of beige imitation fur and a matching Cossack hat. The temperature was in the low teens and a light snow was flurrying. At the Formica tables sat an odd collection of paper-mill workers and cops and after-party people still in their tuxedos and gowns and truckers having a last cup of coffee before heading on into the east Tennessee hills with that morning's copies of the *Tennessean*. Country music played on the jukebox. A couple of old boys played FoosBall. The wide plate-glass window was steamed over.

"I thought you got off earlier," Jaybird said when she joined him at his booth. He had been there for more than an hour and was on his third cup of coffee.

"Fight broke out after my second show," she said. "It was a mess."

"Anybody hurt?"

"Lot of egos, that's all. Cops came. It's all right."

"Hey," Jaybird said, "what's that about Bluejay?"

"Hank told me," she said.

"Is that why you agreed to talk?"

"In a way. At least I know who to tell if you're a bad boy."

"Yeah, Pa may be the best ID card I've got."

"Bluejay Clay. God, when I was a little girl I'd lay awake at night listening to the Opry, just waiting for Bluejay to come on.

Even if you and I don't do any business, I want you to promise you'll let me meet him. Deal?"

"It's a deal," said Jaybird.

They sat there in the booth at Jerry's for nearly two hours, talking about everything, and through it all came a sorrowful picture of Maureen Barksdale. She had been raised on a farm in southern Indiana, one of eight kids, and one night when she was nineteen and working at a Dairy Queen in town she went to a country-music show at the auditorium and met one of the second-line stars—a singer by the name of Lefty Dews—and she followed him to Nashville and they married and she had a miscarriage and he took to beating her and they divorced. "They didn't call him Lefty for nothing," Maureen told Jaybird. "This scar over my right eye, the whole right side of my body, was his punching bag." She tried marriage again, the second time to a drummer who turned out to be a pill-head, and that was it for men. During her fifteen years or so in Nashville she had done a bit of everything to make a living—cocktail waitress, lounge singer, receptionist, Music Row secretary—and now she found herself thirty-five and unable to have children and wary of men and living alone in a little frame house off Lebanon Road and earning $100 a week tending bar and singing at Hank's Pop-a-Top.

"How'd you manage to buy the house?" Jaybird said.

"Royalties off my song," she told him. "Brenda Lee recorded it."

"You said it was *your* song."

"Well, it *is* sort of autobiographical. That how you say it?"

"Uh-huh. Like Pa's song. 'Molly.' "

"I mean, 'Please Be My Cowboy.' I guess I'm still looking for a cowboy to take care of. God knows, I ought to know better. Any time I go to a fellow's place the first thing I do is look around. If I see dirty dishes and clothes all over the place I say to myself, 'Uh-uh, Mo, watch it. He's not ready.' "

"Ready."

"If he can't take care of himself, how's he gonna take care of me?"

"Well," Jaybird said, "I don't think you want to see my place."

He told her about himself—Sixkiller, growing up as the son of Bluejay Clay, Sam, Becky, Robin, TopRank, Kris Kristofferson—and was surprised at how openly they had talked of themselves. He didn't envision anything marvelous happening to her career, such as it was, nor did she, but they struck an informal deal whereby he would take the agent's twenty percent for whatever business he might drum up. They finished off the night with sausage and biscuits and more coffee. He gave her the number for the pay phone in the foyer of his rooming house and she gave him her address and phone number on a paper napkin and it was a few minutes after four o'clock when they stepped out into the eerie chill.

"You make a promise, now," she said as he walked her to her '64 Mustang.

"A promise," said Jaybird.

"Dummy. You're going to introduce me to Bluejay Clay."

"Right, right. Next time he's in town. I promise."

It struck him, as he drove carefully back to his room on the glazed streets of Nashville, that it was possible he had never before opened up his life like that to a woman. The only women in his life, in fact, had been his mother and Becky Rollins. He was too young to have anything to reveal to his mother, Molly Clay, and the things he had shared with Becky in their five years of courting and four years of marriage had been more along the lines of which sofa she thought would go best with which coffee table. When he reached the rooming house he jumped beneath the covers, still in his clothes, and promised himself he would tidy up the room a bit.

CHAPTER V

AMONG the services Jaybird provided for his clients was to produce promotional flyers for them, something he was doing at TopRank before Gordy Mock let him go, and even though there was little evidence that the modest little fold-out biographical leaflets were doing anything for his business, they did wonders for the clients' egos. When he had talked Amos Threadgill into allowing him to become his agent and personal manager, for instance, he went to the *Banner* and got his friend Red O'Donnell to find a back copy of the picture story the paper had run on Amos in the late fifties—"Taking His Music to the Streets" was the headline, with a photograph of Amos and his tin cup and cane and guitar on the steps of Ryman Auditorium—and then sat at a typewriter in the newsroom of the *Banner* to fabricate a bio and wonderful quotes to use in the flyer. Amos, according to the flyer, had grown up on a tenant farm in Mississippi and was born blind and had learned "slave songs" from his great-grandparents and was considered by Chet Atkins "one of the great pure folk guitarists of our time." Even Charley Pride, the first black to become a Grand Ole Opry regular, had great things to say about Amos Threadgill: "If it weren't for Amos' inspiration I'd still be picking cotton." Jaybird made it all up, of course, for Amos on a good day collected five dollars in his tin cup for whapping out vague spirituals in front of the old Noel Hotel at Church and Fifth.

But Jaybird enjoyed the ritual. He would go down to the newspaper on slow Saturday mornings, when most of the typewriters in the newsroom were free, and gaily compose press releases and material for "updated" flyers. Once he conned one of the photographers, when the chief of the photo department wasn't in, to take mug shots of his stable of entertainers in exchange for six tickets to the Opry. Another time, again bartering Opry tickets, he got one of the men in the composing room, when nobody was watching, to set in thirty-six-point Cheltenham type the names of Bama Red and Amos Threadgill and Luciano LaRussa to make the flyers appear more nearly legitimate. Then he would go home to the rooming house and, with scissors and paste and copy paper borrowed from the *Banner* newsroom, lay out the flyers. Finally he would take them to a quick-printing shop next door to a pawn shop on Broadway and they would print up, say, five hundred copies of the Bama Red flyer ("Bookings available through Clay Productions," the title Jaybird had given his operation, with the number of the pay phone in the foyer of the rooming house), making a deal with the alcoholic twin brothers who owned Kleen-Kopi to pay them the next time Bama got work. That was fine with Al and Hal Blount, the brothers, because it made them feel a part of the music industry.

It was while he was putting together a flyer and some press releases for Maureen Barksdale—Hank Elliott had supplied him with a snapshot and agreed to foot the bill as long as the flyer said she was "appearing nightly at Hank's Pop-a-Top Lounge, Music City U.S.A."—that the idea for *The Clay Chronicle* was born. It hit him like a thunderclap. Nine-thirty on a bright but cold Saturday morning found him feverishly at work in the newsroom at the paper, deserted except for a police reporter and a lone editor, reading and clipping from the piles of old newspapers and magazines from all over. From the *Reader's Digest* he clipped a story entitled "The Real Tragedy of Divorce," about the tug-of-war over children when a marriage fails. From *Forum* he found a story about how women use their sexuality as a weapon. The *National Enquirer* offered "I Wanted Love, She Wanted Gold." From the photo department he lifted an eight-by-ten of a father and son holding to each other and weeping—it had run in the *Tennessean* the day before, to illustrate a story about a funeral, but who was to know?—and in the composing room he got his friendly printer to hand-set in Old English type *The Clay Chronicle.* He typed an "editorial," a strident plea for "fathers' rights," and a "lead story" about an unidentified woman withholding an unidentified son from his unidentified divorced father and an "exposé" about the rape of southern hardwood forests by midwestern conglomerates.

At noon, armed with the makings of "Vol. I, No. 1" of *The Clay Chronicle* and the material for Mo Dale (as he and Maureen had agreed to bill her on the grounds that "Maureen Barksdale" was both cumbersome and tacky), Jaybird walked into Kleen-Kopi to begin his career as a publisher. One of the twins was at the front counter and the other, he could assume, was overseeing the press he heard whirring in the rear. He could never tell them apart.

"Well, now," the one up front said, "they let you out?"

"Just for the weekend," Jaybird said. "How you doing, Al?"

"I'm Hal."

"Why doesn't one of y'all wear an eyeshade or something?"

"Shit, Jay, it's easy to tell me and Al apart."

"Damned if I've figured it out."

"He drinks scotch, I drink gin." Hal Blount, who had been hunched over a ledger book trying to figure the week's take, bent over laughing. "Hey, Jay, you hear the one about the astronaut? One that's gonna walk on the moon?"

"No, but I intend to watch," Jaybird said.

"Know what's the first thing he's gonna see?"

"I give up."

"Some old boy with a guitar on his back, asking him which way it is to Bradley's Barn." Hal collapsed in laughter. Jaybird began to laugh, too, and soon they were joined by brother Al. Hal produced a half gallon of Mr. Boston gin from beneath the counter. Al went to the back and returned with a near-empty fifth of Inver House. Dixie cups appeared. The CLOSED sign was hung, it being noon, and as they celebrated the flight of Apollo Eight to the moon Jaybird began spreading out on the counter the raw materials for the first issue of *The Clay Chronicle*.

"You can't do this, Jay," said Hal.

"Who says?"

"The goddam copyright people, for starters."

"Nobody'll know where it came from."

"Yeah, but it says 'Clay' right there on the masthead."

"Hell, Hal, there are Clays everywhere."

"Yeah, but they'll see the postmark. Nashville."

"Got that figured out, too," said Jaybird. "Soon as y'all get it printed up I'll give copies to somebody going out on the road and just tell 'em to drop 'em in a mailbox somewhere. No questions, just put 'em in a mailbox in Iowa or somewhere. I'll already have 'em stapled and addressed."

"Sounds like a lot of trouble to me," said Al Blount.

"It'll be worth it just to see 'em squirm."

"Okay," said Hal. "Okay. How many copies?"

"Eight."

"Come again?"

"Eight," Jaybird said. "One for my ex-wife, one for her parents, one for my Pa. Lemme see. Got two lawyers, the judge down home, and the newspaper. And one for my files. That's eight."

"Godamitey, Jay, we could make five hundred as cheap as eight."

"All I need's eight."

"You're crazy, son. Stark-raving crazy as a bat."

"I've been told that already."

By six-thirty that evening Jaybird was sitting in the front booth of Tootsie's Orchid Lounge, where he had been since three o'clock, waiting for his father and feeling good about *The Clay Chronicle*. Even if it only lasted for one "issue," he figured, it would be worth the trouble. Outside, on Broadway and Opry Place and across the way in every corner of every parking lot, stretching up Opry to the downtown ridge of Church Street and then down Broadway to the sullen Cumberland River—everywhere, like ants—the Opry crowd was gathering. The scene was the same as it was some twenty years earlier when Bluejay had first brought him along to Ryman. There was a collage of bumper stickers, loose Iowa-farmwife slacks, Phenix City perfume, WALLACE FOR PRESIDENT straw boaters, Nebraska license plates, Georgia campers, Rebel flags, phony cowboy hats bought at Hackensack five-and-dime stores, old codgers from Lexington strutting into Friedman's Pawn Shop to buy panties with I LEFT MY ♡ IN NASHVILLE on the frilly bottoms, a bunch of old boys with a sign reading WVOJ VOICE OF JACKSONVILLE on their pickup while they barbecued ribs over grills set up on the asphalt parking lot, the ticket line meandering like a snake in front of the fierce old red-brick Ryman Auditorium for that night's Opry.

"Yo' daddy gon' be here tonight, Jay?"

"Got his name pasted up on the door," said Jaybird.

"First show, I reckon."

"Yeah. Wants to get back to the farm."

Jaybird was sitting with Scoopie Brucie Harper, a semilegendary Nashville character of vague origins who did occasional disc-jockey stints for country radio stations in the small towns ringing Music City U.S.A. during the week and spent his weekends at Tootsie's. Bluejay was, indeed, going to be on the Opry that night and Jay was checking his watch and the door leading in off the sidewalk on Broadway. He and Scoopie Brucie had managed to do a bit of damage to Tootsie Bess's supply of Pabst. The beer bottles were strewn about the table like tenpins, and Geraldine, the waitress, had to keep stopping by to empty the black plastic ashtray of crumpled cigarette butts.

"You hear about Geraldine?" said Scoopie.

"Heard she has cancer," said Jaybird.

"Naw, Tootsie's taking care of that."

"Didn't know Tootsie could cure cancer, *too*."

"Naw, naw. I meant the *story* about Geraldine."

"Christ. Which one?"

"Well," Scoopie said, "one day ol' John Seigenthaler, one at the *Tennessean*, he brings a bunch of editors down the hill to show 'em Tootsie's. Give 'em a little of that 'local color,' you know. Figured maybe they'd catch Acuff playing pinball or something. Didn't know Roy's so big in the church you ain't never gonna catch him playing no pinball at Tootsie's. Not in front of anybody, anyway. So anyhow Geraldine comes back with the beers on this tray and soon's she gets to the table she trips and one of the beers winds up on this writer from *The New York Times*. Guy's halfway up and sopping up the beer from his lap and Geraldine, she—"

"Throws him her apron," said Jaybird.

"You heard it?"

"And she says, 'Hope I didn't spill it on your dick.' "

"Damn," said Scoopie, "how'd you hear that?"

"Geraldine's been telling it for years."

Scoopie ordered two more beers and Jaybird was checking his watch again when he saw his father come into Tootsie's. Bluejay was dressed for the Opry, in the same sequined silver-and-blue outfit and tooled gray high-heeled cowboy boots he had worn on Jaybird's epochal trip to the stage of Ryman Auditorium some fifteen years earlier, descending almost regally down the rickety stairs from the stars' upstairs "back room" rather than through the tourist-infested front door on Broadway. Jaybird scattered the clutter of peanut hulls from the table and popped a mint in his mouth and straightened his collar. His father, he was reminded, still had a certain presence about him after all of these years. Jaybird smiled.

Bluejay waved at Jaybird and Scoopie but first went directly to Tootsie Bess, a high-spirited little woman whose Orchid Lounge had replaced Essie May's Blue Room as *the* watering hole for Opry people when she opened it in the late fifties, and when Tootsie saw Bluejay she let out a whoop and waddled around the cash register (NO BEER TABS FOR NO BODY—POLICE ORDERS read a poster right next to a cigar box holding at least $1,500 worth of IOUs) to give him a bear hug. They hooted and hugged and poked each other in the ribs. Tootsie nodded in the direction of Scoopie and Jaybird. Bluejay enjoined Tootsie in a brief but earnest conversation and then went to his pocket to count out a roll of bills for Tootsie. They giggled and hugged again. Bluejay grabbed the neck of Harold Weakley, Tootsie's son-in-law, a member of the Opry stage band, a grinning good old boy with a rakish toupee who always stood at the end of the bar with a beer until it was time for Grant Turner to welcome the opening act in behalf of Purina Dog Chow, and then he walked through the crowd to his son.

"Blue," said Scoopie, "come here and sit down."

"Scoopie," said Bluejay.

"You know this scoundrel, don't you?"

"Heard about him."

"Hi, Pa," Jaybird said.

"Son."

"We was just talking about Geraldine, Blue. She can probably hustle up a beer if you need one. They got plenty."

"Naw, thanks, Scoopie. I gotta work and scoot."

"Work and scoot. I like that. Which way you headed?"

"Back home. We played Dayton last night."

"Where's the band at?" said Scoopie.

"They're setting up backstage. We're doing the first show."

"How about ol' Sam. He come with you?"

"Naw," Bluejay said. "He's probably back home throwing rocks at bulldozers."

"Bulldozers."

"First goddam bulldozers rolled up Thursday morning."

"You doing work on the farm?"

"Hell, no," said Bluejay. "Goddam Diversified's building some ski slopes up on the hill above Sixkiller. Right up to my land. Even put a fence up next to the family cemetery. Sam's been looking through his war-surplus catalogues at bazookas."

"Sonofabitch," said Scoopie, "I remember the first time I—"

"Scoopie," said Bluejay.

"Naw, really, Blue—"

"I ain't got much time and I need to talk to Jaybird here."

"Gotcha. Geraldine? Catch you later, Blue."

They had only twenty minutes to be together, the father and the son, and even that was a blur. Faron Young, dressed in his tight-fitting Western-cut Opry outfit, chugalugged a beer to applause. Carl Smith came in with Goldie Howard, his new wife since he and June Carter broke up, to stand atop a chair and autograph the wall. Somebody drew boos by announcing he was dedicating the next five plays on the jukebox to Elvis Presley. A wasted straggler in a straw boater came through the front door, taking off the boater as he went, announcing he was soliciting campaign funds for George Wallace, getting more jeers than cash from people who knew a working wino when they saw one. Talking above the din of a late Saturday afternoon in Nashville— the clatter of Broadway, the people begging for Opry tickets, the music flowing from the loudspeakers outside Ernest Tubb's Record Shop across the street, the jukebox within Tootsie's, the backslapping and general hoo-rawing—was nearly impossible.

"What's that about the bulldozers?" Jaybird said.

"That's why Rollins wanted my land," said Bluejay. "They've bought damned near everything around the farm. My hundred acres is going to be like a no-man's-land. Putting up chalets and a ski resort over toward Standing Indian. Don't guess there's much I can do about it."

Pressed for time, shouting over the noise, they tried to catch up on each other. Bluejay said little had changed since Jaybird's abortive Christmas trip, that he had given the Flexible Flyer to Billy Wingo to pass to Robin, that some reshuffling of Diversified executives was going on and he had heard talk that Rex Siebert might go back to the Chicago office, that Robin's horse, Sutalitihi, was ready and waiting for Robin but Becky had told Billy Wingo to tell him that the boy was too young to ride a horse, and that Becky had been paid all of the back alimony out of the Holy Ghost, Inc., fund. Jaybird, figuring his father had already found out the real story about what happened with him at TopRank, talked about Kris Kristofferson and the rooming house and Hank Elliott and Bama Red and Amos and Luciano LaRussa. And Maureen Barksdale.

"Are y'all, ah, how do they say it these days?" said Bluejay.

"Sleeping together?" said Jaybird.

"Yeah, that's it."

"Oh, no, Pa. We just talk."

"What you talk about?"

"Everything. Where she's been, what's happened with me. Robin, Andrews, you. She's a big fan of yours. I promised her I'd introduce y'all sometimes."

"How come she ain't here right now?" said Bluejay.

"Working," Jaybird said. "Hard for her to get off on Saturday."

"Pretty thing, you say?"

"Yeah. Black hair, black eyes. Good figure."

"Good woman?"

"Hah," said Jaybird. "I swear, Pa, you trying to fix me up?"

"Hell, boy, sounds like you've already taken care of that."

"Maybe. Right now I'm just trying to see if I can help her out. You know, with her career. She's not the greatest singer in town but there's worse. Lots worse. If Owen isn't still mad about me wrecking his place I might ask him if he'll listen to a demo. She's got this song she wrote, calls it 'Please Be My Cowboy,' and it's pretty good. Wish you could go out to Hank's tonight and hear her."

"Wish I could, son," Bluejay said, "but I've been away too long. I tell you what, though. Something that might work."

"Want me to bring her down there?"

"Oh, hell, no, ain't you got no sense?"

"Hey, Pa, I've been divorced for five years."

"It ain't that, Jaybird. You'd scare hell out of her."

"I don't follow you."

"Make her feel like you was taking her home so Pa could look her over."

"Well?"

"There's a better way," Bluejay said. "Sam's putting together a little run to Texas. Can't even call it a tour. Fort Worth, maybe Dallas, Abilene, whatever he can work out. How about you and this Mo come along with us? They love them little girls that sing about cowboys out there. Both of y'all come. I'll take care of expenses and pay her a hundred dollars a show. How about it?"

"I can't argue with it. She'll die when I tell her."

"Don't let that happen," said Bluejay.

And then, almost as quickly as he had come, Bluejay was gone. The fans in the bar who had recognized him tried to corner him and make over him but he explained that he had to run across the alley and host the Purina Dog Chow show but maybe they could catch him later at his bus. Jaybird watched his father bound up the steps and was leaving a tip for Geraldine, preparing to go backstage to hear the first show before going on out to Hank's Pop-a-Top for the night, when he was confronted by a squared fifty-ish man wearing white tasseled loafers and a string tie. With the man was a fat bleached blonde, dumpy and hollow from childbirth, and their three rowdy kids. They were blocking Jaybird's way.

"Well, by God. I finally made it," the man said.

"Made what?" said Jaybird.

"Grand Ole Opry. Played three years with the Vols and never made it."

"Look, if you don't mind."

"Name's Cecil Cantrell," the man said, extending his hand. Jaybird limply shook his hand and looked for a way out of this. "They call me 'Stud,' actually, for obvious reasons. This here's the little woman. Used to be Dixie Box. Fella wrote a book about us one time when I was still playing ball. Maybe you read it. Got Dixie all pissed off."

"I don't read much except *Billboard*."

"Are you anybody?" the man said.

"What the hell kind of question is that?" said Jaybird.

"Naw, I mean I seen you sitting there with ol' Bluejay. God-dam. Next to Hank Williams, rest his soul, Bluejay's the best."

"How many do you need?"

"Five." The man's eyes drooled when Jaybird pulled out a handful of Opry tickets. The man punched his haggard wife on the arm. "Hey, friend, anytime you're down in Dothan and want

to play some golf, let me know. I run the pro shop at the Wire-
grass Country Club down there."

"I'll do that. Now, if you'd excuse me."

"You got to be somebody, with all them Opry tickets."

"No," Jaybird said, breaking away, "nobody." He scurried up
the stairs and through the back room of Tootsie's, sidestepped
a gaggle of old women wielding Instamatics at spangled Conway
Twitty in the alleyway behind Ryman Auditorium, was passed
through the door marked STARS ONLY and made it backstage in
time to hear Grant Turner announce his father to the faithful.

CHAPTER VI

Dear Son,

I'm sorry I'm having to do it like this, but there doesn't seem to be any other way for me to get a letter to you. I've written you at least once a month, I guess, since your mother took you away from me. That would mean I've written something like fifty letters to you and as far as I know she hasn't even let you see a single one. It's probably no surprise to you that she's still mad at me. Well, I'm plenty mad at her, too, but I guess that's the way it goes when two people who thought they loved each other grow up to be different and all of a sudden find they can't get along. Anyway, I hope it doesn't upset you when they pull you out of class just to get this letter to you. I'm mailing it to Grandpa and he's giving it to the school principal, Mr. Sellers, who said he thought it's pretty awful what your mother's doing and promises he'll give this to you.

Except that I miss you an awful lot (it almost killed me and Grandpa and old Sam when we couldn't see you on Christmas) I guess I'm doing okay. I've got a real nice apartment on what they call "Music Row" in Nashville. This place has really changed from back when I was your age and used to come up here with him for the Grand Ole Opry. The Opry's still going strong but it's going to be changing a lot pretty soon. WSM, the radio station that runs the Opry, is about to start building a fancy amusement park they'll call "Opryland U.S.A.," with rides and a big motel and a new air-conditioned Opry House. So people won't be fainting from the heat in the old place—Ryman Auditorium's been officially rated as a "firetrap" by the Fire Department for years—and this "Opryland U.S.A." ought to be a lot better for all of the television they're starting to do out of "Music City U.S.A." They're also calling the music "The Nashville Sound" now. A lot of the old-timers like Grandpa don't like it—they think it's too fancy—but it's not called "hillybilly music" anymore.

Let's see, there's so much I wanted to tell you. My business is doing real well since I quit that company I used to work for. It's called TopRank and they represent a lot of stars like Bobby Smart. I used to travel with him and his band all over the country but I just got tired of working for a big outfit. I guess I'm like Grandpa in that respect. I like being my own boss. I'm "personal manager" for several people who're going to be big stars if I have anything to do with it. One of them isn't really a "country" singer (his name is Luciano LaRussa and he's from Rome, Italy). One's a blind black man like Ray Charles, in case you've heard of Ray Charles, and I also represent a comedian named "Bama Red" who's probably as funny as another "Red"—Red Skelton—and I'm trying to make him just as famous. And the best one of all is this girl singer Mo Dale (I'm enclosing a "promotional flyer" I did for her) who's going to be a very big star if I have anything to do with it. She's pretty, as you can see from her picture, and she sings like a robin (no joke, Robin). She's not exactly my "girlfriend," but we like each other a lot. I'm going to fix it so she can make her first record pretty soon and Grandpa says maybe she can go on tour with him and his band.

But what about you? I sent you a card last month for your tenth birthday. Did you get it? The last time I saw Grandpa he said he gave the Flex Flyer sled to Billy Wingo to give you as my Christmas present. And I don't know whether the word got to you, but Grandpa and Sam got you a nice pony for Christmas and broke it in for you. They named it "Sutalitihi" after Sam's great-grandfather, Uwani Sutalitihi, the Cherokee brave Sam told you about one time. Your mother says you're too young to be riding a horse but I say that's a bunch of baloney. You ought to throw a fit about it—now that you know you've got your own horse on the farm, waiting for you—so she'll have to let you stay with Grandpa some weekend.

Grandpa said he heard some talk that your mother and that man she married may have to move to Chicago. Is that true? It's been tough enough getting to see you when you live only about four hours away, but I looked on the map and it's almost five hundred miles from here to Chicago. That would be terrible if you moved up there. Chicago's just about my unfavorite city in all of America. It's cold and big and windy (they even call it "The Windy City") and like a foreign country. I'd raise the Dickens about that, too, if I were you. Grandpa talks a lot about what happens to people when they're taken away from their "roots." I thought he'd never shut up talking about it when I was your age, and he's even worse about it now. But there's something to it, I guess. The older I get, the more I see that a lot of strange things can happen when you move away from the people and the places you grew up with. Sometimes I wish I'd never moved away from Sixkiller. But other times I figure you have to move away to want to move back.

I'm trying very hard to keep from saying terrible things about your mother, son, and it's not easy. The way she's kept me from seeing you—my own flesh and blood, the last of the Clays, as Grandpa keeps putting it—is against the law. I know the papers say I've got to pay "X" dollars every month for you, which I do, but they also say I get "visitation rights." Somebody even told me I have the right to "kidnap" you, as a matter of fact, since a father can't really "kidnap" his own son. But I don't know about that. You're probably having enough trouble as it is, having to be around that bag Mrs. Rollins and that Yankee s.o.b. your mother took up with.

Well, I'm sorry. I guess I shouldn't talk to you like that. I wish I'd never married your mother in the first place, but if I hadn't there wouldn't be a Robin Clay. There's a book out called *Catch-22* and that's what it's all about. A fellow tried to get out of the war because he says he's going crazy and they tell him he can't get out because you *have* to be crazy to be in a war. You're damned if you do, and damned if you don't. That's about the way it is with me and your mother. I just hope you do a lot better when it comes time to find a woman to marry. Your father can give you some expert advice about what we call the "Rocking-Chair Theory" when you're old enough to understand it.

I've got to go now. Please don't let your mother see this letter. But also please hold on to it—surely you've got a special hiding place for things you aren't supposed to have—so you can read it again from time to time. I don't know when I'll be down there again. It depends on whether I can work out a way to see you. We're working on that. Sometimes I think the easiest way is for you to just walk to Sixkiller after school one day instead of going "home" to "Cloudland." Your horse is looking for a rider.

All My Love,
Dad

P.S.—I've got a good picture of you now. I gave Grandpa a good camera for Christmas, one of those with a telephoto lens, and when Sam learned how to work it (Grandpa doesn't know anything about "machinery," as he calls the camera) he sneaked onto the school yard and got a good picture of you. I had it blown up to about two feet by three feet and it's in a frame over the bed in my apartment. You look just like I did when I was ten. More Love, Dad.

CHAPTER VII

MO DALE'S FIRST APPEARANCE on a genuine country-music road show had taken place the night before, for the benefit of more than five hundred red-faced Big Thicket yahoos and their faded darlings at the cavernous Reo Palm Isle Ballroom outside of Longview, Texas, with predictable results. The Sixkillers had played "San Antonio Rose" and "I'd Waltz Across Texas With You" and some other danceable East Texas favorites while the Friday-night celebrants streamed through the wide double doors to get their hands stamped for in-and-out privileges and hauled their Styrofoam coolers to the tiny tables covered with red-and-white checkerboard oilcloths. Then Bluejay came on and did "The Longer You're Gone" and a couple of others, setting the sawdusted dance floor a-twirl with stomping boots and flying calico skirts, before he asked the crowd for "a great big Reo Palm Isle welcome for little Miss Mo Dale, direct from Nashville, Tennessee." When Mo came bouncing out in the same black-and-white outfit she had worn the night Jaybird first saw her the galoots began howling and when she went into "Please Be My Cowboy" they went crazy. She put them to crying with "Faded Love" and she had to encore "Cowboy" three times before they would let her go. Jaybird, watching it all from the wings of the cramped stage, picked her up and twirled her about and kissed her full on the mouth when she came off.

143

Now it was four o'clock in the morning and the bus, which Bluejay had rechristened "Molly," had made the swing around Dallas and Fort Worth on the new Interstate 20 and was rumbling westward toward Abilene. Bluejay was asleep in his "suite" at the very rear of the bus and the others—the Sixkillers, who had been with Bluejay for nearly twenty-five years—tossed in their bunks in the midsection while Skeeter McGahee, the bootlegger and lead guitarist, drove through a sudden June thunderstorm. Jaybird and Mo, still excited over her debut at the Reo Palm Isle Ballroom, sat beside each other in the wide shotgun seat while Ralph Emery's "Opry Star Spotlight" came in over the intercom from WSM in Nashville.

"Say you never been to Texas, little lady?" Skeeter said.

"Lord," said Mo, "I've never been past the Mississippi."

"Well, you ain't seen nothing yet."

"Is it pretty?"

"I don't know about 'pretty,' " said Skeeter, having to shout, "but it might as well be another country."

Jaybird said, "Call it 'West by-God Texas.' "

"Bet your boots," said Skeeter. "Folks are independent as hell out here. Play hell getting 'em to go any farther away from home than Fort Worth. They think Dallas is worse than New York. Best way to find out how the economy of one of these towns out here is doing is to ask how many pickups got sold last month. Music's different, too. Dancing, that's what they like. Mel Tillis says one time they took a break and when some old boy cranked up a John Deere tractor outside six couples got up to dance."

"You're kidding," said Mo.

"Naw, I ain't kidding," Skeeter told her.

"But my songs aren't exactly made for dancing."

"Don't let it worry you. You watch. Out here tonight at Buffalo Gap the boys and the girls are gonna start arriving separately in their GMC pickups. Be dressed just alike. Pearl-button shirts, boots, jeans, big old shiny belt buckles. Those buckles must weigh a pound each. When you get up there and start singing 'Cowboy' and they go belly-to-belly in the 'cowboy shuffle' it's gonna make the sparks fly."

"The 'cowboy shuffle.' What's that?"

"Close-dancing. So close they could get arrested."

As the old Bluebird bus droned on through the wind-swept Texas night, Maureen alternately dozing off on his shoulder and bolting awake when an oncoming eighteen-wheeler would nearly blow them off the road, Jaybird aimlessly chattered with Skeeter and laughed at his carryings-on over the new citizen's-band radio (Bluejay's CB "handle" was "Molly") and pondered what was going to come of this trip. He didn't really need to be along—everybody knew that—and it really wouldn't make any difference to Bluejay's fans in Texas whether there was a perky female singer there as a warm-up act. Everybody knew that, too. But everybody also knew that there might be something budding here between this wasted son of Bluejay Clay and the mysterious woman who had abruptly entered his life. That was why Sam, fooling no one, begged off of the trip, meaning making space on the bus for Jaybird and Mo, on the grounds that there was pressing business at the farm. That was why Bluejay made a solemn promise to his son that he would try to set a personal record of going eighty straight hours without cussing. Maureen Barksdale, and Jaybird with her, was going under the microscope.

It was eight o'clock in the morning, a steamy summer Saturday morning along the undulating hills of West Texas, when Skeeter McGahee finally found the Alamo Plaza Motel on the southern edge of Abilene. When he rolled the bus into the gravel parking lot, the legend on the side announcing BLUEJAY CLAY & THE SIXKILLERS, surprised ranchers and farmers and their healthy women lurched from their breakfasts in the motel dining room and charged. They were strong wind-burned people of the land, people who fought the rain and the wind and the incessant sun all week in order to make it to Saturday night, and they were demanding to have a word with Bluejay Clay. *I know he's in there somewhere/Come on out, now, Bluejay, I want to have a look at you/Wonder who's that purty woman they got in there/ Reckon ol' Sam, that Indian of his, reckon he come along?/Lord, God, ain't this something?* The hubbub and the gentle shuddering of the bus as Skeeter shut it down brought the other Sixkillers out of their bunks. They blinked as they peaked through Ethel McGahee's dainty calico curtains, rushing to get their boots and pearl-button shirts on, and when Skeeter jerked open the door the members of the band—Claude Owenby, farmer/dobro-steel, from Buck's Creek; Floyd Watkins, Diversified mill worker/ drummer, Andrews; Buddy Brumby, carpenter/fiddler, Hayes-ville—stepped into the fray and were followed by Skeeter, the bootlegger/lead guitarist from Tusquitee, and it was as though they had returned from some distant war.

"Y'all hush, now," Skeeter yelled, "Bluejay's trying to sleep."

"What's he doing, getting his beauty rest?" somebody said.

"Hell, he'll be sleeping till Doomsday," somebody else said.

"Well, by dang, he can sleep with *me*," yelled a fat woman in Bermuda shorts and a Texas A&M "Aggies" T-shirt.

"Come on, Skeeter, where's Bluejay at?"

The trip had been a long one—951 miles, exactly, from the Gulf station on the west side of Chattanooga where Maureen and Jaybird had stored her Mustang and boarded the bus—and it showed. The two of them, strangers to the crowd, easily stepped from the bus and melded with the crowd. It wasn't so easy for Bluejay. The minute he showed his face, haggard and lined from trying to sleep, he was swamped. Cameras snapped, women squealed, ranchers whooped, autograph albums and ball-point pens appeared. By the time Jaybird, acting as road manager on the trip, had gotten room keys for everybody and returned to rescue his father he had to literally tear him away. "Guess it's too late for me to go to college and learn a trade," Bluejay said to Jaybird and Maureen, who had run interference for him, as he stood in the doorway to his room and admired the king-size Magic Fingers bed.

By midafternoon Jaybird and Maureen had eaten in the dining room, where it seemed the order of the day was to play nothing but Bluejay Clay records on the jukebox, and caught up on their sleep—in separate rooms, of course, but at least Bluejay had splurged on a motel out of deference to Maureen—and now they were sitting at poolside in cheap ill-fitting swimsuits bought

across the road at the Alamo Plaza Shopping Mall. The only sign
of life from Bluejay's room had come when a waitress took a
tray of hambürgers to the door and an arm reached out and
snatched it. The Sixkillers had left the door open to Buddy Brumby's room, where they had a lively poker game going, and occasionally a Sixkiller would step to the doorway to stretch and
belch and wave to Jaybird and Maureen before ducking back
inside out of the heat.

"Well, how'm I doing so far?" said Maureen. The swimsuit
she had bought was a white one-piecer, small enough to show
not only her ample cleavage but also the scars left on her right
shoulder by Lefty Dews.

"You were great," said Jaybird. "They loved you."

"I don't mean with them. I mean with Bluejay."

"Pa? I wouldn't be surprised if he wanted to keep you on."

"Come on, now, sport. You know what I'm talking about."

"I guess I do." Jaybird jiggled a Wing-Ding cup full of ice
shavings and bourbon, posing as iced tea, and took a long swallow. "I can't say I like it any more than you do, but I don't know
how to stop it."

"He keeps calling me 'daughter.' That's spooky."

"Aw, that's just his way. That's what he calls most young
women."

"Is that what he called your wife?" said Maureen.

"He hardly had a chance," Jaybird said.

"It was that bad."

"That bad. All he had to know was that she was a rich kid
and that was it. He could be the meanest sonofabitch in the
valley around her. Like, Becky's mama was named Genevieve.
Any time somebody dropped the name 'Genevieve,' he'd say,
'something 'bout that name I never could stand.' Right in front
of Becky, he'd say that, and Becky'd swear she was never coming
back and Pa'd say that suited him just fine and why didn't she
just rock it off. It got crazy."

"Rock it off," said Maureen.

"Rocking chairs," Jaybird said. "He's got a thing about rich people and rocking chairs. Says they've got 'em but they're so afraid somebody's going to steal 'em that they chain 'em to the floor. And then nobody can rock in 'em."

"Well?"

"Well, what?"

"Were Becky's folks' chairs chained to the floor?"

"Come to think of it, they were."

She stood up and neatly flipped into the pool, her white suit and flowing black hair slicing soundlessly through the greenish water, while he drained the cup. He went to his room to sweeten the cup with bourbon and when he came back to the pool she had toweled her hair and was braiding pigtails for the show that night.

"Want me to help?" Jaybird said.

"No, thank you."

"What, you don't think I could do it?"

"Pigtails? You could probably learn."

"Why don't you let me try, then?"

"Look," she said. "I do my own pigtails. I make my own house payments. I drive my own car. I fix my own dinner. Okay?"

"Okay, okay."

"But thank you very much, anyway."

Skeeter was right about West by-God Texas. The place they would play that night was the Big Valley Trail House, a huge Quonset building set off of a dirt road some fourteen miles south of Abilene in a rolling backwoods of lakes and buttes and scrub pines known as Buffalo Gap, and when Bluejay's bus slithered up in the mud at dusk the party had already begun. Out in the parking lot were scores of pickup trucks and Winnebagoes and even horses. Ernest Tubb songs were being piped outside while the people—dressed, as Skeeter had promised, in identical Saturday-night outfits of cowboy boots and pearl-button shirts and boot-cut jeans and bandannas and cowboy hats—swirled around comparing notes and catching up on gossip and swigging from bottles and generally warming up for what promised to be a night of hell-raising.

They piled off the bus and ran the gauntlet to the safety of what passed for a dressing room. For this night Bluejay wore a cream-colored Western-cut outfit glittering with ruby sequins and the Sixkillers were in more sedate burgundy pants and pearl-button cream shirts with string ties and burgundy cowboy hats. While Bluejay and the band lolled around the mirrored concrete-block "dressing room" Maureen stayed on the bus to finish dressing in Bluejay's cubicle of a "suite." She had chosen an outfit of her own design and making—fringed red miniskirt, sequined white long-sleeved blouse with MO embroidered over the heart—and when she walked in to join them, wearing white knee-length zip-up boots and a red cowgirl hat over her black pig-tailed hair, the little room went as quiet as a morgue.

"Great godamitey," Buddy Brumby said.

"Well?" said Mo.

"You better watch yourself, daughter," said Bluejay.

"Anything wrong?"

"Naw. That's the problem."

They had two shows to do that night, at eight o'clock and ten, and Jaybird's job included setting up folding card tables in the foyer so they could sell eight-by-tens and albums between shows. By seven-thirty the five hundred or so cowboys and their wives and girlfriends had gone through the turnstiles, getting the backs of their hands stamped and lugging their coolers and pasting back their hair, and now they were encamping at blue-and-white checkerboard oilclothed tables just as the crowd had done the night before in Longview. The first show went quickly and smoothly, as though it were a mere warm-up, and Mo Dale was clearly the hit. When she came out in her tight mini-skirt and flashed her saucerish black eyes, the women in the crowd, hard ranch women with bleached hair done up in beehives, had to keep a leash on their mates. One old boy, just below the apron of the stage, stood on his metal folding chair and waved his cowboy hat and yelled like a Marine charging a beach—"Yeeeeaaaiiiaahhh!"—until his wife knocked him and their cooler of beer to the floor.

At intermission, while some of the men wandered outside to relieve themselves in the bushes and others danced with their wives to the juke's "I'd Waltz Across Texas with You," Jaybird stood behind a table in the foyer and did a brisk business. Eight-by-tens of Bluejay were going for $1.50 and his album, "Best of Bluejay," for five dollars even. Mo had gone out to the bus for a rest and Skeeter had gone with her so he could both guard the bus and answer questions from the fans ("Looks kinda like a motel room on wheels, don't it, Earlene?"). The Sixkillers stayed in the dressing room and now and then stepped outside to mingle with the crowd and sip a beer. Bluejay was seated at one of the tables in the foyer, next to where Jaybird was selling photographs and albums, autographing as vigorously as he could.

"I don't want no goddam picture of Bluejay, I just want me a close look at that little ol' thing. *Real* close." When Jaybird looked up from counting the bills he saw a hulking redheaded cowboy, in the process of getting very drunk, hovering above him.

"I beg your pardon?" Jaybird stiffened.

"That girl. Where's she at?" said the cowboy.

"She's on the bus, resting."

"I'll bet. Who's she resting with?"

"Look, buddy, do you want a picture or not?"

"I heard about them Snuff Queens."

"What'd you say?"

"Rock 'n' roll people call 'em Star-Fuckers."

Jaybird sprang across the card table at the cowboy like a rattlesnake, knocking albums and stacks of photographs and dollar bills all over the concrete floor, but after getting in the first licks he was no match. The cowboy was all over him, punching and kicking and butting and biting, and it took all five of the Big Valley Trail House's security guards to break it up. When Mo, alerted by Skeeter, ran inside from the bus, she found Jaybird a bloody battered mess sprawled out on the floor and dozens of people trying to hustle the cowboy outside to inflict justice in the mud of West Texas. Wet towels were produced. Mo cried. Jaybird moaned. Bluejay and the band stood around, stunned, and then carried Jaybird to one of the guards' car. Mo got in with him and the car slithered away to the motel. The second show went on without them.

It was close to midnight when Jaybird came to his senses. He found himself propped up in bed, stripped to his shorts, his right arm in a sling made of a torn bedsheet and his rib cage taped and his left eye closed shut. Mo sat on the edge of the bed, her white-sequined blouse spattered with his blood, wiping his forehead with a damp washcloth. When he blinked his one good eye he saw his father, frazzled and down to a T-shirt now, sitting in a chair beside the bed and twirling a tea bag around in a cup of steaming water for him.

"Where'd you learn how to do all that, daughter?" said Bluejay.

"What, first aid?" said Mo.

"You act like a battlefield nurse."

"I got lots of practice, being married to Lefty Dews."

"Were you married to that, that—"

"Sonofabitch," said Mo.

"Took the words right out of my mouth," said Bluejay.

"And after that it was Tommy McMillen."

"The drummer? The pill-pusher?"

"The one and only."

"Lord, daughter, you need a vacation."

"I'm on one," Mo said, "a *long* one."

Jaybird, wincing as he tried to prop himself more comfortably amid the pile of pillows Mo had stacked for him, reached for the steaming tea with the arm that still worked. "I hope they made a blood spot out of that shit-heel," he said.

"I should've known it was going to happen," Mo said. "These places can be volatile. Saturday night, all of that drinking, women."

"How's that?" said Bluejay. He and Jaybird were looking at her.

"You're asking for trouble in these places," she said.

"No," said Jaybird. "That word."

"I said, 'volatile.' You know, combustible. Like dynamite."

"Where in the pluperfect hell did a little old girl singer learn words like that?"

"Why, you old fart." Mo slammed a wet towel to the floor. "Two days ago I was all excited about meeting the great Bluejay

Clay and now look at what you turned out to be. What gives you the idea I'm just a 'little old girl singer'? Let me tell you something, *Mister* Clay, you come to my house sometime if I decide to let you see it and I'll show you a goddam library like you never even dreamed of. This little old girl singer not only makes her own clothes and pays her own bills, she's also smarter than any fifteen of you hillbillies put together. Wipe that shit-eating grin off your face."

"My, my," Bluejay said.

"You condescending bastard."

"Oh, my goodness." Bluejay was about to laugh and so was she.

"Get the hell out of here," she said. "I've got to administer to Sir Galahad."

Glum was the word for the trip back home. Bluejay and the band went through the motions on Sunday afternoon at Panther Hall in Fort Worth, Mo choosing to stay on the bus and look after Jaybird rather than perform, and there was a pall aboard "Molly" as Skeeter pointed it eastward and counted off the miles and the towns—Marshall, Bossier City, Vicksburg, Meridian, Tuscaloosa, Birmingham, Fort Payne—until finally, around noon Monday, he stopped at the Gulf station on the outskirts of Chattanooga where Mo had left her car. There were perfunctory goodbyes. The bus cranked and headed east toward Andrews and Sixkiller, Mo's Mustang zipping north toward Nashville. Jaybird dozed off and on until at midafternoon Mo shook him awake for directions to his rooming house and when they got there she got his things for him and helped him walk to his door and when she opened it he collapsed on his bed.

She looked around the cluttered room and said, "God."

"What you see is what you get," said Jaybird.

"Who said I wanted it?"

"Mo?"

"Are you okay?"

"Come here and hold me, Mo."

She pulled back the curtains and opened a window to the

musty room and then she walked to the bed and helped him get comfortable and then she got on top of the covers with him and put her arm around his shoulder and hummed to him until he fell asleep. When she left there was a robin singing outside the window and Jaybird was snoring softly.

CHAPTER VIII

H<small>E HAD BEEN LAID UP</small> in his room for nearly a week and he still felt like a Green Bay Packers linebacker on a Monday. The right arm was out of its jury-rigged sling but he still couldn't manage the most rudimentary acts such as brushing his teeth. About all he had been able to hold down, due to his aching ribs and general fatigue, was helpings from the vat of homemade vegetable soup and the saltines Mo had brought him the day after their return from Texas. Mo, in fact, had saved him from going stir crazy. Every morning she would call to the pay phone in the hall, first letting it ring twice as a signal and then calling again when she figured he'd had time to get out of bed to answer. Every afternoon, before heading on to work at the Pop-a-Top, she would drop by with something to nibble on and the afternoon paper and any bits of gossip she had heard from Music Row. Then she would clean the cut over his eye and change the dressing on his ribs and kiss him on the cheek before leaving him to his devices. Down the hall would come the cursing and strumming of Kris, trying to put away the lyrics to a new song he was fashioning, and Jaybird would lie back and listen with erotic visions of Mo in his head.

On Friday afternoon, just after Mo had left and he had opened to Red O'Connell's column (so unknown was Kris that they were still spelling his name "Kristofson"), there was a knock on the door. He figured Mo had forgotten something—a real kiss, maybe? a promise to come back after closing?—but it turned out to be his lawyer, Flip Hanes, wearing his three-piece uniform and a look of utter bewilderment.

"Well," said Jaybird, "my secretary's out for the moment."

"If you're the winner I don't want to see the loser," said Hanes.

"Boys in Texas take their women seriously."

"You'd better, too, buddy-boy."

"What's up, O Barrister?"

"Your ass. Up a creek. What *is* this shit?"

Flip Hanes flopped into the ratty wing chair, exhausted, and helped himself to a long pull of bourbon from the bottle atop the desk next to the bed while Jaybird raised up to examine the papers Flip had brought. One was Flip's copy of *The Clay Chronicle*—addressed to J. Freeman Hanes, postmarked Winterset, Iowa—another was a Xerox copy of the nine-page handwritten letter to Robin and yet another was an onion-skin court order demanding that he "cease and desist from such harassment." The latter was signed by the new judge in Cherokee County, North Carolina.

"Winterset, Iowa, so that's where E.T. was headed," Jaybird said.

"Jay," said Flip.

"Wonder how they traced it back to Nashville?"

"Jay."

"Damned classy printing job, if you ask me."

"Okay, okay. Talk."

Jaybird told Flip Hanes the whole story about the birth of *The Clay Chronicle* and his frustrations over not getting to see Robin, things he had told him many times since he had fired the original divorce lawyer and hired Flip to get him out of the mess, and about Mo Dale and what happened at TopRank and the Flex Flyer and Sutalitihi the horse and the trip to Texas and everything else about his demise that came to mind. He took a good swallow of bourbon, himself, and was starting to say he didn't understand what all of the fuss was about when Flip cut him off.

"Now it's my turn," said Hanes. "You left a trail like Sherman going through Georgia, my friend, and I've been on the phone all week trying to put the fires out. Among the things they're saying is that you libeled Mr. Siebert when you called him a 'Yankee s.o.b.' in your letter to your kid, that you interfered with the boy's education when you had 'em pull him out of class to give him the letter, that you're behind a plot to kidnap him, that you've caused irreparable harm to Diversified Enterprises in that charming little story you wrote about a big company messing up a mountain town, and so on and so forth. You've also implicated the school principal and Sam Sixkiller and your father in invading the rights to privacy of Robin, and also in the kidnapping."

"Come on, now, Flip, I didn't do that," said Jaybird.

"What matters," Hanes said, "is that they *think* you did."

"Who'd you talk to down there?"

"Everybody. Your father and Sam, the principal, your ex-wife and Siebert, Becky's lawyer, the new judge in Cherokee County, even this Wingo fellow. The security guard where they live."

"Billy Wingo? What'd you talk to him for?"

"Seemed to be the surest way to find out what's happening."

"So?" said Jaybird.

"They're moving to Chicago. He got transferred."

"When?"

"Around September."

"Oh, shit. It's hard enough seeing the boy as it is."

"Yeah, but hold on," said Hanes, "you may have done yourself a favor. That newsletter was the goddamnedest harebrained most childish thing I ever heard of. But it might give you something to negotiate with. The judge and her lawyer down there have about had enough of all this. They wish to hell one of y'all would move to England and the other one to China. But look here. You stop the newsletter right now, just quit with volume one, number one, and in return for that Becky promises you get to see Robin like the decree says you're supposed to. She's already told me that if you stop the *Clay Chronicle* or whatever you call it you can have the boy for the whole month of August. Before they move to Chicago."

"What if I don't stop it?" said Jaybird.

"We don't have a chance in front of that judge," Hanes said.

"I don't see why people can't do what they're supposed to."

"If they did I'd be out of work, Jay."

"All right," said Jaybird, "I'll kill the newsletter. I was starting to have fun with it, though, Flip, no matter what you think. I tore a letter to the editor out of *Playboy* for the next issue about frigid women that broke me up. Damn shame I can't use it."

"I don't think Becky's all that frigid," said Hanes.

"What would you know about that?"

"She's been messing around."

"Becky? Miss Tight-Crotch?"

"They got a hell of a mess down there. First she caught Siebert fooling around. Then he caught her trying to get even. In a way that's why they're moving to Chicago, so they can get a fresh start."

"Jesus."

"Billy Wingo missed his calling," said Flip Hanes.

"Well, well." Jaybird hobbled to the sink for glasses so the two could have a genuine toast to their victory. Dusk was coming and Jaybird decided he would try to get dressed and drive out to Hank's Pop-a-Top so he could tell Mo and then get royally drunk.

"You making any money these days?" said Hanes.

"Not to speak of," said Jaybird. "What's the damage?"

"This one will cost you two hundred and phone calls."

"You'll have to put it on my tab, Flip."

"Unless, of course, you wanted to take it out in trade."

"Flip," said Jaybird, "you've got to be about the worst goddam amateur songwriter I ever heard."

"At least you could listen to it."

"What's the title?"

"Listen to this," said Flip Hanes. " 'Billy Broke My Heart at Walgreen's and I Cried All the Way to Sears.' Hanh? It's got it all."

"And I suppose she gets run over by a train."

"Right. How'd you know?"

"I know my country music," said Jaybird.

CHAPTER IX

THE EVOLUTION of Bradley's Barn into one of the best recording studios in Music City U.S.A. had been as natural and accidental as the development of Nashville's music industry. For years Owen Bradley, the veteran artists-and-repertoire man for Decca Records in Nashville—meaning The Boss—had driven past a dilapidated old barn near Old Hickory Lake where he had a summer and weekend place. When he bought it in the early sixties it was with the intention of fixing it up a bit so his oldest son, who had just begun a modest music-publishing company, would have a place to cut demo tapes. So he patched the cracks and insulated and installed a bar and dug wells and hung baffles and his son began cutting demos in the solitude of the pastoral Middle Tennessee countryside. Before Owen knew it, though, with a shortage of recording studios along Music Row in downtown Nashville, Bradley's Barn had become many of the stars' favorite studio and it was humming nearly twenty-four hours a day. Loretta Lynn, in fact, recorded "Don't Come Home A-drinkin' with Lovin' on Your Mind" and she was followed there by the likes of Bill Anderson and even jazz clarinetist Pete Fountain. "Looks like I lost a party room and gained a recording studio," Owen Bradley mused one day.

So Bradley's Barn it would be, for Mo Dale's first recording session, and no expense was being spared. Bluejay's reasons for backing the endeavor weren't entirely altruistic, of course, for he had taken a genuine liking to her and to the idea of Jaybird and Mo being together. But he knew a talent when he heard one—a little rough-edged, sure, but wonders could be wrought at the controls of a modern recording studio—and through his twenty-year friendship with Owen Bradley he arranged for nothing but the best. Mo would record "Please Be My Cowboy" at the Barn and she would be backed by the best studio musicians in Nashville: four violinists and a flutist from the Nashville Symphony Orchestra, Buddy Harman on drums, Floyd Cramer on piano, Bob Moore on bass, the famous Jordanaires, whose voices always backed Elvis Presley, Charlie McCoy on harmonica and none other than Chet Atkins on lead guitar.

Hank Elliott was beside himself. It was eight forty-five at night, inside Bradley's Barn, and he had even put on a coat and tie to be there. Bluejay had bought the nine-to-midnight slot for Mo to record "Cowboy" and, for the flip side of a 45 rpm, the classic Kitty Wells hit "It Wasn't God Who Made Honky-Tonk Angels." Jaybird and Mo had insisted that Hank be there for the event and it was as though his own daughter were there. He kept telling Mo not to be nervous and asking Atkins and the four Jordanaires for their autographs and peering into the glassed booth to see what Owen Bradley and the chief engineer were doing with all of the dials.

"Can you believe this? Chet Atkins," Hank told Jaybird.

"He and Pa and Owen are all old friends," Jaybird said.

"Yeah, but he's a big shot now, ain't he?"

"Head of RCA in Nashville."

"You mean you can just call him up and get him?"

"He just loves to pick," said Jaybird.

"Reckon he'd do that 'Country Gentleman' for me, Jay?"

"Hell, Hank, can't you see they're busy. Maybe later."

When the clock read nine o'clock, Owen, an amiable middle-aged man in a cardigan sweater who looked more like a neighborly grocer than a big-time record producer, asked for quiet. "We're ready when you are, hon. Just be relaxed." Mo, wearing faded jeans and a Vanderbilt T-shirt Jaybird had given her, felt she would be more comfortable seated on a stool at her mike— Bradley had warned her that they might be a while, eight or ten takes, this being her first session—so Atkins boosted her and she adjusted the headset and gave Owen a sound level as she read the lyrics of "Cowboy" she had scribbled on an envelope just in case she forgot. And she began to sing—

> One day he came to me
> And said 'twas his duty,
> He had to go out on the range.
>   So that night I held him
>   And showed him I loved him,
>   And cried away all of my pain . . .

—and began again and again and again. Finally, on the seventh take, Owen Bradley and the engineer agreed that she had done it about as well as she was going to do it. "How's about we keep that one," Bradley said, thanking the sidemen and making Mo feel like the new Queen of Country Music ("Matter of fact," he told her, "Kitty Wells does all her songs right where you were sitting"). They quickly taped "Honky-Tonk Angels" and stood around drinking coffee and chatting for half an hour before dispersing, giddily, into the warm summer night.

At three o'clock in the morning, still unable to settle down from the excitement of the session and call it a night, Jaybird and Mo sat at the round oak kitchen table of the house she had bought between marriages—into their second pot of coffee now— while she tried to talk herself tired. "I got my scars to remind me of Lefty," she was saying, "and I got this hang-down lamp over the table to remind me of Tommy McMillen. When he moved in I kept bugging him about how I wanted to hang this lamp I'd bought but I didn't know how to get up there and drill a hole for it. So one night he was sitting there, floating around on some pills or whatever it was he took, and he went to the bedroom and came back with this six-shooter he kept. I never knew the thing was loaded. But anyway he reared back and aimed and shot a hole right through the ceiling and said, 'That big enough, hon?' "

"Even I couldn't make up a story like that, Mo."

"It's true. I chased him out. Hung the lamp the next day."

"The Tommy McMillen Memorial Hanging Lamp," Jaybird said.

"Ho, boy," Mo said.

"Some life you've lived."

"Some life."

There was only the drone of the air conditioner in the kitchen window. Jaybird asked Mo if there was any whiskey and she hesitated but produced a near-full fifth of Old Crow bourbon and he poured a good dollop into his mug of coffee and smacked his lips when he drank it. She got up and opened the kitchen door and dumped a sack of garbage in the can outside. While she was doing that, Jaybird, carrying a tea glass and the bottle of bourbon to the living room, found the new Merle Haggard album, "Same Train, a Different Time," a salute to Jimmie Rodgers, and was putting it on the stereo turntable when Mo followed him into the living room. She had brought along a glass of burgundy and, barefooted now, sat in the deep-blue sofa while Haggard sang "I Love the Women."

"Bragging?" said Mo.

"Shhh, listen," said Jaybird.

Jaybird joined her on the sofa and, when she didn't resist, began gently flipping her pigtails with his fingers. "The last line, that's me." He sang it. *Women make a fool out of me.* "Story of my life."

"It's time for some revisionist history, then, ace," she said.

"What say?"

"Hank warned me about Jay Clay."

"Hank Elliott? What the devil does Hank know?"

"He said no secretary on Music Row was safe when you were at TopRank."

"Ah," said Jaybird. "But he didn't ask TiHi Tompkins."

"Come again?"

"TiHi Tompkins." Jaybird had to control his laughter. He hadn't thought about it in a long time. "I doubt if Pa knows to this day what really happened, unless she told Sam and Sam told him. But I was about eighteen, see, about ready to go off to college, and Pa was worried that I was going to rush into marrying Becky just to find out what sex was like. So Sam goes over to Gatlinburg and finds this teenaged hooker and brings her back to the farm so they can get me laid. You know, get it out of my system. And I *was* a virgin. Becky and I were 'saving it.' Anyway, she takes me down to Sam's cabin on the pretense of looking at some of Sam's artifacts, Indian arrowheads or something, and before I know it she's got both the lights and my clothes off at the same time and before I know it I've been deflowered."

"Did it work?" said Mo.

"Work?" Jaybird said. "I couldn't get enough after that."

"What do you suppose Bluejay paid this 'TiHi'?"

"I never thought about that. All I remember is the shit-eating grins they wore at breakfast the next morning. Whatever they paid, if they paid her anything, it backfired."

"Did you ever see her again?"

"Oh, hell, no. When I told her I loved her she ran."

Mo doubled over in laughter, her head falling onto Jaybird's chest, and when she stopped laughing over TiHi Tompkins she stayed there. She stayed there, in fact, until Jaybird picked her up and carried her to the back of the house and placed her on the bed and loosened the braids of her raven pigtails and did something he had never done in his life. He made love.

CHAPTER X

ON THE WHOLE he felt like a diplomat waiting at Checkpoint Charlie in Berlin for an exchange of prisoners. But this was the trim little glass and stone gatehouse at the entrance to Cloudland Knob overlooking Andrews, at high noon on the first Saturday in August, and the prisoner Jaybird Clay awaited was his own son. Becky, who would move with her husband and the boy to Chicago after Labor Day, had relented and would allow Robin to spend August with Jaybird and Bluejay on the farm. Jaybird had just driven down from Nashville in his old Chevy station wagon and now he sat on the curb at the gatehouse with Billy Wingo. Now and then they glanced up Cloudland Ridge Road to see if Becky was coming.

"How the hell did you keep your job?" Jaybird was saying.

"Blackmail," said Billy.

"What'd you do?"

"Found out who she'd been messing with."

"Talk," Jaybird said.

"Well, hell," said Billy, straightening the military creases on his lightweight gray uniform shirt, "all I had to do was keep my eyes open. I reckon it all started when she went down to Atlanta one weekend back in May. Left the boy here. Went by herself. First night, and every night after that, I'd be making my rounds after supper and there'd be this fancy car in the driveway. Tracked it down. Belonged to a rich married lady over at the country club in Hayesville. Well, sir, then Becky comes back and must've found out about it because pretty soon in the daytime while Mr. Siebert's at the plant and the boy's in school there's this air-conditioning truck parked in the driveway. Checked that one out, too. Some old boy named Bobby Trawick from over at Murphy."

"You tell anybody?" said Jaybird.

"Asked Siebert how the air-conditioning work was going," said Billy.

"And?"

"Old man Rollins give me a new pickup truck. Four-wheel drive."

When they saw Becky approach in her black Mercedes coupe, Robin leaning forward in the shotgun seat and peering through the heavily-tinted window, they eased off the curb and walked over to the gravel shoulder. When the car stopped the door flew open and Robin stepped out. He shut the door behind him and for a moment—*an hour? a month? five years?*—the father and the son stood staring across the eight feet separating them. Each took a tentative step forward, not knowing whether the protocol was to shake hands or wave or what, then suddenly they rushed into each other's arms in a blur of whoops and laughs and tears and sentences which barely began. *Well lookit . . . Howya . . . Sonofagun you . . . I'm doing . . . The horse.* They came untangled when Becky gave a short tap on the horn.

Robin, dressed in hiking shorts and a CAMP WINNATASKA T-shirt and old sneakers, went back to the car to take a kiss on the cheek from his mother and pull a suitcase out of the Mercedes and shut the door. While he was walking across the street to the station wagon, returning a salute to Billy Wingo, his father went around to speak with his mother. Becky hit a switch to roll down the window and when Jaybird leaned toward her he could see that she looked awful—housecoat, purple scarf, dark wrap-around sunglasses which failed to enhance her sallow face—as though she had just been jolted awake.

"You're late," Jaybird said.

"He had to do poo-poo," she told him.

"What?"

"I made him go to the bathroom."

"Becky, ten-year-old boys don't 'do poo-poo.' "

"Don't start anything."

"All right," he said. "I promised myself."

"August thirty-first, noon, right here," she said.

"Okay."

"We have to start packing then."

"Have you found a house yet?"

"That's none of your business."

"It is," Jaybird said, "but I won't push it."

"Do you have that girl with you?"

"And that's none of *your* business."

"It is," Becky said, "but I won't push it."

"Well, then," Jaybird said, standing up and stepping aside, "see you on the thirty-first." She rolled up the window and gave a toot on the horn to Robin, who waved halfheartedly from the front seat of Jaybird's wasted white station wagon, and threw gravel as she fish-tailed the Mercedes past the gatehouse and down the hill toward town. He didn't know which town and he didn't care. He had his boy.

To Jaybird and to Bluejay and to Sam and even to Maureen, who would be along later once she finished an arduous tour of one-nighters across the Midwest, the center of the Universe for the month of August would be the streams and fields and hearths and coves and cabins and trees and animals and sounds and smells of Sixkiller. It was an impossible chore, they knew, but in that one month they intended to try and bring the boy back into the fold. The divorce of Jaybird and Becky had marked the one and only break in the Clay circle, if the history of the family as recorded in Molly's Bible could be believed, and now was the time for patching it back together. From Bluejay, the patriarch, the boy would hear of Ulster and King James I; of Elijah and Jubal driving out the Cherokees to carve Sixkiller out of wilderness; of Molly and young Jaybird and the day the lights came on, and of the Clay blood. From Jaybird, his father, Robin would hear of growing up in the valley and stalking deer with Sam and driving off to college in a pickup truck with his name painted on the doors and managing shows in Cobo Hall in Detroit and what it is like for a father to be without his son. From Sam, almost a surrogate grandfather, the boy would camp out under the stars and catch trout and learn to ride a horse and hear the legend of Sutalitihi. In Maureen, the men hoped, the boy would see a woman who understood.

They sat atop the rail fence, Bluejay and Jaybird, watching as Sam released a calf into the lower pasture and Robin raced after it astride Sutalitihi. In only a week the boy, already growing lean and lanky in the Clay manner, had taken to the horse. Sam was shouting instructions as Robin galloped in pursuit of the calf and clumsily swung a lariat over his head in the sticky heat of midafternoon.

"Looks just like you did, son," Bluejay was saying. "Kinda skinny, lot of bones. Think he's got my face and feet, though. Don't reckon we oughta hold that against him."

"He's a Clay, all right," said Jaybird.

"Where'd he get that suntan?"

"Camp and hanging out at the country club, I guess."

"Country club. Shit."

"Leave it alone, Pa," said Jaybird.

"It's been hard as hell, son."

"I know it. Me, too. But what's done is done."

"He saying anything about his mama and that Siebert fella?"

"No. And I don't ask."

"That seems kinda strange, don't you say?"

"What?"

"That he don't talk about his mama."

"I'm not complaining," Jaybird said. "From the looks of her the other day, and what Billy Wingo told me, they're not doing so well. I can't do anything but guess. But it looked to me like maybe he'd been slapping her around. She had some bruises. There it was, noon, and she was still in her housecoat and was driving off somewhere."

Early one morning, after they had finished collecting the eggs and slopping the hogs and repairing a gate, Jaybird and Robin went for a stroll which took them to the family cemetery on the hill overlooking the farm. The sun had burst over the top of Standing Indian, to the east toward the Appalachian Trail, and they found themselves trapped between the serenity of Sixkiller down below them and the groaning and clattering of engines behind them. They sat to rest in the grass of the graveyard where four generations of Clays were buried.

"What's all of that noise, Daddy?" Robin said.

"The bulldozers," said Jaybird.

"What are they making?"

"Ski slopes, chalets, golf courses, you name it."

"Right here next to the cemetery where Grandma's buried?"

"Right here."

"Gah," the boy said. "Will Grandpa have to move the cemetery?"

"No, son," said Jaybird. "One day he'll be buried here, and so will I. It's important to Grandpa."

"I don't understand why it matters where you're buried."

How do you tell it to a ten-year-old? "Neither did I when I was your age, son. I was just about your age when my Mama died and Grandpa and Sam and I came up here with shovels to bury her and what would have been my brother. We were going to call him Robin but he died while Mama was having him and so did she. It was cold and we had to clear the snow away to dig the graves. I helped Sam and Grandpa because Grandpa insisted. I remember crying and digging with the shovel and then helping put the coffins in the ground and finally pouring the dirt into the holes. It looked scary up here. There was all of the snow and the two little patches of black dirt. And then we put up those two headstones you see over there, one for Mama and one for the dead baby, and we walked back home in the snow."

"Is that why I'm called Robin?"

"Yes. Henry Buford Clay III. After me and Grandpa."

"Will I be buried here, too?" said the boy.

"Yes," said Jaybird.

"But we're moving to Chicago."

"Only your things are moving to Chicago, son. That's temporary."

"Well, I'm moving, too."

"Not really."

"You're talking crazy, Daddy. Just like Grandpa does. He keeps talking about 'the Clay blood' and all of that. He gets kinda *weird* when he talks like that."

"So be it," Jaybird said. "It's taken me thirty-three years to figure it out. But come on. Let's go see what Grandpa's up to."

When they got back to the main house they saw that Maureen had arrived. Her Mustang was parked beneath the elms and Bluejay was gallantly hosing off the mud while she lolled in the hammock and chattered away about the three-week tour she had completed with Ernest Tubb and the Troubadours. Her recording of "Please Be My Cowboy," on The Holy Ghost label, had shot to No. 8 with a bullet on the *Billboard* country chart in less than a month and she still didn't know what to make of it.

"Mo," Jaybird said, "meet Robin. Maureen Barksdale, son."

"You been having a good time, Robin?" said Mo.

"Yes, ma'am."

"Please call me 'Mo.' Everybody else does."

"Yes, ma'am."

Everybody laughed, Mo and Robin as nervous as young lovers, and there was babbling beneath the trees while everybody tried to catch up. *Jaybird, Mo tells me that you snore and you take all the covers for yourself/Daddy, Sam says to ask you if he can take me out camping tonight/I tell you, hon, after three weeks on the road like that I don't think I'm cut out to be a star/Pa, I told Robin about the day we buried Mama up on the hill/ Before I leave I want to see the famous TiHi Tompkins Memorial Bunkhouse/Saw something in the paper about Lefty Dews getting out on parole/Sam says he might open up a moonshine stand for the ski folks and serve 'em through the fence/Starting to get a little brisk at night now up on Clingman's Dome, I hear/I don't know, Pa, I just got to where I can't handle it like you can.* Time is what they needed. Time is what they took.

And then, finally, came the last night. Robin would be delivered back to his mother at noon the next day. Mo and Jaybird would go back to Nashville and Bluejay and Sam and the Sixkillers would head out on a month's tour of the Middle Atlantic states, and Sixkiller itself, except for the two men hired to look after the place during the absences of Bluejay and Sam, would be left alone to face the onrushing autumn. That last night, then, was to become a feast akin to a Last Supper. Trout and fried chicken and ham and corn and okra and cornbread. Moonshine whiskey and milk and tea. Mo and Bluejay for homemade entertainment. Sam's Indian legends. Breaking out old Clay family photographs. Jaybird teaching Robin to clog-dance. Full moon rising, cicadas squalling, wild dogs baying in the hills. The home place.

"Daddy?"

"Yes, son."

"Are you going to marry her?"

"I don't know. Why? You like her?"

"Uh-huh," the boy said.

"Then maybe I do, too," said Jaybird.

"If you married her, would I have a brother?"

"No."

"Why not?"

"It's complicated," Jaybird said. "She can't have children. But that's all right. We've got all the Clays we need. Right here in the house. Now hush up and go to sleep. And don't take all the covers for yourself."

BOOK THREE

Robin

CHAPTER I

I T WAS CHAOS, utter chaos, and whoever labeled it the "Friday Nite Follies" had hit it on the nose. Friday night and into the wee hours of Saturday at Boston City Hospital's emergency entrance was guaranteed to either make or break a young intern's mettle. Blood, gore, sirens, knife wounds, gunshots to the belly, wounded manacled to disheveled cops, bloodstained surgical gowns, nurses who hadn't stopped for a cup of coffee in four hours, hysterical wailing of the next-of-kin, bug-eyed street urchins so high on heroin they didn't know there was an ice pick dangling from their chest, more blood and more sirens and more commands and more screaming in one night than most people would know in a lifetime. *Blood pressure?/Shit, we lost him/ Look, Officer, I find it difficult to set his arm when he's handcuffed/Give me a chest tube over here/My baby, my baby, my baby/Hook it up to eighteen centimeters/Oh, my God, here comes another one/Dr. Jamison, Dr. Jamison/What happened out there, where are they coming from?* The Friday Nite Follies.

He had no idea what time it was. He had checked in for his shift at dusk on this, the first Friday night of 1983, and he had barely looked up from open wounds since the instant he donned his gown. Where were the normal sickies when you needed them—*aspirin, liquids, rest*—he thought as he tossed his blood-spattered gown into a hamper and scrubbed and put on his sheepskin

173

jacket and headed for the hospital cafeteria. He felt like Hawkeye
Pierce, the cynical battlefield surgeon from the television show
"M.A.S.H," as he went through the line for coffee and a Danish
and then joined another of the interns at a Formica table beneath
the harsh fluorescent lights.

"I could be wrong, Frank," he said, off-loading his plastic tray
and reaching for the sugar, "but I could swear Vietnam was
behind us."

"Robin. How goes it?"

"No, really, did they just move the war over here?"

"Gotta admit, it makes the supply lines shorter."

"Small favors, small favors."

"Well, you asked for it."

"Indeed I did. 'deed I did."

For Frank Price and Robin Clay, each twenty-four and married and about to be able to put "Dr." in front of their names,
this was the last lap. They were serving their obligatory year's
residency at Massachusetts General, after graduating from Harvard Medical School, but for reasons of their own they had re-
quested temporary duty at Boston City's emergency wing. Frank
Price wanted the experience in trauma surgery because he intended to set himself up in plastic surgery when he went back
home to Baltimore. Robin needed it because he had finally decided, after much tugging between his mother and his father, to
go back to the land where the Clays had originated—the isolated
backwoods of the southern Appalachians—and serve as a simple
old-fashioned "country doctor." In June, once they were certified
MD's, they would go their separate ways.

"It's certainly not any of my business, pal, but I can't help
asking you a question," said Price, mopping up his fried eggs
with a biscuit.

"God, I hate questions that start like that," said Robin.

"But I *will* ask, of course. Devil's advocate, understand."

"Right, right. Search for truth."

"Why are you throwing it away like this? Two years at Sewanee, four years at Harvard, a year of combat at Mass General
and this slaughterhouse. For what? Hold hands with the elderly?

Pass out pills? Demonstrate the proper application of the fail-safe Trojan prophylactic? Anybody can do that shit, Robin, and you know it. Why don't you want to be rich like me? Give Barbra Streisand a nose job. Fix Jim Palmer's pitching arm. Make them happy, make you and Meg happy."

"For Christ's sake, Frankie," said Robin.

"What're you, gonna be Tom Dooley of the Hills?"

"That'd be all right with me."

"Oh, come off it," said Price. "Nobody's that altruistic anymore."

"Look," said Robin, "you're oversimplifying it again. You're not going to be a doctor just so you can drive Cadillacs and cruise the Bahamas. How many Barbra Streisand nose jobs can you do? You're going to be a doctor for the same reason I am, Frankie, and that's because you care about people. Plastic surgery's a noble calling. So's being a country doctor. There's a demand for both of 'em. I choose the latter."

"I still can't figure it out. Harvard Med School degree."

"Sometimes I can't, either."

Price said, "What's Meg say?"

"What do you expect?" said Robin. "Country girl from Vermont. Freaked-out liberal Earthie, blowing a Harvard Law degree to do legal aid for the southern hillbillies. She's rolling in it."

"And your mother. I can't wait to hear what Mrs. Siebert of Chicago is thinking."

"Horrified, of course. Says she's coming over this spring to reason with me. She's already picked out my country club in Oak Park."

"Might as well get 'em all. Your father and your grandfather."

"Ah," said Robin, "here's where I become a genuine folk hero. Grandpa and Sam have already fixed up one of the cabins for us."

"Sam."

"That's the old Cherokee on the farm. I told you about him."

"Right," said Price. "The Renaissance Redskin. And your father?"

"Anh." Robin waggled his hands. "Dad waffles. Nashville

damned near killed him but he can't let go of it. What he really ought to do is go ahead and marry the country singer I told you about and move back to the farm. If he's drunk he says Nashville, if he's sober he says Sixkiller."

"Jesus. You oughta go down there and play shrink."

"There'll be some of that, too, I suspect. That's Meg's forte."

"How is the fair Miz Branscomb? She fat yet?"

"I'm about to go find out," said Robin, glancing at his watch for the first time since he had sat down with Frank Price. "Jesus. Almost six-thirty. Mama calls."

Robin had to beat on the door handle of the '66 Volkswagen Beetle to force it open, temperatures during the night having dropped near zero, and as he testily bumped through the icy streets of old Boston to the Charles River bridge leading to Cambridge he muttered to himself. How he detested having to explain and justify what he had chosen to do with his life to his fellow doctors-to-be. It seemed as though they truly couldn't understand why he would want to take all of that training—that degree from the Harvard Med School, that seven years of schooling, that shingle, all of those "possibilities for greatness" as one of his more hyperbolic friends was wont to say—and become a general practitioner, a mere GP, in the forlorn hollows of western North Carolina where people still referred to any sort of illness as, simply, "the fever." That right there, he would argue over cheap Chianti and spaghetti and garlic bread at candle-lit suppers in Salvation Army student apartments, was enough cause to go. A "Tom Dooley of the Hills"? *Close. Not bad. Got a nice ring to it. Maybe Grandpa could write a song.* He had no problems with the decision, once he had made it, except that he had trouble explaining it to his peers without sounding either morally superior or condescending.

He even had trouble explaining the decision to himself. It probably had its roots in the summers he spent with his grandfather and the old Indian—Bluejay Clay, erstwhile star of the Grand Ole Opry, and the ageless Sam Sixkiller for whom the hundred-acre spread was named—during his early teens. He would spend the school year away at various prep boarding schools, in

Pennsylvania one year and Indiana the next, away from the tumult and philandering and newspaper gossip in Chicago. But then it was on to Andrews, North Carolina, for a summer of doing what a teenaged boy is supposed to do: riding horses with the wind in his face, swimming naked in frigid mountain lakes, camping out with Sam the Indian, going to the picture show with his father when he wasn't drying out at the rehabilitation center in Buttner, on one occasion even riding on the bus to Nashville with Bluejay and Sam and the band as they played the Opry. It was during those summers that he discovered, for one thing, that eating watermelon on the bank of a trout stream is much more inviting than having to wear a coat and tie while dining on *escargots* at the Pierre Hotel.

By the time he was ready to go to college, then, the bill to be paid by his father and his grandfather, it figured he would choose not Northwestern near Chicago but Sewanee (the University of the South) in Middle Tennessee. It was a fine little private school of some one thousand students and one hundred faculty, sort of a Harvard of the South, a place where one could go for four years and not once be asked what he intended to do for a living. Young Robin Clay did well there, only a two-hour drive from Sixkiller, and it was probably at Sewanee that he put his life in order. He was accepted to Harvard Medical School. He met a spunky young woman of the Harvard Law School named Margaret Branscomb—his age, not particularly "pretty" with her long red hair and freckles and bony athletic frame, but bright and inquisitive and herself in search of what she preferred to call "honest work"—and when she became pregnant they married. The real world was upon them.

It was dawn when Robin drove over the Charles River and turned left onto Mount Auburn Street, Harvard Square nearly deserted on a bitter Saturday morning in January, for the quick jaunt to Shaler Lane. It was there, in the upstairs front bedroom of their two-story Harvard Housing town house, that they had conceived in October. "Might as well, kid, before the Provo Papas start talking about you," Meg had said to Robin. Shaler Lane was crawling with kids, Mormon kids, the Shaler Lane Apart-

ments after decades of subleasing being what the boys down at
Cronin's called "Provo East." Robin created a parking place for
the VW in the narrow brick alleyway which was Shaler Lane
and entered the apartment.

Meg, already up and dressed in jeans and a crimson Harvard
sweatshirt and her camper's insulated booties, was curled up in
the sprung-hinged Naughahyde recliner eating an apple and reading a book when he came in. "Well, now," she said, "Dr. Kildare,
I presume?"

"More like Hawkeye Pierce," said Robin.

"Rough, huh?"

"They weren't taking prisoners. Coffee?"

"No thanks, had some. Help yourself."

Robin walked to the cramped kitchen and poured himself
some coffee, hot and black, and came back to shed his coat and
stretch out on the sofa. He had grown as tall and lanky as his
father and his grandfather—the three could interchange clothes,
in fact, if not for the slight paunch Bluejay had developed in
recent years—and his six-foot three-inch frame was a bit too
much for the sofa. It didn't matter. He took a sip of coffee and
lay back on the ragged armrest and said, "News. Give the people
news."

"Let's see," Meg said. "It's Saturday. First one of 1983."

"Recorded," said Robin.

"Cold as a mine shaft."

"Duly noted."

"And, ah, let's see. Ronnie-Baby's still President."

"Okay, barrister, what is it?"

"What's what, boy?"

"That shit-eating grin on your face."

"Whah, ah jes' don' know whut y'all talkin' 'baout, Yankee."

"Come on, come on. What's up?"

"Well, nothing much," said Meg. "You got yourself a new
mama."

"Say what?"

"They got married last night."

"Dad and Mo?"

"No, Kildare, Ferrante and Teicher."

"I'll be a sonofabitch." Robin bolted up in the sofa like an exclamation point. "Tell me. Tell me."

Meg pretended to have a telephone in her hand and plunged into an animated description of the phone call. "It's maybe ten-thirty, see, and you're long gone and I'm waiting up for Johnny Carson and the phone rings and it sounds like eighteen-dozen people trying to talk all at once. Your grandpa must've let Sam talk him into getting some extensions put in. Anyway, finally Mo gets on the line and I can't tell whether she's laughing or crying. It must've been hilarious. Some fellow named Hank who runs a bar in Nashville where Mo used to sing, he gives away the bride and your grandfather is your dad's best man. Mo's wearing your grandmother's old wedding gown. God, it must be, what, fifty-something years old. And Sam marries 'em. Right there in the big room at the big house."

"Sam married 'em?" said Robin.

"The one and only. The Reverend Sam Sixkiller," said Meg.

"He can't do that."

"He can, too. You forget that our guy was stoned."

"Sam's never seen the inside of a church."

"Doesn't matter, sport. He sent off forty bucks and they mailed him a diploma saying he was a preacher."

"Godamitey," said Robin. "Dad and Mo."

"But wait. And they had their wedding night in Sam's cabin."

"I don't believe it. Been living together off and on for a dozen years and they have a wedding night."

"Well," Meg said, "that's the news. I thought I'd never get Mo off the phone. She said something like, 'I know he can be a no-good rotten SOB sometimes, but at least he's *my* no-good' blap-blap-blap. I like her, Robin, I really do. When I met her last year I could feel it. She's tough and she's good. If you don't mind my saying so, I think your dad picked a winner this time."

Robin thought for a minute. Then he said, "Yeah."

CHAPTER II

THE ONLY REASON Robin had for going to the monthly meeting of The Southern Club, a loose association open to anybody at Harvard with a background or an interest in the South, was because the first guest speaker of the new year would be Dr. Robert Coles. Robin detested The Southern Club, feeling it was nothing more than a snobbish collection of tomorrow's southern robber barons, and he had tried diligently to stay away from their meetings—scotch and soda, rep ties and button-down Oxford shirts and navy-blue blazers, practiced cultured country-club drawls, everybody a would-be lawyer or MBA who would go back home to run for office or join a huge law firm in Atlanta or build shopping malls around Charlotte—on the grounds that he had already met the enemy and didn't like him. Dr. Coles, though, might have been Robin's only hero. He was a short, rumpled, humanistic man, a child psychiatrist with the Harvard Health Services, best known as a Pulitzer Prize–winning author of a series of volumes entitled *Children of Crisis*. One of the latest volumes, in fact, was *Privileged Ones*. Coles not only knew the South, Robin reckoned, but he cared for it. For the right reasons. *Maybe he'll teach the ass-holes something*, Robin was thinking as he walked past Harvard Square to the Adams House, but he doubted it.

When he was directed to the room where the meeting would

take place, actually a three-room suite of high ceilings and oak paneling inside Adams House, he felt it was an ironic choice. A bronze plaque on one wall proclaimed that this had been the living quarters of Franklin Delano Roosevelt while he was an undergraduate at Harvard, years before he went on to become perhaps the best U.S. President the Deep South ever had, and on another wall was a framed reproduction of a letter he had scrawled to his wealthy parents upon arriving on the New York-to-Boston train: ". . . and for the first time in my life I was uncomfortable, for the train's brakes made a wheezing sound all night. . . ." The room also had been used as an office one year by a Harvard history professor writing a book about Zapata and a Nieman Fellow doing a book on country music. (Robin, in fact, had some association with *Hillbilly Heaven*, by the writer David Nelson, because both his father and his grandfather were mentioned quite prominently.) So here you had a group of southern country-clubbers gathering to hear an empathetic sociologist in a room once used by the man who delivered electricity to the southern backwoods and by the authors of books on a Mexican revolutionary and the folk music of the mountains.

There were about two dozen of them lolling against the walls of the suite when Robin, stomping the slush from his boots and brushing the powdery snow from his sheepskin coat, entered. It was the same scene he had witnessed when some apologist for the Reagan administration came by to proclaim his man "a populist at heart"—the ruddy cheeks, the button-down Oxfords, the name tags of aristocratic southern scions (J. Willis Pemberton IV, Hartman Townsend), the scotch and soda—and when Robin got a double scotch on the rocks to help him endure the evening he took a seat near the door, beneath the plaque proclaiming FDR, to await Dr. Robert Coles.

Coles' appearance, as he shuffled almost noiselessly into the room, was in counterpoint to that of the men of The Southern Club. He limply returned handshakes and introductions and welcomes as he tried to shed the snow and unburden himself of layers of clothing—sweaters, raincoat, galoshes, mittens, ragged scarf—looking like a man who had bought his last wardrobe during the late sixties at Filene's Basement. "For those of an inquiring nature," he said in his self-deprecatory nasal whine, "the answer is yes. My wife does, indeed, dress me for formal occasions such as this." That served as his introduction and it was the last time anybody in the room laughed. For he had come to deliver a message—that the privileged have an obligation to use their privileges properly—and it was evident to Robin that even Dr. Robert Coles, one of the eminent thinkers in America, was just as frustrated as he that they wouldn't hear the message. *It's not that I expect the rich to give all of the things they have worked for to the poor. . . . Now, golf is a fine game, good exercise. . . . And then the "briarhoppers," as they call them in Dayton and the other industrial cities in Ohio, are left without not only their land but their dignity as well. . . . So what you have, then, is "development," where overnight a peaceful little mountain hamlet becomes a rich man's playground with a name like Raccoon Valley Estates. . . .* When Coles was done forty-five minutes later, and there were few questions, he excused himself on the grounds that there was a plane to catch. They applauded, Robin Clay more than most, and returned to the portable bar set up in the corner.

"Well, I suppose the *theory* is there, but the whole matter is academic. It's not the way the real world works." Robin had just turned away from the bar with a drink in his hand and was heading for his spot near the door, next to FDR, when he looked up and saw a rep tie. The name tag said TY WARREN.

"I'm sorry?" said Robin.

"These academicians. They worry me."

"What the hell did you expect at Harvard?"

"Oh, wait, now." He extended his hand. "Tyler Burton Warren Jr."

"Henry Buford Clay III," Robin said, shaking the hand.

"I just meant that it's easy to sit up here and *think* like that."

"But hard to be rich, right?"

"You're oversimplifying things. My father worked hard to build what he has. But now he has one of the most successful resort development companies in America, if not the world. Now he's preparing to completely remake the face of southwestern West Virginia. Dams, condominiums, chalets, ski resorts, water and power lines, the works."

"That's the Hatfield-McCoy country, isn't it?" said Robin.

"Yes," Ty Warren said. "So you know how poor it is down there."

"Nobody can deny any of that. But what happens to the people?"

"I don't understand."

"The people, dammit, the people," said Robin.

"They benefit more than anyone," said Warren.

"Please tell me how."

"My God, it's obvious. The dams control the flooding. The resorts produce billions of dollars for schools and hospitals and paved roads and things like that."

"Things like that."

"You know, things for a better way of life."

"And the tax rates go up," Robin said.

"Of course," said Warren, "they have to."

"And the people can't afford to live there anymore and they lose their houses and so they have to go to Dayton to work in the Frigidaire plant and back home there's nobody left to enjoy your schools and hospitals and your 'things like that' because the rich people kicked 'em out so they could ski."

"Come on, don't use that old bromide."

"If it's a bromide it's because it's true."

"You're an expert on it, I take it," Warren said.

"You're damned right I am," said Robin.

"How so?"

"You familiar with Cherokee Hills in North Carolina?"

"Of course. Everybody in the business is. One of the finest."

"My mother's father built it," said Robin.

"Well, then, you should understand."

"Oh, I do, I do. Last trout I caught down there was a pushover. Floating down Sixkiller Creek on his back. All I had to do was wade through the shit from eighty-nine-hundred A-frames and pick him up."

It had already reached the childish stage and Robin didn't have the stomach to carry on. He had swallowed his drink and brushed past Tyler Burton Warren Jr. and was walking briskly toward the exit to Adams House, throwing on his coat and wishing he had dramatically pointed to the FDR plaque and given Warren a history lesson on rich men who handled their position the way Roosevelt had, when he caught up with a passing friend and proposed a drink or two at the Wursthaus. Robin needed a Southerner who would agree with everything he said. Will Brooks would do nicely.

Robin had met Will, a Nieman Fellow on leave from the Nashville *Tennessean*, one night at Boston City's emergency room. Will had been out carousing the bars and the strip joints and the X-rated movie houses in the "combat zone," where Boston tried to keep its sin corralled, and when he got jumped by three sailors he was rushed to the hospital for minor repairs and it was Robin Clay who patched him up. When Robin heard the southern twang—Will Brooks, at forty-two, was one of the older Niemans and fit the mold of the cynical career reporter—they talked a few minutes and then, three or four times over the ensuing months, they occasionally met for a drink.

"I would've broken it up but I was enjoying it too much," Will said as they ordered beers.

"You heard the whole thing, then?" said Robin.

"You can't even insult those people. You know that."

"I keep trying."

"I did an editorial jumping all over the people at WSM, that's the radio station down home that runs the Grand Ole Opry. Well, you know all of that. Anyway, I tried to soap-box it and talk about how if they moved the Opry out to the suburbs it'd be the death of downtown and they ought to be ashamed for closing old Ryman Auditorium just like that after all those years and they'd have blood on their hands when Broadway, that's the main drag where the Opry used to be, was turned over to the hookers and the druggies."

"Wait a minute," said Robin. "The Opry's not at Ryman anymore?"

"Aw, hell, no," Will told him. "I thought you knew that."

"Nobody told me. I went there one time when I was a kid. Grandpa, you know, Bluejay Clay, Grandpa took me. And I remember he sneaked me into this saloon they had across the alley. Can't remember the name."

"Tootsie's Orchid Lounge."

"That's it. That was a hell of a place. Is it gone, too?"

"Not quite," Will said, "but give 'em time. Tootsie Bess died when they moved out of the Ryman. Place is just hanging on, now. The streets are crawling with hookers and low-life now, just like I said would happen. Everybody's out at Opryland getting rich."

"What the hell's that?" said Robin.

"Opryland U.S.A. Tacky as turkey turds. Four hundred acres of joy rides and restaurants and gift shops and all that tourist shit. Got a brand new air-conditioned Opry House in the middle of it. Hank Williams probably turns over in his grave every Saturday night."

"Yeah. No telling what Grandpa's got to say about it. Well. So much for the power of the press."

"Like I say, you can't even insult the bastards. Day after my editorial the fat cats hand-carry a letter to the editor refuting me point by point. Ryman's a firetrap. Not enough parking. Heat strokes in the balcony. 'Seedy downtown district.' 'Paving the way for downtown development.' All that shit. Same stuff that kid was trying to pass off on you tonight. Beware of bastards bearing blueprints."

CHAPTER III

FROM TIME TO TIME there would be communiqués from Bluejay, sometimes mailed from Andrews but more often than
not from disparate places out there on the road in America,
and Robin and Meg got so they could make an evening of reading
the latest from Grandpa. The old man, in his mountain simplicity, was a wonderful correspondent. "Funny," he once wrote
them on Johnny Reb Motel stationery from Edna, Texas, "but I
notice them Baptists don't like to drink in front of each other,"
causing them to crack with laughter as they splayed the Rand
McNally out on the floor of the apartment and found Edna and
tried to picture Bluejay Clay & the Sixkillers playing a roadhouse
there on a Friday night. There would be a picture postcard from
Tulsa, showing the stiletto-shaped "Prayer Tower" on the cam-
pus of Oral Roberts University, with Bluejay's observation that
"with ol' Oral as their president the basketball team don't *need*
a trainer." Once there was a Polaroid photograph from Musko-
gee, Oklahoma, near the terminus of the Trail of Tears, showing
Sam Sixkiller jabbing a feathered spear into the grass in front
of City Hall as though annexing it to the Cherokee Nation.
Bluejay's missives, sometimes including ragged tearsheets from
newspapers along the way ("I'm so old I'm about to reach *re-
tardment*," he told the Baton Rouge *Advocate*), were like un-
lettered versions of John Steinbeck's *Travels with Charley*.

Then, one afternoon around the middle of January, there came a short note from Bluejay on Holiday Inn stationery in Akron, Ohio, hurriedly scribbled, as usual, with a ball-point pen. "Working your way," it read. "Play Boston 24th. See you 23rd." That was all it said. There had been nothing in the Boston papers about a show starring Bluejay Clay & the Sixkillers. The only radio Robin and Meg listened to, when they did, was the National Public Radio station. They knew of no transplanted redneck fighting-and-dancing roadhouses around the city. So Robin phoned the Boston *Globe* and got somebody on the entertainment desk.

"Oh, yeah," a man said, "we're running the ad Sunday."

"Bluejay Clay *is* going to play here, then," said Robin.

"Sunday night the twenty-fourth. Boston Symphony Hall."

"Boston Symphony Hall?"

"Andrés Segovia Saturday night, Bluejay Sunday."

"Bluejay at Symphony Hall? I can't believe it."

"Where you been, pal?" said the man at the *Globe*. "It's already damned-near sold out and the ad hasn't even run. Bluejay's become a cult figure. Folk hero, you know. They can't even keep his records in stock over at the Harvard Co-op. The kids are nuts about him."

"I'll be damn," Robin said. "Where are they staying?"

"Sorry, but we shouldn't give that out."

"I can understand that. But, see, I'm his grandson."

"Yeah, sure, and you didn't know he was coming."

"No, really. I'm Robin Clay, Harvard Med School. We just got a note from Grandpa saying he was coming, but that's all he said. What do you want, his shoe size? Come on."

"Okay, okay, wait a second." The man at the *Globe* yelled at somebody and came back on the line. "They're booked into the Sheraton-Plaza downtown on Saturday the twenty-third. Hey, look, you aren't that kid in that song are you? 'Molly,' that song he does."

"That's my Dad."

"Well, look, maybe we could get a photographer and—"

"Naw, I don't want that. I just want to see my Grandpa."

Not even Will Brooks, his Nieman Fellow friend from the

Nashville *Tennessean*, was aware of this abrupt latent "discovery" of a man who had been singing "The Longer You're Gone (The Harder It Gets)" off-key for nearly four decades. "The South shall not only rise again," said Will, "it shall rub their noses in it." Robin and Meg toyed with the idea of inviting a gaggle of Bostons and Harvards to their apartment to meet Bluejay and eat turnip greens and the like—Derek Bok? Robert Coles? John Kenneth Galbraith? Ted Kennedy?—but in the end, when even Will said he couldn't make it because of a skiing weekend in Vermont, they settled on trying to get Grandpa to come by the place to eat fried chicken and talk family. There was plenty of each.

On the prescribed Saturday afternoon, a gloomy late-January day in Boston, Bluejay phoned the apartment the minute he and Sam and the band arrived at the Sheraton-Plaza downtown. The next night, he told Robin, would end a twenty-day tour which had taken them to places like Philadelphia and Washington and Hartford and even Manhattan. They were seeing packed houses everywhere, he said, and one night they got a check for more than $10,000. He was dead tired from it all, and glad to be ending it, and "supper at y'all's place" sounded fine. No, don't bother to pick me up, he said, Sam wants to be able to say the bus went to Harvard.

They came at dusk, simply rolling up and parking the new luxury Greyhound afforded by this recent eminence down the street from the Mount Auburn Hospital—BLUEJAY CLAY & THE SIXKILLERS, "The Longer You're Gone" & Other Hits, Stars of Grand Ole Opry—adjacent to the icy Charles River and scant blocks from the office of Dr. Robert Coles. Bluejay and Sam emerged, and then the others, many of the band members being young replacements for the Sixkillers they had met the summer before, and there was a backslapping reunion right there on the sidewalk which had Mormon mamas calling to their children sledding on Shaler Lane. *You oughta seen ol' Sam driving this thing in New York City/And this here's Buck Brumby, Buddy's boy, plays fiddle for me now since his daddy died/We'll be down there about the first of June, Grandpa/Lord, I never seen so many people in my life/And that White House, looks just like the picture postcards.* The Sixkillers wanted to nap in a real bed before going out on the town, and Sam had to find somebody to administer to the bus, so they rolled away in the gathering mist and Bluejay Clay clomped down the brick alleyway behind the last of the Clays in a place he never dreamed he would see.

Over fried chicken and turnip greens and rice and sawmill gravy and biscuits, in a shabby apartment furnished in what Meg called Early Depression, they caught up as best they could. Bluejay looked thin and pale and ragged, a condition he blamed on the nature of playing one-nighters for nearly three straight weeks, but his spirit prevailed.

"Any fish in that river y'all got out there?" he said.

"The Charles River? I doubt it," said Robin.

"Pretty thing, though, ain't it?"

"Go ahead, Grandpa. I know you're dying to tell it."

"Well, sir," Bluejay said, wiping grease from his mouth, "I told Sam y'all lived on the river so while we were driving around looking for your place I saw this old boy standing on the corner and I figured I'd ask him for directions. Funny-looking fella. Had one of them Sherlock Holmes pipes and a sissy-looking umbrella. So Sam stopped the bus and I leaned out the window and I said, 'Hey, buddy, wonder if you can tell me where the Charles River's at?' He looked kinda upset. Took that pipe out of his mouth and said, 'My good man, here at *Hah-vahd*'—that's the way he said it, '*Hah-vahd*'—says, 'here at *Hah-vahd* we *nevah* end a sentence with a preposition.' So I thought about it a minute and then I told him, 'All right, I'll put it another way for you. Wonder if you can tell me where the Charles River's at . . . you *ass-hole.*' Sam like to died laughing. Thought the fella was gonna swallow his pipe."

"Obviously he won't be there tomorrow night," Meg said.

"Don't reckon he will, Granddaughter, but you never know," said Bluejay. "I can't figure out what the hell's going on."

"You've become a folk hero, Grandpa," said Robin.

"That's what I read. Said that in *The New York Times.*"

"Where'd you play in New York?"

"Place called the Lone Star Cafe. Kinda looks like home."

"Oh, yeah," said Meg. *Très chi-chi*. Urban cowboys."

"Would you tell me what the Yankee girl just said?"

"Trendy, Grandpa," said Robin. "They think you're, oh, *amusing*."

"Way they paid me they must think I'm funny as hell," Blue-jay said, covering the chicken bones with his napkin. "Do y'all know that I was singing these same songs back there twenty-five years ago, about the time y'all were born, and maybe I'd get five hundred dollars if I was lucky? Damned if I can figure it out. Now I might get five *thousand*. I know what you're saying. You watch 'em tomorrow night, these educated Yankees, they'll get all dressed up like they was us. Cowboy boots, blue jeans, maybe cowboy hats if they can find 'em up here. Try to say 'yawl' but never quite get it right. And they'll act like they just love ol' Bluejay Clay. What do they call that, Granddaughter?"

" 'Condescension,' " said Meg.

"I got an answer for that."

"What's that?" said Robin.

"I may be dumb, but I'm too rich to quit."

Meg went to the kitchen to slice and serve up the apple pie and ice cream, Bluejay using the occasion to visit the bathroom, and when he came back to the table he moaned and reached for the small of his back as he maneuvered into the rickety chair. The doctor came out in Robin.

"How long have you been like that, Grandpa?" he said.

"About seventy-one and a half years, I figure," Bluejay told him.

"No, seriously. Your back been hurting?"

"Riding that damn bus all the time."

"And you look like you've lost some weight."

"Don't see how. You saw me put it away tonight."

"Well, maybe you're right," Robin said. "You've been on a tough schedule. You ought to try to stay home and rest for a while."

"What I'm gonna do, son, what I'm gonna do. Me and a barrel of Sam's finest whiskey." Meg came in with the dessert. "But lookie here, now," said Bluejay, "Granddaughter, you gonna bring me a great-grandson? Damn, I never thought about that. A *great-grandson*."

"We could know soon if we wanted to, Grandpa," said Meg.

"What do you mean, if you wanted to? They got a test?"

"Sure. It's not exactly recommended, but there's a test."

"You mean just like that? They can find out ahead of time?"

"They can," said Meg, "but we want to be surprised."

"Surprised?" Bluejay blinked. "Well *I* sure as hell want to know."

"Why's that, Grandpa?" said Meg. "You don't like suspense?"

"Naw, naw," said Bluejay. "But if it's a boy we need to know damned fast. We need all the time we can get. I've about run out of bird names."

He said he would just as soon stretch out on the sofa for the night, even if his long bony feet did dangle, and in the morning they made the mistake of walking up to a diner on Harvard Square for breakfast. Bluejay, appearing to enjoy every second of it, bantered with the Harvard students and signed autographs and even sang a few bars of "The Longer You're Gone" when one of them asked. He gawked at Widener Library when told how many books it held ("I know everything that's in every book in every library in the world," he said; "words") and had Franklin Roosevelt's old room at the Adams House pointed out by Robin and watched people ice-skating in parks where the fire department had flooded the low places. And then, at midafternoon, they all cleaned up and headed for the hotel so Grandpa could transform himself into Bluejay Clay for the amusement of five thousand Yankees.

The show was a success, as all of them along the trail had been, and no sooner had Bluejay closed with a triple encore of "Molly"—they actually *cheered* the sappy recitation—than he and Sam and the band were on the bus, shedding costumes and getting back into rumpled jeans and sweatshirts, ready to blow all the way back home. Fans were crowding around the bus, parked in the rear of the Boston Symphony Hall, and Robin and Meg arose from the fold-out table in the front cabin to hug Bluejay as Sam fired the bus and prepared to take it on the Boston-Washington leg.

"Know that cabin y'all stayed in last year?" Bluejay said.

"Uh-huh," said Meg. "Uncle Newt's cabin. With the peg-leg holes."

"That's gonna be your place. We put in a dogtrot."

"We can't wait to see it, Grandpa. It'll be June."

"Baby can stay on one side, y'all on the other," Bluejay said.

Meg said, "You old rascal."

"Painted it blue for you. Baby's room, that is. But if, you know, if things turn out different . . . well, you know, we can always paint it another color." Somebody turned on the stereo speakers in the bus and the music began to flow—*It started in the mountains/Spread all over town/Went all the way to Boston/Can't keep a 'billy down*—as Sam gunned the bus and headed south. *That playing the road,* Bluejay liked to say, *is like robbing banks. You ride in, take the money, and ride out.*

CHAPTER IV

ACCORDING TO the Nielsen ratings for the second week of February 1983, most of America was eschewing the bars and the restaurants and the movies to go to bed early with a bottle of wine and some cheese and crackers in order to bundle and watch a "mini-series," as the television people called them, entitled "The Winds of War." It was an eighteen-hour drama about the two or three years leading up to the beginning of World War II and it starred several near-forgotten Hollywood actors and actresses. One of them was Robert Mitchum, sixty-five, known best as a rollicking barrel-chested don't-give-a-damn masculine hero in roles such as the commanding officer of a submarine in a movie entitled *The Enemy Below*. Another was Polly Bergen, age officially unavailable but probably pushing fifty, trying to make a comeback after getting rich from sponsoring "beauty aids." Yet another star of the movie, and easily the most interesting, was a forty-three-year-old woman named Ali McGraw. Ali McGraw's high point as an actress had come about a dozen years earlier when she played the "love interest" in a sappy movie (*Love Story*) written by a Harvard professor about a young Harvard couple, starring Harvard. Ali McGraw, playing a "Jennifer Cavilleri," Radcliffe music major, was properly flippant in *Love Story* (always referring to her blue-blood-rich boyfriend Oliver as "preppie," throwing out lines to him like, "Love means never having to say you're sorry," even laying that one on Oliver as she was dying), and the best thing Ali McGraw had done in her career was to perfect the Preppie Pout.

Robin and Meg couldn't resist holing up in bed to watch the spectacular grand opening night of "The Winds of War" on television, any more or less than could Paul and Akiko Miloni, owners and operators of a roadside diner-gas station-souvenir shop on the banks of the Arkansas River in Texas Creek, Colorado, Pop. 2, Alt. 6,734 Ft. All of America, it seemed, was swept up with the promise of this spectacle. The fact that Robin and Meg Clay, unlike Paul and Akiko Miloni, had read the novel by Herman Wouk made no difference.

"You ever see *The Enemy Below?*" said Robin. The opening scenes had just flashed on their $78 twelve-inch black-and-white set bought at Filene's Basement. They had bought a bottle of cheap Beaujolais and laid in some saltines and cheddar from Buddy's Bottle Shoppe and it was nine o'clock on a Sunday night, first February Sunday of '83, and they were snuggled like bear cubs in their Salvation Army bed upstairs.

"Ummm," said Meg. "Say what?"

"You ever see *The Enemy Below?*"

"Met him one night. Absolutely frightening."

"Big sumbitch, was he?"

"Terrifying, Preppie, terrifying."

"And where'd you meet the enemy below?"

"Below."

"And did he fire torpedoes?"

"None of your goddam business, Preppie."

"Admit it. He fired repeatedly, with great *vigah.*"

"Well," said Meg, pouting like Ali McGraw, "if y'all want to put it *lack thayut.* I have to *admeeyut* it *wawas* an absolutely *terrifyun tahm* o' *mah lahf.* Ah mean, my Mama *nevah* tol' me it was gonna be *lack thayut.*" Now, on the flickering television screen, Luftwaffe fighters were strafing Polish soldiers on horseback, the Polish soldiers dandily bouncing along in all of their armor, Poland's Finest, escorting hordes of ragged Jews trying to get the hell out of there before Hitler got dead serious, and here was Ali McGraw and her boyfriend running along with the refugees, and ABC-TV with a closeup on Ali McGraw and all of America awaiting her next words and Meg Bransford, in an upstairs bedroom in Cambridge, Massachusetts, saying, "Okay, Preppie, here it comes."

"Here comes what?"

"Watch Jennifer McGraw."

"*Ali* McGraw?"

"Well, whatever they're calling her here. All right, here it comes now, here it comes, the Luftwaffe is strafing the Poles and the Jews and the dirt's flying all over the place and if the Jews get out of this one they'll convert. Okay, here it comes. Ali what's-it looks up at the German planes and, right here now—ah, shit, she blew it."

"Blew what?"

"She was supposed to say, 'Love means never having to say you're sorry.' They call it 'type-casting,' Preppie."

The phone rang. Robin wanted to see how Pug Henry (Robert Mitchum of *The Enemy Below*) would handle the situation with Winston Churchill. But duty called. He peeled out of bed and fumbled for the phone atop the dresser.

"Mr. Mo Dale?" said the operator.

"No. I know a Mo Dale, but—"

"Sorry. Collect call from Mo Dale for Mr. Robin Clay."

"This is Robin Clay. I'll take it."

"On the line. Sorry."

"Me, too," said Robin.

Crackling over the line was the hysterical voice of Mo Dale. It was impossible for Robin to break in on her. "Oh, Robin, he's dead. I know he's dead. They got him nailed to the wall with all these wires and they put these casts all over him and he can't even talk. . . . The doctors won't even let me go and try to talk to him . . . Lord, I love that man, Lord I love him . . . You've got to come, Robin, you've got to come . . ."

When Robin finally got Mo Dale off the line he sat in the dark on the floor near the dresser and tried to sort out what had happened. Or what he could guess had happened. For starters his father, Jaybird, was laid up in traction in Finney County, Kansas, in Garden City. The Great Plains. All right. Right about now they had a string of one-nighters starting in Little Rock and more or less following the Arkansas River all the way to Leadville, Colorado, in the Rockies. Now Robin remembered a note from his father, typing errors all over the place, telling of how they would be in the car for about three weeks, trailing along as a warm-up act for Ernest Tubb & the Texas Troubadours, working clubs and gymnasiums and roadhouses for the ranchers and farmers along the route. They were having a terrible winter out there, he had read, and he was guessing that Jaybird was drunk and trying to drive through the snow and the night to save time and money. Bluejay, Grandpa, was somewhere on the road in Indiana and Mo hadn't been able to find him. Now the boy, Robin Clay, was being brought into combat. Not in Poland, nor in Berlin, nor even Manila of "The Winds of War," but in the middle of the only discernible metropolis in the Great Plains of Kansas. To father his father.

"Bad, hunh?" Meg said when Robin got up to his feet.

"Bad," he said.

"What can I do?"

"Where's that Gold Card they sent?"

"I think I can find it. I put it under 'R' for 'rich.' "

"You got any cash?"

"Maybe twenty. Twenty and some change."

"Okay. I've got forty somewhere. We gotta move, kid. Can you throw some clothes and things together? Jesus Christ." Meg had snapped off the television and turned on the lights. They flurried for an immediate departure. Sixty-eight dollars in change, the Gold Card, socks, underwear, toothbrush, change of jeans, sweaters and longjohns for Kansas in February, P-coat, the cowboy boots, phone numbers. A rush to Logan through the light snow, dented vintage Volkswagen tooting along the back streets of that tired old New World city, through the tunnel, paying the toll to some toothless old son of Ireland, quick kisses at the United gate, flashing the Gold Card, smoking or nonsmoking, strains of "The Longer You're Gone" ringing in the ears for inexplicable reasons, young Robin Clay of the mountains going to somewhere on the plains. At two o'clock in the morning on a flight from Boston to Chicago, somewhere over Lake Erie, thirty-eight people huddled beneath blankets and not talking at thirty-two thousand feet, over the headsets came the words of a song which bolted Robin awake for a moment before he snuffed and shifted and waited until a stewardess would jiggle him awake to change planes.

> One day he came to me
> And said 'twas his duty,
> He had to go out on the range.
>   So that night I held him
>   And showed him I loved him,
>   And cried away all of my pain.

"You can't talk loud, now, and don't talk too long, because your father's hurtin'." Robin, at dawn, clopped in his cowboy boots down the waxed linoleum floors of the Finney County, Kansas, Memorial Hospital. His father was in intensive care, they had told him, but with time he would be all right. *Good thing nobody else was involved,* a doctor said, *because he was plenty drunk. Just lost it on the ice and flipped. Lucky man, mighty lucky. Lord seems to protect 'em sometimes.* Robin followed the nurse down the corridor to his father's room.

"Amphyl," he said.

"Sir?" said the nurse.

"The disinfectant."

"Oh, that. Smells great, doesn't it?"

"Works."

"They make it in Toledo."

"I know."

"Are you a doctor?" the nurse said.

"Gonna be."

"Not many people know about Amphyl."

"If they've taught me anything at Harvard," said Robin, "they taught me how to spell Amphyl. Spell it and smell it."

When Robin was shown into the room his father was asleep and Mo, who looked as though she had walked through a mine-field and lived to talk about it, sat in a straight-backed aluminum chair beside the bed. Jaybird's condition was as bad as he had feared, given Mo's hysteria over the phone the night before, but Robin's limited experience as a doctor told him that his father would be all right with peace and quiet and a lot of time. Broken were a leg, a wrist and the collarbone. The leg, in a cast from the ankle to the thigh, was suspended in traction. His eyes were black and his face was scratched and his scalp was covered in bandage. In a corner of the room was a bloody heap of his clothing and his torn boots.

"How about you?" Robin said after hugging Mo for a moment.

"Physically, okay," she said. "Mentally, a wreck."

"They put you on something?"

"They let me bathe and they gave me a shot. Whatever it is, they ought to put it on the market."

"They do. Right on the streets of Boston."

"I'm sorry about last night. I was hysterical."

"It's understandable."

Robin pulled up a chair and listened while Mo recapitulated. They had already been on the road for nearly two weeks, playing Little Rock and Tulsa and Hutchinson and a lot of places in between as part of a package show with Tubb and the Trouba-dours, and the night before they had played the annual Steer Ropers' Stampede in Dodge City. The next date was in Salida, Colorado, on the eastern slope of the Rockies, and they were having to drive all night in the new Dodge station wagon. The roads were barely passable and Jaybird had been drinking with the cowboys after the Stampede in Dodge City. She should have been driving, she knew, and she had intended to take the wheel once U.S. 50 took them around Garden City. But she was napping in the back seat, bushed from doing a medley of her songs ("I did four encores of 'Cowboy' "), when suddenly he lost the car. Nobody knew how many times the station wagon flipped. Everybody knew they were lucky to be alive.

"Oh, and congratulations," said Robin.

"Same to you," said Mo. "We should have made it a double-ring ceremony right there at the farm. Me and your father, you and Meg. How'd yours go?"

"Okay as far as shotgun weddings go. We did the Harvard Earthies number. Field of grass, in more ways than one, with a freaked-out divinity student doing the honors."

"When's the baby due?"

"July the Fourth."

"Come on, you made that up."

"No, really. Gonna be an All-American kid."

Jaybird was beginning to stir. "This is going to be a setback for him," said Mo, "but I tell you, Robin, I never thought I'd see Grandpa so happy. He told us about the trip up there and how much he likes Meg. I think he's always felt good about me. So here we are. His boys are married well, the way he sees it, and a baby's coming and we're all going to be back home together as soon as y'all finish school."

"What?" said Robin.

"This did it," she said. "We're going home."

A nurse came in to check on Jaybird. They were giving him heavy sedation to ease the pain of the busted ribs but when he saw Robin standing beside the nurse he asked her to prop him up in the bed. Mo said she would go to the hospital cafeteria and try to eat something for breakfast. Robin sat down beside his father's bed.

"Kinda drunk out last night," said Jaybird.

"That's what Mo says," Robin told him.

"No amount of AA meetings can do what this did. That's it."

"Dad," said Robin, "Mo says y'all are going to go home."

"Yes."

"How're you going to make a living?"

"About the same. She can work out of Sixkiller as easy as she can out of Nashville. She's wanting to cut back, anyway. Mo's a farm girl at heart. What she really wants to do is take care of me and Pa."

"How bad off is Grandpa?"

"You're the doctor, son, but I'd say he's plenty sick."

"Has he had a checkup? Is he on any medication?"

"Medication. Hah. He won't take it."

"I don't guess I'm surprised."

"Says he went seventy-two years without even taking aspirin and he's not about to start now," said Jaybird.

"But you, Dad, what'll you do?" Robin said.

"Write a book."

"You? A book?"

"Me and Sam. 'Blood in the Hills,' by Sam Sixkiller, as told to Henry Buford Clay Jr. Think we're going to get a contract with one of those publishing houses in Nashville. Sam ought to be home talking into the tape recorder right now. Dedicating it to Uwani Sutalitihi."

"Well, I'll be damn."

"That's what I was thinking."

In the afternoon, when it was clear there was nothing he could accomplish by hanging around, Robin said his good-byes to Mo and Jaybird and was lugging his bag toward the front door of the hospital when he was flagged by the receptionist at the admissions window. She had a question about his father's bill.

"It'll be taken care of," he told her.

"Oh, I'm sure. We just received a wire for $5,000," she said.

"From Andrews, North Carolina?"

"Why, yes."

"The money's good, then."

"Yes, it is. We checked with the bank."

"So," Robin said, "is there a problem?"

"Well, no, of course not. We were just all curious."

"Curious."

"First there was a call from Cambridge, Massachusetts," she said.

"My wife, checking up on me."

"Yes. But then it got crazy. The next call came from some-body in Valparaiso, Indiana, who said his name was Bluebird or something and he wanted to talk to a Jaybird or a Robin or a

Modell. No sooner had we gotten rid of him than we got a call from an Indian who said his name was Sam-something. Sixkiller, can you imagine? Sam Sixkiller. And he said The Holy Ghost would take care of everything. Can you tell me what's going on, Mr. Clay? Do you represent one of those religious cults?"

"Sort of," said Robin, bolting toward the glass doors to catch his cab to the airport and Meg.

CHAPTER V

ONE FRIDAY AFTERNOON in March, not long after Bluejay's visit to Shaler Lane, Robin lay flaked out on the sofa in the living room. Meg had taken the car up to Manchester, New Hampshire, to audit an abortion clinic for a paper she had to write on welfare programs in depressed areas. So essentially, except for an informal lacrosse match on Saturday morning against the staff surgeons at the hospital, he had a long weekend stretched out before him. He looked it. Ty Cobb, the cat, was kneading his chest. The half-read *Boston Globe* was in a heap on the floor open to the story on the sports pages about how the Atlanta Braves had not only agreed to pay one of their star sluggers $1 million a year but were also including a "fat" bonus of some $7,000 for every time he showed up for a Friday weigh-in at 215 pounds or less. A pot of homemade vegetable soup was steeping in the kitchen. The television set was humming, with some buxom young blond nurse telling the chief surgeon of "General Hospital" that soon he would be a father whether he wanted to or not, and outside there was a Mormon mama lecturing her brood. Robin was pondering whether to comb his hair before sundown, before his cohort Sammy Weisberger came by for soup and Scrabble, when the mail came.

Mr. Pendergrast, the postman, had stomped onto the landing and stuffed the mail into the box, rattling the screen door and saying, "Mail call," before continuing down the lane. Robin eased up, rustled his hair and checked his crotch before sliding across the linoleum floor in his socks to open the screen door and collect the mail. Marilyn Morrison, the one next door with the three kids, was already on the stoop going through her mail while Hiram, age two, rattled around on his Big Wheels.

"Morning," said Robin.

"Morning? It's almost four o'clock."

"Well, the cat's away."

"Gone again?"

"New Hampshire. They're killing babies up there."

"What?"

"Kidding. Just kidding. Interesting mail?"

Marilyn waved one letter she had opened. "Big offer from IBM." She looked again at the letter. "My God. We could have *eighty* kids with this. Dale's at Widener now. He'll die when he sees this."

For Robin and Meg there was the usual. American Express had a personal computer. BMW making "an offer you can hardly refuse" for a convertible. British World Airways, in a one-time-only "sacrifice," practically giving away a round trip for two to London. Life insurance, credit cards, luxury cars, Caribbean vacations, book clubs, investment loans, sailboats, Brooks Brothers charge accounts, surgical knives. Once a month the brotherhood of med school grads held a bonfire on the banks of the Charles River to burn the month's mail. Robin would have added all of this to the pile but for one thing. There was a crumpled brown envelope and it had a handstamped postmark which said, "Andrews, North Carolina." Robin, letting the screen door slap behind him, shuffled back to the sofa and threw the junk mail onto the floor with the *Globe* and sat down to open the envelope.

Boy. Forgot this till got home. This fella and I had fun. Long time ago. Maybe he's still up there. Tell him Bluejay still kicking.

Grandpa.

That was on a piece of paper—Bluejay's stationery, BLUEJAY CLAY, STAR OF GRAND OLE OPRY, "The Longer You're Gone (The

Harder It Gets)," Decca Records Recording Artist, Nashville, Tennessee, navy-blue letters on pine-shaded stock—in a hurried longhand. Enclosed with it was a crinkled yellowing tearsheet, several pages, in fact, of a profile from the October 18, 1944, issue of *The New Yorker*. The story, simply entitled "U.S. Journal: Appalachia's Wilds," began, "Deep in these smoky blue hills of America's Southern Highlands even such a celebrity as Henry Buford Clay, better known to thousands as 'Bluejay' Clay of the Grand Ole Opry in Nashville, Tennessee, never thinks twice about the daily amenities enjoyed by most of his countrymen. On this day Mr. Clay and I are astride Sally, the family horse, as we ride back into the hollows . . ." The article went on for nearly 10,000 words, with a tight focus on Bluejay Clay and his life and times in Sixkiller Gap, and it was signed by a writer named Sean Shaughnessy.

Why his grandfather, in all of his ramblings about the history of the Clay family and the mountains and the Scotch-Irish and anything else pertaining to bloodlines, never talked about being lionized in *The New Yorker* back there in '44 was a mystery to Robin. After rereading the article he was struck with a whim. *Why not?* he thought. He found the Boston phone book and began flipping through the scores of Shaughnessys until he located a Sean S. Shaughnessy. He was right there in Cambridge, around the corner on Brattle Street, if that was the right one. He dialed. On the first ring a voice said, "Shaughnessy here."

"Mr. Sean Shaughnessy?"

"Yes. And who is this?"

"Did you once write for *The New Yorker*?"

"Now and then. Who is this?"

"Oh. Sorry. My name's Robin Clay."

"Who?"

"Clay. Robin Clay. I'm a medical student at Harvard."

"Clay. I know a Turnbull Clay. Vermont. Damned fine poet."

Robin said, "No, sir, no relation that I know of. I'm sorry to catch you like this. I mean, you don't know me from Adam." *Adam Clay? No, sir, it's Robin Clay.* "Let me explain," said Robin, and he did, and after some mumbling and going off to check his files Sean Shaughnessy asked Robin how he felt about lunching on Saturday at the Faculty Club. "Just tell Victor you're meeting me and he'll direct you to my table," Shaughnessy said. When Robin hung up he went next door to ask Marilyn if Dale had a proper sports jacket, size forty long, he could borrow.

It had been a long time since Shaughnessy had rolled out of Boston on a train for New York and then the Philadelphia-Baltimore-Washington-Richmond run, this phlegmatic Easterner, this Harvard man, on assignment for *The New Yorker* because they paid him enough money to keep up the taxes on Abigail's Victorian along Brattle Street; Shaughnessy going away more for that than for any feelings about people who lived in the Southern jungles, as he called Appalachia, his despair growling in his stomach as the train in that summer of '44 turned westward and began following the ridges and valleys of the Blue Ridge Mountains through the bleak huddled towns of Durham and Greensboro and Winston-Salem and Asheville. He had been a promising young man then—not yet thirty, a former Nieman Fellow, house on Brattle, entrée to the Faculty Club in Cambridge, an agent in New York who regularly finagled choice assignments for him with such magazines as *Collier's* and *The Saturday Evening Post*—but much had happened during the thirty-nine years since. His marriage to Abigail, never a marriage of any noticeable passion, had ended with some notoriety in the early sixties when she was shot to death and her lover turned the pistol on himself in a room at the Holiday Inn on Massachusetts Avenue. Sean and Abigail never had any children. To occupy himself he went to cover the war in Vietnam as a columnist for *Newsday*, the newspaper on Long Island, and while there he stepped on a Claymore mine and lost his right leg one morning with the Marines near DaNang. By the time he had recuperated, more or less, he found himself to be tired and lonely before his time. His best moments these days were spent at lunch.

Robin made a point of arriving at the Faculty Club early, about ten minutes before noon on Saturday, and when he told Victor, the *maître d'*, that he was to meet Mr. Shaughnessy he was directed to a corner table next to some windows. "Mr.

Shaughnessy is always nervous about not being on time for a meeting," Victor said, and Robin walked over to introduce himself. Shaughnessy stood up to shake hands. "Handsome jacket, perfect for a lunch," said Shaughnessy. Robin, who had never seen the inside of the Faculty Club before, thanked Shaughnessy and waited for him to sit first. Shaughnessy took *The New York Times* from under his arm and, with a slight moan, positioned his wooden leg and plopped into place at the table and slapped the *Times* next to his water glass. He had been reading about the American military's latest adventures in the Middle East.

"War," said Shaughnessy. "Terrible waste."

"I've got a lot of friends who say that."

"Believe me. I know personally."

"Yes, sir."

"Had no business going. Fifty years old."

"Yes, sir."

"So," said Shaughnessy. "Enough of that. It's over for me. God knows. At any rate. After you called I went back into my files and found the piece I wrote on your grandfather and the Appalachians. Didn't realize it had been that long ago. Godamighty. In '44 I was still just a boy. Not that much older than you are right now. Lot happens over the years. I remember an awful train ride down there and old Bluejay meeting me at the station on his horse and an Indian he had pouring me full of moonshine whiskey and a woman who seemed to cook all day and a lot of old log cabins all over the valley. And there was a boy around the place. I remember testing some of the whiskey with your grandfather and the Indian, and then the boy joined in and we played what amounted to lacrosse. That boy, now, who was that?"

"That's my Dad," said Robin.

"Had a strange name, as I recall."

"Jaybird. Grandpa named him Jaybird. Dad never liked it."

"That's it," Shaughnessy said, "Jaybird. Bluejay and Jaybird. And now there's Robin."

"Yes, sir. Bluejay, Jaybird, Robin."

"Got a nice ring to it. Reminds me of Jack Kennedy the first time as President he heard the Marine band play 'Hail to the Chief.' He leaned over to Kenny O'Donnell, I think it was, and said, 'Got a nice ring to it, don't you think?' Bluejay, Jaybird, Robin. Nice ring. But come on, fill me in. Old reporter here. Facts, dates. Sure you won't have a Bloody Mary? Victor makes the best."

"No, sir, thank you. I'll wait a while."

"Well. At least you *look* like your grandfather."

Throughout lunch, for more than an hour of tuna-fish sandwiches and chips and pickles and Bloody Marys and iced tea and sun streaming through the civilized windowpanes of the Harvard Faculty Club, Robin Clay told Sean Shaughnessy what had transpired over the forty years since his visit to Sixkiller. Grandma, Molly, had died in stillbirth during the winter storm of '45. Grandpa, Bluejay, wrote a song about it that did okay on the *Billboard* charts and he was still living there at Sixkiller. So was Sam, the Indian, Sam Sixkiller. Dad, Jaybird, had divorced his mama and he'd had some problems but he was doing all right now and he and his new wife were back living on the farm with Grandpa. He and Meg planned to move back to the homeplace, too, once they finished their schooling in May, so they could set up their careers and await the baby.

"As a matter of fact," said Robin, "you just missed Grandpa."

"Bluejay?" said Shaughnessy. "Here? In Boston?"

"Yes, sir. He played Symphony Hall a few weeks ago."

"I guess he *has* become a sort of folk hero to the kids."

"He doesn't quite know what to make of it."

"And your father, now," Shaughnessy said. "Did he go into the music business?"

"He did. Yes, sir. In the business end of it. You know, a 'personal manager.' I'm afraid alcohol and the divorce from my mom got him messed up for a while. But he's remarried now to another singer. It's a long story. His new wife is named Mo Dale. I doubt if you'd know about her. Anyway, they had a bad wreck out in Kansas and he got torn up pretty bad and that about did it. He and Mo are living on the farm now."

"And the farm. Forty years must have brought some changes."

Robin said, "Not with the farm itself. Grandpa's got what amounts to a principality down there. He still has his hundred acres but it's all but surrounded by barbed wire. About thirty years ago a conglomerate came in for the timber and then they branched out and bought up more land and now there are chalets and ski slopes and all of that. Grandpa and Sam, the old Indian, just sit there and refuse to budge. When Meg and I move down there it'll be a family compound, more or less, with three generations of Clays holding down the fort."

"That's a hell of a story, boy," Shaughnessy said.

"Sir?"

"A family staying together like that."

"Seems the natural thing to do," said Robin.

"Natural, you say."

"The generations staying together."

"Exactly. Exactly."

Shaughnessy summoned Victor to the table and told him that they wouldn't be wanting dessert, to put the bill on his account, that they had to be somewhere that afternoon. There was a pall of great sorrow across the old man's face as he struggled with his artificial leg. "You should know," he said to Robin, "that the best time I ever had in my life, now that you've reminded me of these things, was when I got drunk with your Grandpa and an Indian and played lacrosse in a pasture full of cow dung." Shaughnessy then called a cab for Brattle Street while Robin began the walk back to Shaler Lane.

CHAPTER VI

A T ONE O'CLOCK in the afternoon, she having gone by her room at the Ritz to change into something suitable for lunch at Locke-Ober's on a glorious spring day, they sat at a cozy table next to a window so they could take in the sun and have a quiet talk. She wore a white silk dress imprinted with violets, complemented with lavender stockings and matching high-heeled sandals and a pearl necklace and a glistening ivory bracelet her late husband had bought for her in Kenya, and he thought she was trying a bit too hard not to look forty-seven years old. He was loosely dressed in a blue-striped seersucker suit, white Oxford-cloth button-down shirt but no tie, and a pair of black loafers. When the waiter came she ordered another martini, he another Perrier.

"I'm so sorry Margaret couldn't come," she said.

"She's not feeling so good these days," he told her. "It's her seventh month. And she's under a lot of pressure to get her degree."

"Can't she, well, *do* something for herself? Those *clothes.*"

"Mother, she's pregnant. Don't you remember how it was?"

"I try not to. That awful duplex in Nashville. Your father out all night chasing women while I'm at home having his child."

"Mother, please."

"I'm sorry, Robin dear, but I'll never forgive him."

209

"It doesn't do any good now to talk about it," he said. "I don't know why you persist. Dad's been through his own kind of hell, too, but at least he's managed to put it behind him. It's like he's been born again."

"With that little floozie to help him," she said.

"Not true. She's a strong woman and she's good for him."

"And your mother wasn't? How *dare* you."

"I'm not going to touch that."

"I should certainly hope not. After all I did for you."

"Yes," he said, "the best boarding schools available."

Their salads came. Through the window, on the sidewalk, businessmen in rolled-up shirt sleeves and young secretaries in pleated skirts enjoyed the April breeze. A fellow in a clown's costume, in an old-fashioned baseball promotion, had sandwich boards slung over his shoulders announcing that afternoon's game between the Red Sox and the Yankees. Robin, given a choice, would take Fenway Park over lunch with his mother at Locke-Ober's. But Mrs. Rebecca Rollins Clay Siebert gave him no choice.

"I just can't figure it out," she was saying. "A country doctor. My son, with a degree from the Harvard Medical School, passing out pills to those pitiful illiterates."

"You're not the only one, Mother."

"And what does *she* intend to do? Besides have babies."

"Her name is Margaret. 'Meg.' "

"Whatever. Well? What'll she do with *her* degree?"

"Legal aid. Union work. ACLU. Something like that."

"Good God, Robin, it was people like that who brought that horrible lawsuit against your grandfather and Rex," she said. "Don't you remember that? It cost Diversified millions of dollars just in legal fees."

"Come on, Mother, they were running a sweatshop," he said.

"A 'sweatshop'? Those people had nothing before the company came."

"They had trees and land and clean air. They had some dignity."

"Dignity? You call living in a shack with eight kids dignity? I went to that high school, remember? I grew up with those,

those wretched people. That two-bit sheriff, that horrid Wingo man. My God. Those Southern *creatures*. They came right out of an Erskine Caldwell novel."

"We could argue this all day and get nowhere," he said. "Our minds are made up. Grandpa's already got one of the cabins fixed up and waiting. Dad's about recovered from the wreck and he and Mo are already living on the farm. Sam—you remember, the old Indian—he's still there sort of taking care of the place. Grandpa's coming up on seventy-two and I'm afraid he's pretty sick. So that's it. We're going. We need them and they need us."

"But you could do so *well* in Chicago, Robin."

"Mother," he said, "I don't *want* my office at a country club."

"There you go again," she said.

"Seven years, for what? Diagnosing tennis elbow? No thank you."

"You're impossible. None of my friends can understand it."

"That's their problem," he said.

When she shifted in her seat to stir yet another martini, her third, the sunlight caught her face and he could see through the liberal blush and mascara and lipstick that his mother had become one of those women who once was pretty. There were lines now, hard lines, and the eyes alternated between being dull and being angry. When he chomped on a piece of ice she jumped.

"What about you, Mother? Are you okay?"

"Rex was a good provider," she said.

"I'm sure of that," he said.

"The poor dear. Heart attack and only fifty-two."

"You weren't calling him a 'poor dear' before he died."

"I know. I know. Sometimes one must, oh, *endure*."

"Endure."

"Certain unpleasantries," she said. Sunlight flashed from her diamond rings as she brushed at a wisp of her streaked hair. The waiter brought their lobster and they began to dabble at lunch. He made the assumption that she was paying for the lunch.

"I have a very good life," she said.

"I'm glad," he told her.

"I have the house and my friends. There's the club."

"Grandmother and Grandfather, do you see them?"

"In the winter I go out there. Arizona's nice in January. Better than Chicago. My phone bills are atrocious, though."

"I can imagine," he said. "But what do you *do*, Mother?"

"*Do*?"

"I mean, you're not but forty-seven. Surely you get bored."

"Dear son," she said. "Me? Bored? You don't know me very well."

"That's a fact, I'm afraid."

"The reason I can't see you graduate next month is London. I'll be in London with a friend. He was a friend of your father's."

"My father doesn't have friends who go to London."

"I mean *Rex*," she said. "I'm sorry."

"I hope so."

"It was just a slip."

"Mother." He toyed with a cocktail napkin. "I can forgive you for almost everything. The things you did and the things you didn't do. I'm grown up now. I'm not little Robin anymore. But sometimes, at the weirdest times, I still wake up shaking and remembering the night you and Rex very nearly got me to sign that piece of paper changing my last name. A frightened, badgered, crying ten-year-old boy, Mother. You ought to be ashamed of yourself."

She paid for lunch with her American Express. He offered to walk her to the Ritz, only a few blocks away, but she said she would take a cab. She apologized for not being able to treat him and Meg to dinner that evening because there were friends she hadn't seen in a long time. He was able to catch the last four innings at Fenway and spilled a beer on his suit when Carl Yastrzemski, beginning his last season in a baseball uniform, won it in the ninth with a homer off Goose Gossage.

CHAPTER VII

THE YARD SALE, conducted with cavalier insouciance by Will Brooks right there in the middle of the alleyway which was Shaler Lane, had turned out to be not only a success but also a rousing good way to say farewell to Harvard (or, as Robin put it, "clear the base"). "And now folks, the most treasured item of them all," Will would say to the gaggle of curious treasure hunters standing in the soppy morning heat, he wearing a straw planter's hat and red suspenders for effect, Robin and Meg watching in bemusement from the stoop of their apartment, "an original iron bed upon which young Henry Buford Clay IV was conceived on the fateful evening of October the fourth, nineteen-hundred and eighty-two. A rare collector's item, folks." It brought eighteen dollars, worth one good pig-out feast of hamburgers on the 984-mile drive from Boston to Sixkiller, so when they rolled away that afternoon they didn't have to pull a U-Haul and they had more than enough cash for the road.

"Eat, gas, motel," Robin said as he dragged a handful of McDonald's French fries through a gob of catsup. They were propped up in bed, waiting for the "Tonight Show" to come on, at a cheap mom-and-pop motel somewhere between Philadelphia and Baltimore. Meg was still debating whether the Magic Fingers on the bed would damage her eight-month-old fetus.

"I think the eighteen-wheelers have gotten to you," she said.

213

"It'd make a hell of a book, though. Life on the road. Willy Loman, circa '83. Eat, gas, motel. Day after day."

"Oughta get your Dad to do it with Grandpa."

"I'll mention it. Be a nice sequel to 'Blood in the Hills.'"

Meg said, "Is that what they're going to call it?"

"Yeah," said Robin. "I tell you, it could turn out to really be something. If Dad's as straight as he sounds and Sam can still get it up after eighty-three years, I could even see a best-seller. We're talking about a lot of history here. You know it's been almost two centuries since Sam's great-grandfather killed all those settlers?"

"Well, look out, Sixkiller. Here comes some more settlers."

They were somewhat surprised at the ease in which they had made their getaway from Harvard. Receiving their diplomas, he as a doctor and she as a lawyer, had been anticlimactic after all of those hours and years in libraries and lecture halls and earnest discourse. If that hadn't been the Real World they didn't know what was. But now, as Meg kept saying, came the *real* Real World. No longer would they have to explain to their peers, most of them aghast that they were "throwing away" their training, why they were doing what they were doing. It seemed to them quite enough to live simply and work quietly and honestly at what they did best. They were, in short, ready to quit talking about it and get on with it.

And so they rumbled southward in the trusty little black '66 VW, Meg feeling horribly fat and uninteresting in her eighth month of pregnancy and Robin trying doggedly to keep a smooth and steady pace, leaving the interstates in Virginia so they could make a symbolic approach to Andrews through the twisting hills of Southern Appalachia. On the car radio around Roanoke they heard a country station playing one of Bluejay's songs—*Started in the mountains, spread all over town*—and gaily they went through Grandpa's entire forty-year repertoire of songs from "The Longer You're Gone" to "Molly" and the rest, munching on peanuts and sipping from Dr Peppers bought at country gas stations, feeling the excitement as they drove deeper and deeper into the mountains and the coves of North Carolina until finally, after three days and two nights, they found themselves bumping beneath the archway proclaiming SIXKILLER.

It was not until they unloaded their things and settled in at the farm that Robin began to see how absolutely correct he had been when he remarked to Sean Shaughnessy, on that day at the Harvard Faculty Club, that Sixkiller would become what amounted to a "family compound." The Kennedys and other wealthy Eastern families were cloistered in places like Cape Cod or Penobscot Bay or the tip of Long Island while the Clays of North Carolina were gathered about, celebrating the bloodline apart from the rest of the world, in much the same way. The steady reminder for Robin was the fence. Part of it had been put up by Bluejay and part of it by Diversified Enterprises. It followed the lines of the Clays' one hundred acres precisely, a ten-foot chain link fence running across a ridge here and dripping through the bed of Sixkiller Creek there, reminding Robin and Meg of the ridiculous "running fence" some avant-garde "artist" calling himself Cristo had strung up over miles of undulating land in northern California a few years earlier. Cristo had had some difficulty explaining the "statement" he was trying to make with *his* fence, but the statement of the fence surrounding Sixkiller was quite clear. Keep Out.

Now, with the arrival of Robin and Meg, it was a family compound in the purest sense. What Elijah Clay had begun before the turn of the nineteenth century—with a simple clay-chinked log cabin slapped down in a hardwood clearing wrested from stray Cherokees—had inexorably grown into a backwoods principality. Newt's original one-room cabin was now a sprawling disjointed "big house" occupied by Bluejay Clay, Newt's great-great-great-grandson, who wandered alone through rooms where Clays had been born and Clays had died; rooms which had been patched and painted and wallpapered and then stripped before the process began all over again; rooms full of ghosts and family Bibles and such memorabilia as arrowheads and antlers and crinkled photographs and Bluejay's framed gold records; rooms preserved in memory. The same was true throughout the valley of Sixkiller, a place so old that the SEE ROCK CITY paint job on the main barn seemed as trendy as yesterday's fad even though it had been there for forty years. Bluejay could sit and rock on the front porch of the main house, which is the way he was spending most of his time these days, and when he looked out across the lush green valley of his ancestors he saw the only thing he deeply cared about anymore. He saw Clays in the nearest cabin, a roomy cottage where his grandson and his wife awaited the birth of his first great-grandchild; and beyond that he saw another cottage, the outgrowth of a log cabin built by his great-great-grandfather Buford Clay, now occupied by his own son and the woman who had salvaged that son's life; and beyond that yet another dwelling, this one little changed during the century except for a modest front porch and an extension in the rear for use as an "office," the home for nearly eighty years of Sam Sixkiller.

In the afternoon Robin sat with Sam on the front porch of the cabin beside Sixkiller Creek. They were propped back on chairs Sam had fashioned from barrel staves and birch limbs and baling wire, watching Monarch butterflies cavort in the June breeze and bumblebees nip at the honeysuckle, having to raise their voices whenever the heavy machinery cranked up beyond the family graveyard and the chain-link fence on the ridge above it.

"My God," Robin said, "they're right on top of us."

"Almost skiing season," said Sam. "Finishing the lifts."

"Cherokee Hills?"

"They wanted to call it 'Sixkiller' but we took it to court."

"Hah," said Robin. "Meg would've enjoyed that one."

"She'll have her chances," Sam told him.

"They got man-made snow up there, I suppose."

"Everything. I was thinking about a moonshine stand."

"Grandpa told us about that but I didn't believe it."

"Maybe I'll still do it. 'Paleface want firewater? Fresh firewater, two hours old, right out of pot.' They pay a dollar seventy-five for a martini at the lodge and it takes eight to get drunk. If they did business with me they could have their toes curled by a real Redskin for a dollar."

"Why don't you do it, then?" said Robin.

"Too old."

"Come on, Sam. Too old for what?"

"I'm about to make it through life without a liquor license."

Two jaybirds had teamed up and were strafing a striped cat. When the machines on the hill shut down for the afternoon, apparently having plenty of time to complete their work on the lifts before the skiing season began in mid-October, Robin and Sam could hear the gurgle of the creek. They couldn't fish the creek for trout anymore because it had been condemned as polluted. Sam was tired of talking about it.

"Sam," Robin said.

'You want a drink?" said Sam.

"Maybe later. Sam, I want to talk to you."

"I know."

"It's about Grandpa."

"I know."

"He's gong to die, Sam. Before we know it."

Sam barely blinked. "When?"

"It's cancer of the pancreas," said Robin. "He finally let me have a look and that's what it is. I got a second opinion. I don't know when it started but it usually takes six months. First, it's hepatitis."

"And then liver failure," said Sam.

"You've been reading again."

"When he started looking a little yellow."

"Well, then, you know it's irreversible. There's nothing."

"Yes," Sam said. "Did you tell him?"

"I did."

"What happened?"

"He said, 'Don't tell Jaybird because he'll want a drink.' Can you imagine that, Sam? A man finds out he'll be dead by winter and his only comment is that it might get his son messed up. Can you imagine that?"

"Yes, I can," said Sam.

CHAPTER VIII

WHEN Boone Clay went out to the barn to do his milking on the morning of July the Fourth, 1908, he found a runaway Cherokee boy wrapped in a horse blanket and asleep atop a pile of hay. The boy, dressed in buckskin and moccasins, appeared to be about eight years old. He was hungry and tired and still wet from an all-night rain, a frightened urchin with fierce blue eyes and raven hair and taut bronze skin stretched over a wiry frame as hard and straight as an arrow, and he knew few words in English except "eat" and "they die" and "mountain." He was like a spy who had come in from the cold, one who had already wearied of the fight, so Boone Clay and his wife took him in as their adopted son. As the boy became "civilized" and began to pick up English the story of his beginnings came into focus. He was a descendant of the fabled Uwani Sutalitihi, the obstinate Cherokee for whom the valley of Sixkiller had been named, and when his mother died at childbirth and his father fell into alcoholism far up in the hills he simply walked away from it. Boone and Elisabeth Clay named him Sam Sixkiller—Sixkiller for Sutalitihi and Sam because they liked the sound of it—and made the decision, for the record in the family Bible, that his birthdate was July the Fourth, 1900.

And so once again the Clay clan came together in celebration of Sam's birthday, this time his eighty-third, and not in recent memory had there been so much to celebrate. Nobody could recall the last time there were three generations of Clays living permanently at Sixkiller. Soon, with the birth of Meg Branscomb Clay's child, there would be a fourth. The son, Jaybird, had made it to hell and back. The grandson, Robin, could look ahead to a long and productive life as "the doctor" to all the families in the valley. Only Robin and Sam and, of course, Bluejay himself knew that this would be the last time the patriarch would sit at the head of the long pine dining table in the great room of the main house and hold forth on Sam's birthday.

"You setting up your clinic down there where Jack the Clipper Barbershop used to be, Robin, sort of reminds me of the time the Martians landed here," Bluejay was saying. The entire family was there, Bluejay and Sam anchoring opposite ends of the table at dusk, swapping stories as they finished a whopping meal.

"I don't think I've heard that one, Grandpa," said Robin.

"Oh, hell, it made big news, boy. Right, Sam?"

"I'll say," said Sam, pausing over a drumstick.

"Tell us, Grandpa," said Meg.

"Well, sir," Bluejay said, "me and Sam were sitting there at the barbershop one day passing the jug around when Hink let on that he'd won this monkey in a poker game and didn't know what to do with it. That must've been somewhere around 1955 because Jaybird was off at school and everybody was talking about these UFOs from Mars landing in cornfields and letting out funny-looking little men and stuff like that. Well, to make a long story short, Hink ran home and got his monkey and brought it back to the barbershop and Jack shaved off all his hair—"

"Oh, no, don't tell me."

"—while Sage ran down to the hardware store and bought a can of spray paint off of old man Floyd and we painted that little booger green. Oh, yeah, and Jack tied a scarf around his neck. Sage and Hink were drunk as skunks so they put the monkey in my pickup and drove him out toward Marble and let him out on Highway 19 and then came back here and called the state patrol and told 'em the Martians had landed. Damnedest mess you ever saw. Dog catcher, Billy Wingo, state troopers, even the

TV station from Asheville went rushing over there. Chasing that monkey through Jimmy Lee Townsend's cornfield. Didn't anybody know anything for sure until one of those fellows from that Center for Disease Control in Atlanta flew up and caught him with a net and the paint came off in his hands."

"See there, Pa, I told you college was a waste of time," Jaybird said.

"How's that, son?"

"Taught me not to believe in foolishment."

"Reckon you're right," said Bluejay. "Reckon you are. Man needs to believe in things like Santa Claus and ghosts and Easter bunnies now and then. Keeps a man from going crazy. Like me, right now, I'm believing that Granddaughter here"—he nudged Meg, bloated from her full-term pregnancy, at his side—"she's gonna have a big old strapping boy and she's already figured out what she's gonna call him. Ain't that right, Granddaughter?"

Meg blushed. "But you don't know for sure, Grandpa."

"Sure I do," said Bluejay. "Gonna be a boy. I *believe*."

"You want me to tell everybody?"

"Couldn't think of a better day than today. Right now."

"Okay, then," said Meg. "On the outside long-shot *infinitesimal* possibility that it's a girl, we'll name her Molly."

"Here, here," said Jaybird.

"What the hell's that *infinitesimal*?" said Bluejay.

"Means there ain't no way, Grandpa."

"All right. Go on. And when the *boy* comes."

"We'll name him Sam Sutalitihi Clay," Meg said.

"Sammy," said Robin.

"You wouldn't kid an old man," said Sam. Nobody, not even Jaybird and Bluejay on the morning of Molly's death nearly forty years earlier, had ever known Sam Sixkiller to cry. He didn't this time, not quite, but he was close. He arose majestically from his seat at the end of the table. He brushed the graying cowlick from his forehead. He cleared his throat and poured a liberal shot of moonshine into his tea glass from the jug at his end of the table while everybody else, except for Jaybird, did the same. They all stood, waiting for Meg to heave herself onto her feet, and raised their glasses. Then Sam said, in all solemnity, "It's about time."

On the front porch of the main house, as darkness fell and the fireflies and cicadas performed their last show of the evening for them, they drank and talked and then instruments appeared— guitars for Bluejay and Mo, a dulcimer from the closet for Meg, a harmonica from the mantel for Jaybird, a penny whistle from Robin's pocket, Sam's hands slapping a washtub for a drum— and they made music. There was, of course, "The Longer You're Gone" and "Molly" and "Hillbilly Fever" by Bluejay, and "Please Be My Cowboy" and her others by Maureen Barksdale (Mo Dale) Clay, and scores of other songs until the chill of night came and Bluejay took to his favorite rocking chair and was wrapped in a wool blanket by Sam and they all sang "Peace in the Valley" as though it had been orchestrated. They left Bluejay there where he wanted to be, snoring softly in the rocker on the front porch of the only home he had ever known, and they slid away into the darkness to their own places.

"That may be the most wonderful night I've had in my whole entire life," Meg told Robin as they snuggled in the old hickory four-poster crafted by Bluejay's father at the turn of the century. " 'It's about time,' Sam says. Can you believe it?"

"I thought he was going to break," said Robin.

"How's he taking it about Grandpa?"

"I think it's killing him. He's a stoic, but he's not *that* tough."

"I still think you ought to tell your dad," said Meg.

"No," Robin said. "I don't think he can handle it yet."

"But look, hon. It's a whiskey disease, right?"

"Uh-huh. Pure and simple."

"Well, my thinking is, for what it's worth, you sit him down and spell it out. Tell him Grandpa might've lived forever if it hadn't been for the drinking. Scare the hell out of him again, remind him that he can't drink anymore, just like what happened in Kansas."

"It's not that simple, Meg."

"Maybe not. I don't know diddly about alcoholism."

"I'm a doctor and I don't know, either. But I've got to watch it."

"You," said Meg. "*You?*"

"That's something else they think might run in the blood."

"Uh-oh."

"What?" said Robin. "Nobody can prove it, but—"

"No," she said. "Here. Feel it. There it is again. Here we go, pal. The Indians are coming."

It was, unlike in the old days, an orderly process. Robin Clay, the doctor, turned on the bedside lamp and timed his wife's labor pains. While she got up and laid out some things in an overnight case he called the Cherokee County Memorial Hospital—no doctor to call, because he would help bring his own child into the world—and then called the cabins of Jaybird and Mo and then Sam. Sam said he would go up to the main house and tell Bluejay and sit up with him. Jaybird said he and Mo would go to the hospital in order to welcome his grandchild—Molly? Sam?—into the fold. And so Robin helped Meg into the Volkswagen ("Don't they still give you a new VW if your kid's born in one?" she said) and they puttered to the hospital and in very short order they were doing business. *Okay, hon, the epidural ought to be working now/Lord, it's gonna be a whopper/All right, now, remember the Lamaze/Good Godamitey/Here she comes, here she comes/What?/Just a figure of speech/Wake me when it's over/Well, now, what do you know about that?/What've we got, Ace?/We've got a Sam Sutalitihi Clay.*

CHAPTER IX

WHAT y'all are going to see tonight's a long way from what it was like that time Jaybird sang with me on the Opry," Bluejay was saying from the shotgun seat of the new bus as Jaybird maneuvered it around Chattanooga and picked up the interstate which would take them to Nashville. "What year was that, son?"

"Must've been about '54, Pa," said Jaybird.

"I didn't know you played the Opry, Dad," Robin said.

"Oh, just that one time, son. Pa did 'Molly' for the first time."

"Did you sing?" said Meg.

"Mainly I shook in my boots."

"He done good," Bluejay said. "He done good. I don't think Jaybird cared much for my kind of music back then. Everything was changing fast. All the kids wanted to hear was that 'nigger music,' that 'rock 'n' roll' crap, and I sorta figured if maybe I got him out there on the stage at the Ryman it might change his mind. Didn't do a damn bit of good. That's the night he met Bobby Smart. Didn't recover for fifteen years."

"Bobby Smart the singer?" said Meg.

"One and only."

"Did you work with him?"

"Represented him off and on for maybe ten years," Jaybird said. "He was hot stuff for a while. That was in the sixties when

223

I was with an outfit called TopRank. But he kept on singing rock 'n' roll and the times left him just like they left Pa. He couldn't take it anymore, so he killed himself."

Bluejay said, "Lot of 'em are dead now. I always figured I was gonna die on the road somewhere, just like Jaybird and Mo almost did out there in Kansas this year, busting butt to get to another show. Cowboy Copas, Hawkshaw Hawkins, Patsy Cline, Jim Reeves. All of 'em, killed trying to make it to the next show. What's that saying we got? 'Playing the road is like robbing banks—you ride in, take the money and ride out.' If the road don't get you the pills or the whiskey will. Hank Williams, he's another one. Had that song, 'I'll Never Get out of This World Alive.' Died right after that, all juiced up from something in the back seat of a Cadillac, trying to make it to Canton or somewhere."

This was on the Saturday of Labor Day weekend and they were going to Nashville for what would be the last appearance of Bluejay Clay on the Grand Ole Opry. Everybody knew that except his son, Jaybird, but even he could sense that the old man couldn't make it much longer. Bluejay, his back relentlessly aching and his skin yellowing from hepatitis, was in constant pain now. The last time he had performed, in fact, was back in January at the Boston Symphony Hall. These days he spent his time rocking on the front porch with Sammy, his great-grandson, or sitting by the fire listening to tapes of his own songs or the Grand Ole Opry when they could get WSM on the radio or driving the others' patience to the limit as he babbled and repeated his stories. *One day poor ol' Billy Wingo came by and said he had a warrant for Sam's arrest. . . . Shorty Hunsinger, now, he was just plain sorry. . . . And then, like that, the lights came on. . . . This funny-looking dude came down from Boston to do a story on us hillbillies. . . . The day the Martians came. . . .* It was Mo Dale who had called Bud Wendell, the overseer of the Opry, and gotten a special fifteen-minute spot on the Purina Dog Chow portion of the Opry at 10:15. The entire family would be on stage—Meg had found an old woman to baby-sit Sammy, Robin had found a registered nurse at the hospital to cover his handful of patients, and although Sam at eighty-three couldn't drive the bus anymore he could certainly rattle a snare drum on the stage of the Opry—and this was, for all intents and purposes, Bluejay's dying wish.

"You sure you're gonna just give it up, Daughter, just like that?" Bluejay said to Mo as they began to see exit ramps for Nashville. It was dusk. They had plenty of time to get something to eat at Linebaugh's and hang out at Tootsie's, for old times' sake, before motoring on out to the new Opryland U.S.A. complex. Mo, her raven pigtails showing streaks of silver here and now, was already dressed in a fringed buckskin miniskirt and tight knee-length boots for the show.

"I'm not exactly *quitting*, Grandpa," she said.

"Lord, you haven't played the Opry since Sammy was born."

"I know, but Bud says I'm okay if I play fifteen a year. I just don't want to go on the road unless somebody's crazy enough to pay me a lot of money. I want to be with Jay and I want to help out with Sammy when Meg sets up her practice. Sammy's like my surrogate son."

"Talk English, Daughter."

"Surrogate. That means 'in place of.' My play-like son. The one I never had."

"Well," Bluejay said, "you women can work that out. Don't matter."

"You old fart," said Meg.

When Jaybird parked the bus in an All-Rite parking lot catty-corner from Tootsie's Orchid Lounge, at the intersection of Broadway and Opry Place, he sat at the wheel for a few moments in stunned silence. Only he and his father could fully appreciate what had happened in the eight years since WSM and the National Life & Accident Insurance Company had moved the Opry out of old Ryman Auditorium and taken it to the suburbs. It was dark now and a quick rain had squalled up, the wind gusting dust and scraps of paper against the old buildings of downtown Nashville, and there was the eerie feeling one has when a tornado is about to strike. It was as though this corner, which for more than thirty years had been the very heart of country music in the whole world, was closed for repairs. Ernest Tubb's Record Shop, across Broadway from Tootsie's, was open but only the clerks were inside. Linebaugh's Cafe, where scores and maybe hundreds of country songs had been scribbled on napkins by destitute young rainbow chasers, was boarded up. The grenade screens were pulled tight across the windows of Friedman's Pawn Shop where secondhand guitars and Opry baubles gathered dust. The last tourist of the day had paid his dollar to wander through Ryman Auditorium, now a museum, sad as a red-brick beached whale.

And then there was Tootsie's Orchid Lounge. The place had been an institution since the March day in 1960 when a brassy little forty-year-old woman named Hattie Louise Tatum finally put together enough money to open a beer joint around the corner from Ryman Auditorium. She was a hard country woman from Hohenwald, about seventy miles southwest of Nashville, and already she had been around the block. Her first husband had called her "Tootsie" and her second husband was named Jeff Bess. She and Jeff had traveled about a bit as "Big Jeff and the Radio Plowboys," she serving as ticket seller and singer and comedienne, and when the marriage broke up she opened the bar.

The timing was perfect. The sixties marked the last fine hour for pure knee-jerking beer-drinking howling-in-the-night country music as Bluejay Clay knew it. Those were the years when the music was ruled by Hank Williams and Roy Acuff and Kitty Wells and Bluejay Clay and, later, Del Reeves and Webb Pierce and Carl Smith and finally the John Hartfords and Johnny Cash and Kris Kristofferson. Tootsie's Orchid Lounge was the last pit stop en route to Hillbilly Heaven—the stage of Ryman Auditorium—and it was made purposely shabby. There were pinball machines and a four-by-six Confederate flag above them and the latest futuristic jukebox and cold long-neck beer and unforgettable chili and country-fried steak and, behind the cash register, a cigar box holding some $1,500 in unpaid tabs being held for down-and-out writers and singers. NO BEER TABS FOR NO BODY—POLICE ORDERS, said a sign. She was a mama and they were "my babies," as were the back-street barmaids and hookers she had nursed through illnesses of the mind and the body. She fed them and clothed them and cajoled them—barmaids, stars, starving would-be's, anybody with a reasonably honest face and a good story—and she became the Mother Superior of country music.

A weekend night at Tootsie's in those days was a joyous celebration of life in the emergency lane. Upstairs the stars were ducking across the alleyway from the stage entrance of Ryman for a quick beer and some chili between shows, their buses and Cadillacs parked nearby so they could split for a Sunday matinee in Akron as soon as the Opry ended. Coming through the door with a guitar case was a tired kid fresh off the bus from Waco. Tourists would be everywhere with their Instamatics. More than a thousand autographed pictures of stars, most of them as wrinkled and faded as the stars themselves, were pinned to the walls. The jukebox would be blaring "Your Cheatin' Heart" and an old drunk would be sitting in a corner booth crying into the sleeve of a moth-eaten World War II army jacket. Maybe the toilets in the unspeakable rest rooms were working and maybe they weren't. Movies had been made there. Willie Nelson had called his agent from the pay phone there. Geraldine the barmaid had spilled a beer in the lap of a *New York Times* reporter there (*Oops, did I spill it on your dick?*) and even a younger Jay Clay had been hit up for Opry tickets by a wasted old minor-league baseball player named Stud Cantrell and his wife, the former Dixie Lee Box. That was Tootsie's Orchid Lounge.

What the Clay entourage saw now, as they lurched in from the rain on this night twenty-three years after the birth of the place, was another matter. When WSM held the last performance at Ryman Auditorium some ten years earlier, moving the Opry out to a 110-acre complex costing $28 million, it more or less killed Tootsie's and Linebaugh's and everything else around Ryman. Tootsie died of cancer four years after that and what Bluejay and Jaybird were seeing on this night wasn't really Tootsie's. It was a morgue.

"Would you look here at what I see coming through that door? My God, it's the Holy Ghost. Come here, Bluejay Clay, so I can hug you." Mary Williams, the good friend who had nursed Tootsie Bess until the last second of her life, came around from the bar and rushed up to Bluejay to make over him. The only other people in the downstairs part of the place were a young bartender and a longtime barmaid named Wanda, dangling gold earrings and black wig, trying to shake off a wasted old geezer who kept trying to buy her a beer.

"And Lord, if it ain't Jay," said Mary. "Come to pay his tab."

"You remember my wife, don't you, Mary? Mo Dale."

"Do I? Mo, we still got 'Be My Cowboy' on the jukebox."

"Looks like you don't have anybody to play it, though, Mary."

"I'm going to take care of that right now." Mary took a fistful of quarters from the cash register and began playing every Mo Dale and Bluejay Clay on the jukebox. When everybody had ordered a beer—Jaybird's request for a club soda drew a quick glance from Mary and a nod from Bluejay—they lined the bar and listened to the music while Sam refined his pinball game and Mary caught up.

"Shoot, Bluejay, I thought you was *born* a great-grandfather."

"Naw," he said, "I just look like it."

"How's your health? You don't look so hot."

"Just tired and old, that's all."

"And all of y'all are gonna be on the Opry tonight, you say?"

"Kind of a farewell performance," said Bluejay.

"Shame I can't just run across the alley to see you," said Mary.

"Not the same, I reckon, since Tootsie died."

"Nothing's the same anymore, Bluejay," Mary said. "When they moved the Opry that did it. Scoopie Harper's a security guard up the hill at National Life and sometimes he comes in for a beer when he gets off. Somebody said Willie Nelson sneaked in one night but nobody noticed him. Onie Wheeler, the one that whistles on 'Wabash Cannonball' for Roy Acuff, he comes in now and then. But that's about it. Lot of people read about the place in that Nelson fellow's book and they come in to buy a souvenir and buy a beer just so they can say they drank a beer one time at Tootsie's. Y'all oughta go upstairs while you're here.

Got a few people up there listening to Del Gray and the band."

They walked up the rickety stairs to the upper room, where Bluejay had drunk many a beer between shows at the Ryman, past a table holding mementos of Tootsie's (ashtrays for $3, bumper stickers $1, T-shirts $7, a 45-rpm record of Del Gray's "Tootsie's Orchid Lounge" for $1). On a precarious stage beneath a notice proclaiming BAND PLAYS FOR TIPS ONLY, for an audience composed of three drunk good old boys in cowboy boots and two hookers who had come in out of the rain, Del Gray and his three-piece Orchid Loungers acknowledged Bluejay by doing "The Longer You're Gone" and then closed their set with their one song, "Tootsie's Orchid Lounge."

It took Jaybird forever, it seemed, to find a place to park the bus at Opryland U.S.A. The bus was clearly marked BLUEJAY CLAY & THE SIXKILLERS, and there were cops in rain slickers all over the labyrinthine parking lots, but he would have chosen running over fans behind Ryman Auditorium to this. The place was foreign to him and too big, sort of a poor man's Disneyland with its amusements and rides and thousands of cars, and he hoped the bustle of it all wouldn't be too exciting for his father. But park the bus he did, and they were escorted through the stars' entrance leading into the spacious, carpeted and air-conditioned new Opry House, and shown into a fluorescent-lighted dressing room they really didn't need (out of habit they had dressed on the bus), and it seemed that only minutes passed before they were in place behind the sweeping curtains listening to Grant Turner's replacement, a younger announcer by the name of Hal Durham, make the introduction to the house packed with 4,400 people who remembered when they had to sit on hard church pews with funeral-parlor fans at old Ryman Auditorium.

"Ladies and gentlemen," Hal Durham, the emcee, was telling the thousands in the Opry House and the millions out across the land listening to WSM on their radios, "this is one of those moments that have made the Grand Ole Opry what it is today. It was almost forty years ago, to the day, that the young man I'm about to introduce first set foot on the stage of the Grand Ole Opry. Since that time he has become truly a legend in country music, ranking right up there with Jimmie Rodgers and Roy Acuff and Hank Williams and the handful of others we acknowledge as being true 'superstars.' His hit songs could fill a jukebox and he has remained true to the roots of what makes country music great. Tonight, in what he insists will be his final appearance on the Opry, he has brought with him his entire family. The Clay Family Singers, including a star in her own right—the lovely Mo Dale. So if you will, please, make a great big Opry welcome to the one and only, the legendary . . . BLUEJAY CLAY."

The curtains flew open and the crowd went to its feet and they went to work. They opened with "The Longer You're Gone," Sam Sixkiller in his buckskin slapping away at the snare drum and Meg strumming the dulcimer and Jaybird accompanying on guitar and Mo working the tambourine and Robin doing his best on a harmonica, while the mostly new Sixkillers took the song along and the crowd sang with Bluejay. Hal Durham tried to cut in for a Purina Dog Chow commercial but they encored "The Longer You're Gone." An engineer in the booth overlooking the stage was frantically giving Bluejay the "cut" signal but Bluejay never even looked up. They moved right on into "Molly" and encored it twice, the crowd wanting even more, and now Durham rushed out onto the stage and stood beside Bluejay in hopes that he could cut in with a thank-you-very-much. But it didn't work. Nothing was going to work. It was going to take security guards to get them off the stage until they had finished. Now Bluejay was giving a long sappy spiel about generations living on the land, and describing little Sam Sutalitihi Clay—*My God, he's going to start in on the Trail of Tears, Hal, get him off*—and introducing Mo, who sang "Please Be My Cowboy," which got the crowd going all over again, and they didn't quit until they had overrun the schedule by eighteen minutes—screwing up WSM's radio schedule for the rest of the evening—and somebody suddenly deadened their microphones and jerked the curtains closed. Bluejay was still trying to part the curtains when Robin and Jaybird gently took him by the elbows and dragged him inside.

Exuberant, whooping, hugging, stomping their boots, they

moved off the stage and headed down the polished hallway of the new Opry House toward the exit and the bus out back. They could still hear the crowd buzzing behind them, saying a giddy good-bye to Bluejay Clay, when they were confronted by a WSM executive in a three-piece suit. He was shaking a mimeographed copy of the minute-by-minute radio log in his hand and he was red in the face.

"Eighteen minutes over," he was shouting, "eighteen minutes."

"That all?" said Bluejay, huffing and wheezing.

"Is that all? You just blew the schedule for a week."

"You mean we only did thirty-three minutes? Felt like ten."

"We had to cancel Bucky Boozer," said the WSM man.

"Little piss-ant can't sing, anyway."

"Bluejay, godddamit, next trip do it on your own time."

"Tell you what, you ass-hole," Bluejay said. "Got an easy solution."

"Yeah, and what's that?"

"Why don't you put it on my tab?"

Bluejay, of all people, was the only one other than his boys who couldn't sleep on the drive back to Sixkiller. His son had to drive and his grandson, the doctor, had to stay awake to make sure the old man didn't collapse from the excitement. The rain continued to slash as Jaybird hunched over the steering wheel and Robin nodded and Bluejay, looking as though he had come back from the dead, kept fiddling with the radio dial to see who was being interviewed on "Opry Star Spotlight" that night.

"Yo, Robin," said Bluejay.

"Yeah, Grandpa, right here," said Robin, jolting awake.

"Remember that time I went up to see y'all at Harvard?"

"Sure I do. You played Boston Symphony Hall."

"I ever tell you how Sam almost got lost?"

"I'm not sure, Grandpa."

"Well, see, I knew you lived somewhere on that Charles River, and when we saw this funny-looking fellow with one of those Sherlock Holmes pipes I made Sam stop the bus and I leaned out the window and I said, 'I wonder if you can tell me where the Charles River's at?' and he says, 'My good man, here at Harvard we never end a sentence with a preposition,' so then I tell him—"

"Grandpa, you really ought to get some rest," said Robin.

"I thought he was gonna swallow his pipe."

"He probably did, Grandpa. Probably did. I don't think Harvard was geared for Bluejay Clay."

CHAPTER X

IN little more than four months, working out of the old brick building on Main Street which for years had housed Jack the Clipper Barbershop, Robin had taken on all he could handle as "that new young doctor" in town. Already he had delivered seven babies—not counting his own—and performed hours of surgery and spent countless nights consoling terminally ill patients at the new Cherokee County Area Hospital. (He wasn't surprised when he learned that it had taken eleven referendums to build a new elementary school, given that the average voter's age in the county was sixty-one, but only one to get a modern hospital.) There was more than enough work to occupy the town's two other doctors, older men accustomed to working nine-to-six days at their offices adjacent to the hospital, freeing Dr. Clay for what he had in mind when he left Harvard. Once he had set up his office and hired a receptionist nurse, an older woman named Mona Hatfield who had spent some thirty years on the hospital staff, he bought a new four-wheel-drive Jeep in order to negotiate the ragged back roads in the county. His ministry, if that is what it could be called, was tending those who for various reasons couldn't—or wouldn't—come into town. *What're you, gonna be Tom Dooley of the Hills?* Why not, Robin would think, dressed in crisp jeans and boots and sheepskin coat as he maneuvered his Jeep down an old logging road to a lonely cabin. Somebody had to do it.

Minnie Bottoms was a classic example. She was ninety-three now, a widow since the day thirty years earlier when Henry Bottoms dropped dead of a heart attack while plowing their twenty-three acres back in Otter Cove, and arthritis and a litany of other old-age infirmities made it impossible for her to leave the 120-year-old cabin she shared with her seventy-year-old son Henry Jr. There wasn't much Robin could do for her besides allay the pain, maybe bring her a magazine or some hard candy from town when he went out to check on her, or simply just talk. Like his own grandfather, Bluejay, Minnie was just biding her time.

"What you got for me this time, Robin?" It was late on an October afternoon when Robin bumped up to the cabin and saw Minnie Bottoms rocking on the front porch amid the dozen or so cats she kept.

"Gifts from the Orient, Minnie," he said.

"That anywhere near Chattanooga?"

"You're pulling my leg again. What would you say if I told you I had some perfume from Hong Kong?"

"Henry'd probably drink it. I'd settle for a Rock City birdhouse."

Robin took his black bag from the Jeep and joined her on the porch. Henry, she said, was up on the slopes collecting ginseng and hunting squirrels. It had been peaceful in the cove since Labor Day, she said, once Diversified closed down the swimming pool and the amusement park it built on the land after her husband's death. Robin, while Minnie chattered, probed her joints and checked her vital signs. The cats scrambled when a bluejay made a screeching run on the rickety porch.

"How's your grandpa doing, Robin?"

"I think it's just a matter of time, Minnie."

"Must've been that liquor."

"It didn't help him any," said Robin.

"Lord, why don't men leave it alone?"

"Nobody seems to know. My Dad was the same. It almost got him."

Minnie said, "I heard about that. A body can learn almost everything if you're on a party line. Yessir. I think that's real nice, all of y'all being back together like you are on the farm. New baby and all. Seems like families just don't stay together anymore like they used to."

"That's the truth," said Robin.

"I've got some grandchildren I've never even seen."

"Great-grandchildren, too, I suppose."

"Oh, sure. Got eighteen of those the last I counted."

"Where are they?"

"Everywhere," said Minnie. "California, Texas, Pennsylvania, Ohio. Even got one in England. I can hardly keep up. Seems like when the first man left the mountains to find work the rest of 'em followed him. Then the Company came in and started buying up the land. Grabbed all but four acres of ours so they could put up that silly park over there. I don't cuss much, but that damned Diversified didn't do us any favors around here. I know that was your mama's folks, ones with the Company, but I can't help it."

"It's all right, Minnie," said Robin. "I feel the same way."

"But I sure am proud of Bluejay for hanging on to the farm."

"He's going to die a happy man because of it, I think."

"Bluejay Clay," she said. "Dead. I won't believe it."

"Nobody will," said Robin, snapping his bag shut and getting up to leave. "Now just don't you be in too big a hurry to join him. And take those pills when you need them."

"Tell your grandpa I'm rooting for him, Robin."

"I'll do that, Minnie."

A light snow had begun to flurry, the first serious-looking snow of the fall, and Robin hurried along the rutted road to Sixkiller at dusk. He saw the lights were on in the big house, Bluejay's place, but first he drove the Jeep to his and Meg's cabin—now, with the addition of a modern kitchen in the rear, it could be called a cottage—to get something to eat. Meg was giving Sammy a bottle when he came in. She was not humming to the baby as she usually did at feeding time.

"I think now," Meg said.

"Grandpa?"

"Uh-huh. Yellow as squash. You better go. He's talking crazy."

Robin, still in his sheepskin coat and boots, trotted across the yard to the main house and left his tracks in the light sheet of snow. Far off in the hills he could hear an owl warming up for the night. From the barn came the low moaning of the cows and the jittery whinnies of the horse. The black October sky was getting ready to unload. It would make the people at the Cherokee Hills Ski Lodge very happy, he thought, because now they could shut down the snow-making machinery and enjoy the real thing. He stomped the snow from his boots and opened the heavy front door and entered the main room. Jaybird, his father, had built a roaring fire that looked like it could burn all night. Bluejay, as pale as Meg had said, was stretched out to his full length on the sofa beneath a colorful quilt made by his wife nearly a half century earlier, before Jaybird was even born. It was the same quilt, in fact, which had been used as swaddling for Molly's only child.

"Okay, Grandpa?" Robin said.

"Hurts like a sonofabitch, boy," said Bluejay.

"Let me give you a shot."

"It's about time *somebody* offered me one."

"Well, Dad doesn't know how to do it."

"The hell he doesn't. Just pour it in some hot tea."

"Now, Grandpa, dammit, I told you whiskey'll make you sicker." Robin glanced at Jaybird, who sat on the edge of a rocker next to the sofa, and Jaybird threw out both hands in exasperation. "You'll just throw it up."

"Hell of a waste of good liquor, but I'll take my chances," said Bluejay. "And while you're up mixing my last toddy how 'bout helping me up out of this goddam deathbed. And turn on some music. Turn it up loud so that goddam Shorty Hunsinger can hear it. I want that no-good sonofabitch to hear 'Molly' the way it was supposed to be done. Hell, Jaybird, you knew Shorty. I ever tell you what that ass-hole tried to do to me that time? Hell, you knew Shorty."

"Sure, Pa, sure," Jaybird said. "Here we go. Let me help you."

Jaybird eased his father from the sofa to the rocking chair and tucked the quilt around his arms and shoulders and legs. He stoked the fire and put on a stack of albums, all of them Bluejay Clay albums, and then sat on a footstool beside the hearth. When Robin came back from the kitchen he handed his grandfather a big coffee mug filled with equal parts of bourbon and steaming hot tea. For ten or fifteen minutes they said nothing. The stereo filled the room with the old man's music.

> The cold wind was a-howling
>   On that awful winter's night,
> The night the devil came
>   A-spoiling for a fight.
>
> The three of us were happy
>   For soon we would be four,
> But little did we know
>   What the devil had in store . . .

Finally Bluejay said, "Downright prophetic, if you ask me."

"Prophetic," said Jaybird. "I never heard you use that word before."

"Got a smart-ass Yankee granddaughter that taught me."

"It *was* prophetic," Robin said. "Now there *are* four."

"Yeah," said Bluejay, "but 'little did we know what the devil had in store.' Gonna be back to three pretty soon."

"Grandpa," Robin said.

"It's all right, boy, I told your daddy."

"You two must've thought I was crazy. Anybody could tell."

"He made me a promise, Robin, and I want you to make damned sure he keeps it. He can look at liquor and he can smell it and he can even help Sam make it if he wants to. But he better not ever have another drink. That's one legacy I don't want to leave behind me. That what they call it? Legacy? Damned little ol' Yankee girl taught me that one, too."

"I promise, Pa," said Jaybird.

"Don't promise me. Promise Mo. I won't be here."

"Don't say that, Pa. You're 'the holy ghost.' Remember?"

"Damned if I ain't." Bluejay took a sip from the mug.

"The father, the son, the holy ghost."

"Oh, shit"—Bluejay winced and grabbed his side—"goddam that hurts. Whew. Yeah, I remember when I came up with that 'holy ghost' thing. Me and Sam was sitting down at his place sipping whiskey and talking. Remember he had some lady professor spending the night, claimed she wanted to know all about the Trail of Tears, and I reckon ol' Sam gave her a lesson or two. Yeah, and that was the day he got that book from somebody. Book called *1984*. All about how the government was gonna take over and start running everybody's life for 'em. Well, hell, the Clays knew that when they were still in Scotland. Good thing I didn't need to wait until 1984 to find out how it came out. Oh, shit, goddam sonofabitch, there it goes again. Damn if I even know how to die right. Y'all help me back on that sofa, will you?"

Again they moved him, this time taking off his slippers and adding another quilt and pillow, and while Jaybird threw on some more hickory logs Robin turned down the music. "Hillbilly Fever" was playing—*Can't keep a 'billy down*—as the son and the grandson took up their positions beside the fire and waited for the old man to slip away. The music droned and the fire popped and the owls hooted.

"Jaybird." Bluejay shouted the name.

"What? What?" Jaybird jumped like a geyser.

"Goddamit, I ain't a ghost yet. Sit down."

"You want something, Pa?"

"Naw," Bluejay said. "Well, yeah, I do. In that family Bible there, those pages where we put stuff like date-of-birth and son-of-so-and-so and all that, would you write something down there about how they had to chase me off the stage of the Grand Ole Opry one time? You're the writer around here. I'd kinda like to be remembered for that. Galled the hell out of the bastards."

EPILOGUE

All through the black Appalachian night the wind, messenger of death, howls and shrieks and circles like some giant mythical Ulsterian vulture, raging against the ageless log house, hurling hickory limbs and pine cones at the skittery tin roof, rattling frail windows, cartwheeling loose pails across the yard, tearing gates from rusty hinges, throwing icicle darts at the creaking barn, blowing its hoary breath at terrified animals cowering in the naked orchard, demanding a word with the survivors. *Let me in, let me in, I have news, I have news,* says The Messenger, absent for nearly four decades, furious this time, crying out with malevolent glee, howling, moaning, cackling, circling, beating his great black wings against the fortress of tree and clay. Clay. *One more, that's one more.* And then, finally, he retires, as he has many times before, soaring away to his lonely aerie high above the valley, far away on the bleak ridges of Clingman's Dome, leaving only his calling card of stark white nothing.

At dawn the grandson, the doctor, comes back from the hospital where during the night he has delivered a new life to the world. There is a high blue sky and dazzling sunlight, already, and a thick blanket of snow left by the storm. He parks beside the main house and stomps the snow from his boots and enters the big room. The fire is nearly out. The stereo is still playing. His father is asleep where he had left him, in the rocking chair

241

beside the hearth, and the old man is still sprawled out on the sofa. At first the young doctor tries to awaken the old man but then he takes off his mittens to feel for a pulse. There is none. The boy shakes his father.

Dad. Dad.

Fell asleep. What time is it?

He's gone, Dad. Grandpa's gone.

Oh, my God, I thought I'd be ready.

He was. That's what counts.

What do we do?

We live. You and me and Sammy.

The others are summoned, including the ageless Indian and the mother and her baby, and there are few tears. There is business to be done. A body to be removed and prepared. Pieces of paper to be signed, a hole to be dug, a box to be nailed and closed forever, flowers to be found, marble to be cut, words to be said, Bibles to be read, hymns to be sung. Amazing grace how sweet thou art.

They gather on the distant hillside the next day, beside the marker which says Molly O'Hare Clay 1911–1945 and the one saying Boy Baby Clay 1945, and it is a curious sight. While the son and the grandson and the Indian take turns shoveling the black loam and piling it against the stark snow, with a woman in black pigtails and a younger woman holding a baby standing by, they are being watched in silence by dozens of strangers from the other side of the chain-link fence on the ridge above the family cemetery. The strangers are wearing ski caps and snow goggles and mittens and brightly colored snowsuits, having just dropped from the ski lift and plodded across the snow on their skis, and they peer in silence at something few have ever seen. The baby cries but is silenced by his mother. The three men lift the heavy box and settle it into the hole they have dug. Then they cover it with the black dirt, patting the dirt into a hard mound, before topping it with a marble headstone carved in the shape of a bluejay taking flight. The headstone reads, Bluejay Clay 1911–1983.

Then the woman in pigtails clasps her hands at her breast,

her large black eyes beginning to water now, and on the hill
beyond the fence the strangers blink and whisper to each other
as she raises her face to the cobalt cloudless sky and begins to
sing.

> Amazing grace, how sweet thou art,
>   That saved a wretch like me;
> I once was lost, but now I'm found,
>   Was blind but now I see . . .